ALMOST NORMAL HORROR

Christine Morgan

Madness Heart Press
2006 Idlewilde Run Dr.
Austin, Texas 78744

Copyright © 2022 Christine Morgan

Interior Layout by Lori Michelle
   www.TheAuthorsAlley.com

This is a work of fiction. Names, characters, places, and incidents either are the product of the author's imagination or are used fictitiously. Any resemblance to actual persons, living or dead, events, or locales is entirely coincidental.

All rights reserved. No part of this book may be reproduced or used in any manner without written permission of the copyright owner except for the use of quotations in a book review.

For more information, address:
   john@madnessheart.press

               www.madnessheart.press

With thanks to all the editors who gave these tales a chance

COPYRIGHT INFO

They Wait—originally appeared in *Dead Bait IV,* 2017

The Reaching Wall—originally appeared in *Horror Between the Sheets: Best of Cthulhu Sex Magazine,* 2005

Fin Check—originally appeared in the 'Fuck Cancer' chapbook and *Where There Are Dragons,* 2019

Dumpster Diving—originally appeared in *Shifters,* 2013

Taggers—originally appeared in *Tales of the Seelie Court,* 2014

The Naughty List—originally appeared in *Bad Seeds,* 2013

Don't Look Back—originally appeared in *Fear of the Unknown,* 2004

With Blackest Moss—originally appeared in *Cucurbital 3,* 2012

For Bobby—originally appeared in *The Nightside Codex,* 2020

The Suitcase—originally appeared in the 'Fuck Cancer' chapbook

Eating for Two—originally appeared in *Dreaded Pall,* 2006

Window Dressing—originally appeared in *Mannequin: Tales of Wood Made Flesh,* 2019

The Humming—originally appeared in *Short Sharp Shocks 2: Stomping Grounds,* 2014

Eye See You—originally appeared in *Double Barrel Horror 3,* 2020

Haunted Heist—originally appeared in the 'Fuck Cancer' chapbook

Derpyfoot—originally appeared in *Tails of Valor and Terror,* 2018

TABLE OF CONTENTS

Foreword by Lee Murray i

They Wait 1

The Reaching Wall.. 11

Fin Check 24

Dumpster Diving 28

Taggers 46

The Naughty List 70

Don't Look Back 91

With Blackest Moss 106

For Bobby 119

The Suitcase 132

Eating For Two 136

Window Dressing 153

The Humming 167

Eye See You 186

Haunted Heist 197

Derpyfoot 202

FOREWORD

WHEN IT COMES to Christine Morgan's writing, I admit to being late to the party. I knew her first as a literary commentator, an articulate, informed reviewer offering sharp yet unspoilery insight across a range of dark fiction genres. If Morgan recommended a book, it was undoubtedly going to be well worth the read, her preference, like mine, for gritty, pacy, *spattery* thrillers, confronting unapologetic horror, and macabre cross-genre mashups. She wasn't afraid of blood, of monsters, or the monstrous. Through her reviews, I recognised a kindred, and slightly deviant, spirit.

It wasn't until five short years ago, however, that I discovered Morgan was an also author. What? Face palm. How had I not realised? Those perceptive reflections, that in-depth understanding of story craft; it all made perfect sense. Recognising the error of my ways, I resolved to explore her books, a rewarding endeavour since Morgan has created an impressive body of work: novels like spatter western *The Night Silver River Run Red*, supernatural disaster horror *The Horned Ones: Cornucopia*, sex-demon new-pulp *Spermjackers from Hell*, and deep-sea monster horror *Trenchmouth*. Primaeval, visceral, brutal stuff, Morgan's books are darkly immersive, keenly researched, and filled with engaging authentic characters and hard-hitting relevant themes. Edward Lee (*City Infernal*) claims her spin-off title, *Lakehouse Infernal*, is the "coolest, ball-bustingest, most outrageous, and most entertaining horror novel you're likely to find in some time," and we're all aware Lee knows a thing or two about horror. So, you can imagine my delight when offered this opportunity to preface Morgan's *Almost Normal Horror*, a short story collection comprising sixteen of Morgan's chilling tales plucked from a career that has spanned close on two decades.

Bring it on!

I had three books half-read and waiting for review; I ignored them, diving right into *Almost Normal Horror*, devouring page after page, all the while thinking I had Morgan's measure, and yet this collection is not at all what I'd expected. There is little here of Morgan's trademark confrontational in-your-face extremism. No smushed entrails or sawn-off genitals. Instead, *Almost Normal Horror* is exactly what it says on the box, 'almost normal,' perhaps because rather than being drawn from the depths of hell, its stories are dredged up from the soupy detritus of our quotidian, including tales of the old and the ignored, the othered and the outcasts. There is Cindy, a displaced teen struggling to fit into a new town after her father is sent down ("The Reaching Wall"), Rachel, a homeless woman, who is beyond the notice of authorities ("Dumpster Diving"), and Maude, a grandmother still caring for her feckless brother as per her mother's dying wish ("With Blackest Moss"). There are stories set in amusement arcades, strip malls, and housing estates. Inside schools, beside airport carousels, and on workday commutes. Stories set in ordinary neighbourhoods just like yours.

Almost Normal Horror, a quieter, more contemplative selection of stories than I would have expected from Morgan, is testament to her writing skill. Here, Morgan deliberately dials down the temperature on the sex and gore while still delivering a strong sense of unease and more than a hint of the uncanny. There are brushes with the supernatural and the surreal. There is blood and brutality. Fans of Morgan's work recognise her penchant

FOREWORD

for the bizarre. But there is also an accessibility to this collection that, in my view, will have broad appeal to readers of all ages. I hope it will explode her into the mainstream, where she will happily corrupt the masses.

Every story in *Almost Normal Horror* is a gem, but three in particular resonated for me. "They Wait" is a stand-out, its rare first-person narrative taking an unusual point of view which only highlights its real-world horror. I don't want to spoil the story for readers, suffice to say the humanity of this one is startling, making it the perfect opener.

Morgan's "The Naughty List" is a blast from the past for eighties teens like me. It's your darkest *Breakfast Club* nightmare, with students Minda, Jimmy, Candy, and Derp, and Christmas princess Jolene, breaking out of detention to create their own version of the Christmas pageant. Gruesome and gleeful Yuletide fun.

"Eating for Two" was another highlight. Poignant and chilling in the light of Morgan's recent personal battle, it tells of a woman's alienation, which becomes extreme over the course of her pregnancy. Family dynamics are front and foremost in this story, which examines themes of fertility and mental health.

Now that it's my turn to be the reviewer, I thoroughly recommend *Almost Normal Horror*; it is a collection for the invisible everyman, for the derpy-footed who walk to a different tune, for those of us who have had the misfortune to misstep or miscalculate. Which, of course, is all of us. I invite you to read on. I am certain you will love this collection as much as I have.

Lee Murray
August 2021

THEY WAIT

DIVING IS THE BEST
No matter how awkward we might feel on land, how heavy and clumsy, the moment we're in the water, we become sleek grace and weightlessness. Each supple turn, each rippling roll, pearly bubbles streaming up in long glimmering trails . . . such beauty, such freedom, such wonder and joy.

Leo bumps me. A friendly gesture, but there's flirtation behind the playful affection, and I know it.

It isn't that I mind Leo; Leo's okay . . . he's cute, a great swimmer . . . catches lots of fish when he puts in some effort . . .

He likes me, but Selah likes him, and Selah is my cousin.

Anyway, I like Pip better, though Pip is with Jaya now. They'll probably be king and queen of the beach this year.

I shouldn't be jealous or disappointed. I'm sure I'll find someone. It isn't as if I'm going to end up with one of those scrawny losers who lurk around the edges of things, hoping for a lapse of judgment from the lonely or desperate.

Leo nudges me again. I look over, and he's goofing around, doing twists, showing off. Selah's below us. I see her watching him too. Watching him show off for me, anxiety dulling the dark shine of her eyes.

So, because I'm a good cousin, I splutter a rude string of bubbles to indicate the degree to which I am unimpressed, then arch my body and dive deeper. I skim over the rocky ledges—teeming with life, stars and spiny urchins, wavering fronds, crabs creeping sideways on skinny legs—toward the drop-off.

We know, of course, not to swim too far. We know the dangers, what's down there, what's out there. What waits, always hungry. Gaping maws. Gaping jaws. Rows of sharp teeth ready to rip and to rend.

We know, but we're young, we're confident, we're having fun. We're sure nothing bad will happen, not to us. To others, maybe. The careless or unlucky. Or, like Big Ro, the stupidly brave. Thinking he could take on a shark and win, was it any wonder he ended up shreds of gristle?

Shreds of gristle, adrift in dispersing blood.

A memory I could have done without.

A memory easy enough to shake from my head as I propel myself onward. The water parts around me and I am one with it. I'm not wallowing on the shore, trying to get comfortable, heaving my bulk around.

I am sleek, effortless, limber grace.

This is better.

Diving.

Diving is the best.

Selah paces me, and Leo brings up the rear. We are well away from the beach now. Well into the bay, slipping through liquid indigo silence.

Silence, but for distant whalesong thrumming and warbling from the deep. The serenades of mating, of mothers calling to their calves, of bulls sounding challenges. It is their music, their melody. Oceanic arias in a cetacean opera.

Peacefulness. Serenity.

If only we could stay here forever.

But, sooner or later, we will have to surface. We are not fish to swim eternally while drawing with gills. We must breathe, and are limited to what air we can hold.

Our bubbles stream and trail and glimmer, rising from us, vanishing. I bump Selah and she bumps me back. We

THEY WAIT

twirl around each other, play-fighting with slaps and swats. Leo joins in. We are a tussling tangle of flippers and slick wet fur, noses bristling with tickling whiskers.

I break from them first, disengage as they wrestle and roil. A small school of herring flit by. I dart and snap and catch one. It wriggles in my mouth. I bite. Fine scales and soft meat and a quick burst of juices. Gulp, gone. I want more, but the school whirls away and a constricting pressure in my ribs tells me it's about time to ascend.

The sea-ice hangs thick overhead. Pale arctic silver, shades of pure glacial blue. Its underside forms inverted canyons, ridges, and ravines. Sunlight beams down in shifting, wavering shafts from jagged cracks and smooth-edged holes.

Up and up, I swim toward the shining gleam. Toward the promise of air, of life-giving breath. I exhale more wobbling bubbles, a billowing cloud of them, seething around me in coursing undulations.

My muzzle splashes up into the bracing cold. I puff out a last pluming gust, my own little imitation of a mighty whale.

White, it is so white and so bright after the beautiful gloaming in the depths! The sides of the hole are sloped, ridged with marks made by others before me who've scraped and scoured and dug to keep it from closing over. I add my own contribution, the stubby claws at the ends of my flippers gouging at the ice even as my lungs swell with–

I see the sudden lunging shadow and twitch with shock, recoiling.

The twitch saves me.

Something deadly shears past my face, close enough to flick my whiskers. It crashes into the icy edge. There is a miniature blizzard of flying hail, but I am already dropping, dropping straight down rump-first with my hind-flippers tucked and my front-flippers folded against my chest.

The shadow looms, menacing, furious, uttering some horrible noise. I curl in a somersault; I dive as fast as I can.

Leo and Selah . . .

. . . are not wrestling anymore but rising themselves, rising side-by-side in tandem. They look good together. It is their moment. Like a dance. A thing of beauty.

Which I ruin by plowing right into them, but I don't care. I don't care that Selah actually snaps at me in irritation, or that Leo gawks at me as if I've been chewing on the kind of anemones that make bulge-heads swim in circles.

Selah pushes past me. I grapple at her, prod her with my nose. She spins, and this time it is no play-fighting slap. It's slowed by the water; if we'd been ashore, she would have bowled me over.

Throat-grunting his amusement, Leo slings his muscular body upward. The silvery sheen of his belly-fur flashes. I squeal, but he must think I'm fooling. A strong flex of his hindquarters propels him into the wavering light.

Again, Selah pushes past me. Again, I grapple at her, and again, she snaps and slaps at me. Her muzzle wrinkles, black lips peeling back to bare teeth in a snarl, nostrils sealed to shut slits.

I plead with pup-cries like I haven't done since we lolled on the ice-floes waiting for our mothers to bring sweet milk and half-chewed fish. Selah hesitates. Her head tilts. I see a grey face in her glossy eye, and realize it is my own.

Then she shakes me off, batting impatiently at my grasping flippers, and surges up after Leo.

He has nearly reached the breathing-hole.

My squeal is so loud and shrill the whales probably hear it in the deep. Selah flinches, glancing down at me.

But Leo pops his head up through the hole in the ice.

The shadow lunges. There is a sound, a terrible sound— a grisly, meaty kind of crunch—and a dark tide of blood floods the water. Leo thrashes, flippers flailing, all his sleek grace and strength gone in a writhing and desperate struggle to escape.

THEY WAIT

More blood gushes, a great spreading cloud of its hot, thick red stink. Leo screams. No, Leo shrieks. His bladder and bowels add more hot floods of fluid. The space beneath the air-hole is a vile, churning turbulence.

There is a second terrible crunch. Leo's shrieking becomes a gurgle. He convulses. His flippers beat madly at nothing, then go slack. The bulk of his body is yanked from above. It lodges in the hole, caught on the blood-rimed edging of ice. The ice cracks and crackles.

Whatever's up there gives another tremendous yank. Blubbery skin squeaks as the widest part of Leo is squeezed through. The rest follows. I have a final glimpse of his hind-flippers, a claw snagging briefly, and then he is gone.

Gone, but the shadow . . .

Gone, but the sounds!

The grisly, meaty, crunching, rending sounds.

And the blood. More blood. So much blood. Running like spring meltoff, spring meltoff in steaming, stinking scarlet.

I turn to Selah. Now I see my face in both of her eyes, her eyes so wide they're like round sea-polished stones. Her muzzle contorts. A thin, tiny whine issues from her throat. It is accompanied by a thin, tiny line of bubbles.

She needs to breathe.

She needs to go up.

Up there? Up there where blood stains the ice? Where torn skin and gobbets of blubber plop into the sea as the thing that's killed Leo—there can be no doubt!—is . . . what? Ripping him to pieces? Eating him?

But Selah needs to breathe.

We swivel, gazes searching the contoured, frozen underside for another opening, finding none. We've swum a long way, too far for her to swim back without a fresh lungful of air. She'd never make it.

I jerk my head at the hole above, encouraging her. If she goes now, while the deadly thing is busy with Leo, she can gulp a quick breath. Then we can flee far enough to find safety.

CHRISTINE MORGAN

She shrinks from me, wrapping her flippers around herself. She's trembling, quivering with fear and distress. I don't blame her. The prospect of surfacing through the warm red salt-wash of Leo's blood, the way it would feel coating whiskers and fur, the way it would taste . . . it's too much. Too much even without risking a similar, violent end.

What is it? What can it be?

I know of sharks, of course. I know of the orca, those lethal black-and-white kindred of the gentler whalesong behemoths.

None of them could be on top of the ice.

Something else is.

A death-bear?

I know of them, have even seen them from a distance. They are big and shaggy, white as the snow. They are land-creatures, but they can swim—unlike us, we are sea-creatures who can go ashore. And they will gladly kill and eat us if they can.

Death-bears are sly too. They'll charge us when we're on rocks or pebbly beaches, when we're at our slowest and most ungainly. They'll slide into the sea and paddle with only their snouts and wet backs poking up, slinking alongside our ice-floes as we're trying to bask, looking like ice-floes themselves.

If they've figured out our system of air-holes . . .

We have to surface, we have to breathe.

All they'll have to do is wait.

Selah warbles a small, pitiful sound.

Urgently, almost frantic, I jerk my head. I swat and nudge at her, trying to force her upward, but she resists. She's too scared. She knows something's up there. Waiting, just waiting for the next silly seal to stick its nose up.

I find a place where the ice forms an inverted basin, a kind of hollow. I exhale some of my own breath into it and it catches there, held, suspended, a jiggling air-puddle. I push Selah at this instead, working my head and torso

THEY WAIT

under her to boost her the way our mothers did when we were pups having trouble resurfacing on our own.

She finds the pocket of air. It may not be the freshest, but I feel her gasping. Her flipper pat-strokes at me, desperate gratitude.

Desperate, possibly doomed gratitude, because now neither of us have enough breath to last long.

We explore the underside, claws ticking and scraping, hoping to find a spot we might be able to gouge through. But the ice is too thick.

There's no other choice. If we're going to make it, if we're going to live . . .

I squint up into the hole's murky brightness. I don't see any looming shadows. I don't hear any more menacing growls or awful feeding-noises.

Maybe it's satisfied and has already gone?

Maybe it took its . . . kill . . . with it. Dragging Leo's mangled corpse away, leaving only a long gory smear. To its lair. To its mate or its hungry young.

Maybe it's all right now. Maybe it's safe.

Maybe just the briefest of bob-up-bob-down peeks, to check. To make sure nothing's up there . . . poised and patient . . . waiting.

Selah won't do it. I don't want to, but what else can we do?

A lot of the blood has diffused, so, there's that.

Of course, sharks and orcas may have scented the bloodspill and be coming already, strong tails whipping sinuous side-to-side or flexing powerfully up and down.

Their jaws. Their teeth. Coming at us out of the blackest depths.

Sharks and orcas won't wait.

Danger below. Danger above.

Dead either way.

I gather myself. My heart pounds, my muscles tense. Selah watches me, so much fear in her eyes . . . Leo is dead, and I've already given her my breath, and if I die too, she'll be all alone.

Nothing moves. Nothing makes a sound.

Cautiously, as a test, I blow a few bubbles and hang beneath them as they wibble and wobble to the surface.

No shadow. No noise.

Up!

The water thins, the light brightens, the red-stained ice sparkles and shines. The cold air hits me like a rogue wave. My nostrils flare and my mouth gawps; I suck in as much as my lungs will hold.

The sight almost knocks the breath right back out.

Leo. His belly split open from gullet to tail, layers of blubbery skin folded back to reveal sodden crimson meat and purplish innards. His head hangs back, upside-down, his frost-glazed black eyes staring dead and blank into mine.

The things around him—

They are not death-bears.

They are big, yes, and shaggy, but their pelts are of many mingled kinds and colors. Luxurious ruffs encircle their round, mud-brown flat faces. They have curved claws like sharp stones, slicing dripping dark hunks of liver-meat to gnash at with short white-ivory nubs.

One of them sees me. A female, I think; it seems to have a pup or youngling clinging to its furs. It thrusts a claw toward me and garbles a loud call. The others whirl. Meat in their teeth, blood on their chins, they rear up on hindlimbs and waggle weird forelimbs.

Then there is a stick, a stick with a claw or a tooth of its own, jabbing at me. I flinch like before. And, like before, the fierce shearing strike passes close enough to tweak my whiskers.

Unlike before, there is another claw-tooth-stick and there is pain!

A vicious, brutal, biting pain!

I squeal.

THEY WAIT

No, I scream. I shriek like Leo did.

I try to drop but am snagged, snagged on the claw-tooth, and it digs and it grinds and I feel it shudder against bone and my blood pours down into the water as I thrash my body every wild which-way.

A pull.

A pull, and the claw-tooth catches firm, it is barbed, it is hooked, it has me. My flesh tears, my flippers smack rapid panic on the sloped, wet, bloodied ice. I am sliding, sliding upward, out of the sea, out of the hole, I am being dragged up to where Leo is a cold, gutted carcass.

I will be next, they'll open me from gullet to tail, they'll peel off my fur in silver-grey strips to add to their own monstrous minglings of pelt, they'll eat my liver while rimes of frost ring my dead eyes–

With another shriek, and another agonizing wrenching of my body, and another even-more-agonizing deep-inside slashing of pain, I am suddenly loose.

Loose and floundering on the ice, splashing in blood-slush. Clumsy and heavy, galumphing, awkward, as all around me the killers bellow and roar. Another claw-stick pierces my flipper. I heave myself forward and the grey webbing-skin shreds.

The hole!

I lunge for it. Headfirst, flippers scrabbling, hunching, and flopping. They grab at me. But–

In I go, down I go. The sea closes over me. My sleek grace returns, or as much as my bleeding wounds will allow. I try to dive.

The cold numbs.

The salt stings.

I do not so much dive as sink, but I sink fast and deep. I cradle my hurt flipper to my chest and try to curl into a ball, as if it might meld my injured flesh together again with itself.

Above me, there is commotion. One of the strange-furred killers has fallen in. A big male, a bull. What was my escape and return to grace is the opposite for him. He is not made for swimming. His own pelt hinders and entangles. His broad-set nostrils do not close.

And Selah streaks out of the dark waters. Her jaws, made for nothing much larger than cod, clamp around one of the bull's hindlimbs. She drags him far below any reach of the air-hole, whipping her torso savagely, like a shark rending prey. Enormous bubbles erupt from the bull's gaping mouth.

She is in a frenzy, my cousin, a maddened rage. Blood seethes in a cloud, half-obscuring her from my view. She is a dark shape in the red gloom, a death-shape, and she releases the land-creature's hindlimb only so she can go for his underbelly and face.

Just as abruptly, Selah halts her attack. She loops away from her still-struggling victim—his bubbles have nearly stopped, and his remaining eye bulges with terror—and comes to me. She nuzzles me, rubs her sleek side along mine, makes concerned and inquisitive clicks.

The best I can manage is a mewling kind of cry. Selah, with a gentle care, burrows her head under my wounded flipper to help steady and support me.

I don't want to move, I don't want to swim; it hurts, everything hurts. The next-nearest breathing-hole is still so far away . . . and even if we could reach it, what's the use? Wherever we go, we'll never be able to surface safely again! Not with them up there, waiting!

But Selah is insistent. Even urgent. She will not leave me. She'll push and tug and haul me through the water if she has to. Because she knows what I should have known, what I did know but forgot.

All that blood.

All that spreading bloodspill scent, hot and enticing.

The first ominous outlines of fin and fluke have already begun to appear.

And they do not wait.

THE REACHING WALL

THE VINES
Like long, strange hands with long, strange fingers. Branching out and curling, twining.
Reaching.
Cindy forced herself to stare into the sink basin as she brushed her teeth. Down, down, at the smooth bowl of porcelain. Her wide, darting eyes made note of every minute detail.

She studied the halo of rust stain around the chrome drain hole, the cap of the stopper, a glop of blue-white foam that had dripped from her toothbrush. Curds of soap residue were stuck in the ridged depression where the half-used bar of Ivory rested. The faucet was a silver arc spouting from between seashell-shaped knobs with H and C embossed on them in gold.

Her eyes chanced higher, briefly catching a glimpse of the section of wall between the top of the sink and the bottom of the medicine cabinet. But that was okay because years' worth of backsplash had dulled the paper into non-threatening faded ivory.

She finished brushing, spat, rinsed, spat again, and deposited her toothbrush in another seashell, this one flattened with four holes in it, that jutted out of the wall above the faucet.

Reaching . . . the vines . . . closer, closer now!

Cindy, questing blindly toward the top of the toilet tank for her zippered makeup bag, froze in place.

"Nothing's reaching," she said, and though it was quiet, barely more than a whisper, she hadn't meant to speak out loud. It startled her so that she bumped her makeup bag and almost knocked it into the john.

She grabbed it cat-quick and balanced it on the rim of the sink. The clatter of lipsticks and cosmetics masked any other sounds.

If there had been any other sounds to be heard.

Which there weren't.

With the door shut, she couldn't hear Kevin and his geeky friends downstairs arguing over their stupid game, and it sure wasn't as if she was hearing anything *else* . . . nothing like a stealthy whispering slithering sound of vines like fingers stretching out toward the back of her neck . . .

Her skin prickled in anticipation of that first alien touch of tendrils. She jerked her head forward—so she could see to put on her eye shadow, that was all!—and almost smacked her forehead into the glass.

Nose to nose with her own reflection, she still couldn't help seeing the blurred and wavering shapes of the vines in her peripheral vision. Even with her gaze fixed firmly on her own mirrored blue eyes, groping into her makeup bag and selecting by feel, she was aware of them.

But they weren't moving. Weren't reaching. Weren't creeping and lifting themselves out of the yellow body of the wall . . . undulating toward her with sinister, slithery motions . . .

Concentrate, dummy, or you're going to put it on all screwy, she told herself.

Her tongue poked into the corner of her mouth as she carefully applied the shadow, then a bit of liner and mascara. Her hand kept wanting to shake as she was doing the latter, wanted to jab that bristly black spider-leg into the vulnerable orbs.

She somehow got through it with unjabbed orbs, and dusted on some blush to give color to her cheeks. Not too much; it was the funny lighting in here that made her look

THE REACHING WALL

so pallid despite a summer at the pool. If she let that be her guide, she'd overdo it for sure.

Her hand grew steadier as she put on the lipstick.

A few pumps of gel and some artful primping gave her blond hair just the right lift, and Cindy was finally satisfied.

Everything was perfect. Her clothes, her hair, her makeup. Perfect.

No one would be able to tell her otherwise. No one would dare laugh at her, or ignore her.

It was nice to be popular. To be one of the in-crowd. Admired and envied, sought-after.

The party tonight would be the final proof.

And here she was, ready in record time!

It would have taken longer if she'd had to take a shower, but she'd done that at school after PE this morning. Showering at school was easier. She didn't have to hassle with Kevin over who got to go first; she never ran out of hot water. It certainly had nothing to do with being naked and vulnerable with only a thin sheet of white vinyl shower curtain between her and the . . . and the rest of the bathroom.

On the weekends, she took long soaks in the tub in her mother's bathroom downstairs. Because she enjoyed it.

Cindy put her makeup bag away. She kept her gaze on the floor as she headed for the bathroom door. It was marbled-green linoleum worn paler in a path that ran from door to shower stall, commode, and sink. Not great, but not as creepy as the wall.

Her elbow rubbed against something fibrous and scratchy.

Cindy gasped, jumped, and hugged herself with both arms. She knew what she'd see even as she whirled to face them. Oh, yes. A snaky tangle reaching, reaching from the wall, done teasing her and ready to *grab* . . .

Nothing. Two-dimensional vines frozen in their endless climb on the patterned paper. She'd brushed against the towels hanging on the rack, that was all.

A nervous laugh escaped her.

Only the towels. Come on!

Though . . . she *had* been keeping to the direct middle of the path worn in the linoleum, with her arms close at her sides because she didn't want to bump into the . . . into anything. With her feet dead-center, her elbow couldn't have . . .

It was the towels! she thought vehemently. *Or maybe I can just skip the party and drive on out to Ivybrook and see if they've got a jacket I can borrow. A straitjacket! How would that look in the yearbook?*

She looked squarely at the wall to prove that it was just wallpaper, just ugly vine-covered wallpaper that had probably been here in this dismal wreck of a house for thirty years.

No big deal. Mom had promised they would fix everything up once they caught up with the bills. Weren't they already planning how they'd remodel the whole house? Bye-bye vines, bye-bye horrid country blue kitchen cabinets, bye-bye that goshawful orange carpet in the master bedroom where Mom slept alone.

Cindy touched the doorknob, and it came alive, rattling under her palm in sudden frantic half-turns.

She uttered a short, high screech and stumbled backward.

Her outcry was echoed by someone on the other side of the door.

"Cindy? Are you in there?"

Kevin. He'd been trying the door, that was all.

"Don't you *knock*?" she snapped.

"I thought you left," he said.

"I was about—" Her words broke off abruptly as she realized she was leaning, *leaning* against the wall. She'd stumbled back into it and was propped up as casually as if she was waiting for a boyfriend to cruise by and pick her up after school, leaning on those vines, right up against her!

THE REACHING WALL

She yelped and bounded away, grabbing for the doorknob. Locked, she'd locked it against just such an eventuality as this, her doofus brother barging in on her without knocking. On purpose, most likely, trying to catch her naked because he was a pervert, a horny kid, sixteen going on twelve.

What a charge he'd get out of it, and he'd tell the rest. He probably already had made up some lie, given the way they all looked at her and grinned, then laughed together when they thought she wasn't listening.

"Cindy?" Kevin knocked.

Cindy didn't look back, in case the vines, cheated from the missed opportunity, were uncoiling toward her even now. Ready to wrap around her arms and legs, noose her neck, snare her hair, bind themselves across her mouth like a gag, and pull her, pull her into the wall . . .

She twisted the lock and yanked the door open. The corner of it skidded across the top of her shoe, would have stubbed into her toes if not for the slightly sunken dip of the floor and the way it hung less than perfectly on its hinges.

Kevin barely got out of her way as she exploded into the hall. His myopic brown eyes goggled at her from behind his thick glasses.

"You okay?" he asked. "See a spider or something?"

"I'm *fine*, jerkazoid! What do you want?"

"To pee, if that's all right with you," he said in the tone of voice she really hated, the one that was half condescending and half whine. "Troy's using the one downstairs. He's got the runs."

"God! Like I needed to know that." She swept him with a scornful glare, wondering once again how in the world she'd ended up with *this* for a brother. And a twin at that.

Not that it showed. Kevin looked as immature as he acted, was as dark as she was blond, as pasty as she was tan. Just a stick-thin geek-boy who'd never be with the popular people.

CHRISTINE MORGAN

The clock down in the living room chimed seven. The party would already be starting. Everybody who was anybody was going to be there.

Well, she'd be fashionably late. It wasn't like things could get going without her.

She hurried down to the first floor. To her left was the living room, where everybody who was *nobody* had turned the normally neat room into a tornado-remnant of potato chip bags, empty soda cans, books, papers, funny-shaped dice, and tiny metal figures.

"Garion Winterfox does not surrender!" a porky kid named Fred said as Cindy reached the bottom step. "His honor would never permit it!"

"Yeah, but you can't take out twenty goblin henchmen by yourself." Lewis was nineteen, in college, and sort of cute, yet here he was with the dweebs. "Pretend to surrender and buy us some time. We'll need Garion's sword skill to get past the Warden of the Blades."

"Garion Winterfox doesn't pretend either!"

Cindy groaned. The losers heard her, looked, and instantly got that goggle-eyed look like they'd never seen a girl up close before, least of all a pretty one in a sexy new party dress. As she hurried for the kitchen, she heard one of them laugh in a way that made her think of that baby vulture on the old Bugs Bunny cartoons.

The kitchen was dark and cool, but a long rectangle of light was thrown on the tile from the door of the small utility room that doubled as her mother's home office.

The gift-wrapped item she'd purchased last week at the mall was sitting on the kitchen table next to her purse. She picked them up and stuck her head around the corner. "Hey, Mom. I'm leaving now."

A small desk was wedged between the washer-dryer and the water heater, the shelves over it crowded with computer programming and run-your-own-business books. Her mother glanced up from the spreadsheet on the screen with a tired smile.

THE REACHING WALL

"Okay, honey. Have fun. Back by eleven?"

"Mom, it's Friday night. And it's Jeanette's birthday. Midnight at least, please?"

"I'd hate to make you miss out on all the fun with your new friends. All right. Midnight, twelve-thirty at the latest." Mom pushed her hair behind her ears. It was as dark as Kevin's, but there were streaks of grey that hadn't been so prominent a year ago when Dad was still with them. "I told you things would be better once school started."

"I'm sorry I was so rotten about moving," Cindy said, eyes downcast.

"It's been hard on all of us. But we'll get through it, honey. You'll see."

"Do you think . . . when are we going to be able to start fixing the place up?"

"If I don't pay off the dentist first, they're going to come repossess your and Kevin's teeth. And the holidays are coming. Maybe in January."

"January! But, Mom—"

"Cindy, it's only three months. Unless you want new carpeting for Christmas."

"No, guess not." *Wallpaper!* her mind shrieked. *We need new bathroom wallpaper first; who cares about the dumb old carpet?*

"Besides, it's not that bad," Mom said in a tone that meant she was trying to convince herself as much as Cindy. "Not as nice as our old house, but it could be a lot worse. Is Brett picking you up?"

"He said he'd meet me there. His car's in the shop, and anyway, he lives on the same block as Jeanette."

"So when do I get to meet him? Before Prom Night, I hope."

"Nobody drags their boyfriend home to meet their mother anymore."

"Because their boyfriend has tattoos on his tongue and a ring through his eyebrow and plays drums for a band called Festering Skin Disease?"

"Mom!" Cindy laughed. "He's on the debate team! His dad's a banker! And if I don't show, he's going to think I dumped him."

She went out the back door to avoid having to face Kevin's friends again. It just figured. For her brother, the move was the best thing that had ever happened to him. He'd found an entire group into all the lame things he liked.

Cindy supposed that as far as Kevin was concerned, it was worth everything they'd had to lose in order to end up here.

Even Dad . . .

Not that Kevin cared much about that. He and Dad had nothing in common but their last names. Dad had been athletic, a high-school baseball hero, known and loved by everyone, blond and handsome and popular.

A lot like Brett Evans. Cindy was honest enough to admit to herself that part of the reason she'd been so attracted to Brett was that he reminded her of her father, or what her father had been before the . . . well, *before.*

She got in the car, the present for Jeanette resting on the passenger seat. It had been expensive, and Cindy felt a twinge of guilt when she thought of Mom working so hard to make ends meet. But it was perfect for Jeanette . . . exactly right for her. Just what she needed.

Pine Hill was on the other side of town. It was a neighborhood far nicer than theirs, and one look would have made Mom understand why Cindy could never invite Brett over. Not until they fixed things up. There were no orange carpets in Pine Hill, no faded linoleum . . . no reaching walls.

Cars lined the curb for three blocks around Jeanette's house. As she drove past, looking for a parking place, Cindy could hear the music of a live band and smell the hickory smoke of a barbecue. People were dancing on the big brick patio in the backyard. The pool was lit from within and looked like a huge shimmering sapphire.

THE REACHING WALL

The party was fantastic, a fabulous evening, wonderful in every way.

At least, that was how it looked from the other side of the fence, from the alley where Cindy parked in concealing darkness.

She waited until everyone else left to give Jeanette her present, surprised her in her room with it.

Jeanette was so excited that she actually screamed when it came out of the box.

But she only screamed once before Cindy helped her try it on.

It was a perfect fit.

Red always was Jeanette's color. It went so well with her complexion, and it fit her like it had been painted on.

Cindy left Pine Hill at midnight and headed for home, pulling to the side of the road to let a police car and an ambulance roar past in the oncoming lane, wondering where they were going at this hour. An accident, maybe.

She was much more tired than she'd expected to be. All she wanted was to fall into bed and dream of how gorgeous Brett had looked on the dance floor. Every girl had watched him and wished she was his date.

Bed would have to wait a little longer. She'd spilled something on herself and was all sticky . . . and Mom would already be asleep . . . so she would have to shower upstairs.

The house was dark and silent. Cindy went to her room and got out of her damp party clothes. She dumped them in the hamper, then wrapped herself in her robe and headed for the bathroom. Her steps faltered.

Maybe she should skip it . . .

No, she had punch or something all over her. It was in her hair, turning the blond to auburn. It was all over her arms, clear to the elbows. She could even feel spots of it drying on her face.

She locked the bathroom door and turned on the shower, opening the tiny window high in the stall to keep the steam from filling the room.

CHRISTINE MORGAN

The hissing of the spray masked any other noises . . . not that there *were* any other noises, but if there had been, the hissing of the spray would have masked them. Once she was in the stall with the water beating down on her head, she could hear nothing else.

Opening her eyes to get the shampoo from the shelf, Cindy saw a shadow twining across the thin white shower curtain. Long and sinuous.

Her breathing sped up.

She firmly told herself there was nothing there.

Walls didn't reach for people, didn't try to grab them and pull them back inside, keep them trapped forever. Vines didn't move unless stirred by the wind. Like the ones all over the grey stone walls at Ivybrook, for instance. Wallpaper vines never moved at all.

She poured shampoo into her cupped hand and massaged it into her hair, making a face at the clotted, mucky feel of it. Yuck.

Was it fruit punch? Catsup? Barbecue sauce? Whichever it was, it made a gross swirling red whirlpool around the drain.

Cindy scrubbed and scrubbed until the lather was white and foamy, then rinsed it clear and worked in some lilac-scented conditioner. She soaped herself while the conditioner set, paying special attention to her hands and forearms. It took the stiff-bristled brush to scour the places that the red stuff had grimed in, on her knuckles and under her nails.

More redness splashed across the walls and curtain in a flood.

This redness didn't rinse away. It was red light, whirling through the small window in pulses.

Very dimly and distantly, even over the sounds of the water, Cindy heard a thumping. No, a hammering, a pounding. The front door? Who'd be knocking on the front door this late?

They'd wake up Mom, who needed her rest. Didn't

THE REACHING WALL

people understand how hard it was for her to have been thrust into the role of a single mother? Not by anything so ordinary as divorce or clean as death either.

Determined to give whoever it was a piece of her mind, Cindy stepped out of the shower and reached for a towel.

A vine braceleted her wrist.

She stared at the flat green paper band against her skin. Yes, it was paper. Flat, two-dimensional . . . and already growing sodden as it soaked up the beads of water rolling down her arm.

The wall was moving, stirring, shifting.

Reaching.

It reached for her as she stood stunned. More and more vines peeled themselves loose with faint ripping sounds as the glue backing of the wallpaper gave way.

Cindy saw strips of another design underneath, once-cheery sunflowers turned by time and decay into hideous yellow eyes.

The eyes rolled to fix on her, and in them she read a terrible mindless hunger.

She tried to shriek. It came out in a high, thin wail that barely even carried to her own ears.

More vines settled onto her in streamers, wrapping her like a mummy.

Her strength returned in a sudden terror-inspired burst. She lunged for the door. The wettest of the strands tore away with sickening ease, but others pulled taut. They stopped her with her desperate hand clutching for the doorknob six inches away.

It reached . . . it caught . . . raspy tendrils around her waist, her breasts, her hips. They coiled and slithered over her like snakes. One pasted itself, its underside sticky with glue, over her mouth as she found her voice to scream. Only a muffled moan emerged.

The yellow eyes in the wall blinked. A dozen eyes, twenty, more and more as the vines . . . except they weren't vines anymore, were they? They were tentacles, a Medusasnarl of writhing snakes. They ripped free with sounds that weren't so much papery as scaly, and settled onto her body.

The wall was alive, and it hungered. It wanted her.

She knew what would happen next. She'd be pulled back, taken into the wall, never to be free again . . .

Just like Dad . . . locked away behind the ivy forever and ever. Behind the walls and the bars. At the mercy of the attendants. He told her how they abused him, sobbed and begged her to help before the cruelest one, the one they called Bull, could hurt him again.

The vines, the tentacles, constricted and dragged Cindy away from the door. Her wet feet skidded on the marbled-green linoleum, and now *it* was coming alive too, seething and rising up to wrap her legs.

She saw mouths among the sunflower eyes. Mouths like suckers, slurping eagerly. The reaching wall pulled her toward the mouths. Vines were all over her, vines were doing things to her that she couldn't stand to think about. She could *feel* them working into her. Dry and scratchy and thick.

The one over her mouth bunched and forced itself in. She bit, tasted paper and glue and a rancid sap. Spitting out a chewed wad, she found her breath and finally screamed.

A thick vine drew tight around her throat, cutting off her scream. She clawed at it, but it was slick and strong and her fingernails couldn't rip it. Not papery. Rubbery, reeking of vinyl and mildew.

Cindy grabbed for the edge of the sink. Her hands slid on the cold porcelain. Her heel came down in a puddle, and she fell.

The vine around her neck pulled chokingly tight. She heard a series of popping sounds that seemed to come from far away. The vines pulled her toward the wall. Struggling, her knee slammed into the undercurve of the sink basin.

Heavy rapid thunder banged the door. It shuddered, and a long, jagged splinter leaped from the inside panel.

THE REACHING WALL

The vines were all over her, rasping, slithering, violating. She couldn't breathe. The yellow eyes and puckered rings of mouth watching from the wall leaped out at her in silent black bursts.

The door flew open. She had a dizzying impression of people, unfamiliar men in police uniforms, her mother's horrified gape, Kevin's wide-eyed stare.

Cindy tried to cry for help, but her lungs burned with acid and fire. Her mother started shrieking that she was hanging herself, they had to stop her, she was killing herself just like her father had tried to do.

The policemen came at her, yelling to each other. The things they said made no sense—cut the *shower curtain*? Couldn't they see it was the *vines*, the whispering greedy *vines* coming from the reaching *wall*?

Too late.

The reaching wall drew her into its papery, rustling darkness.

FIN CHECK

I DON'T KNOW why I still do it, but I always do. Any time I'm passing a sizable body of water, whether it's the ocean, a lake, a man-made reservoir, a wide river . . . I always, always do.

Fin check.

Fin check, head check, tail check. Scanning for some shape to break the surface. A rising triangular fin or tapered head upon a sinuous neck, a bump with spouting blowhole, the flat paddle of a tail, the ominous moving-bulge wake of something big.

As a kid, I was fascinated by stories of lakes and lake monsters, leftover dinosaurs, legendary denizens of the deep. Each year when family discussion came 'round of where to take our summer vacation, some such lake or another was unfailingly my enthusiastic vote.

A vote no one else ever seconded, of course. Not when there were theme parks; was I crazy? Who wanted to be stuck in the foggy cold by some murky lake when there were roller coasters and thrill rides and snack bars and souvenir stands and girls in short-shorts?

Once, I tried to be clever, suggesting a trip to Hawaii. Golden sandy beaches, surfing, hang-gliding, volcanoes, hula dancers, luaus. My plan then, also, being to wheedle in a whale-watching excursion or glass-bottom boat . . . but, no . . . Hawaii was too expensive. And if Hawaii was too expensive, that Atlantis place was out of the question.

Other times, I'd angle for going on a cruise, Alaska or

FIN CHECK

Mexico or the Caribbean maybe, and still get the same answer. I started to wonder why our parents even asked. Why open it up for discussion if they already had a limited selection of driving-distance destinations picked out? To let us think we had any actual power?

So, yeah, summer after summer, it was road-trips, fast-food, and motels. I'd spend the long hours in the car, mashed into a corner by my brothers, peering out the window whenever blue water glimmered. Hoping to see . . . something, anything . . . different and special. It didn't have to be the whole dang Loch Ness Monster or a ginormous killer prehistoric shark. Just . . . something.

What I mostly saw was speedboats and jet-skis. Yet I never got over the habit of looking. Habit? Habit, nothing. Urge. Compulsion. Obsession. Whatever it is, I haven't gotten over it. Still haven't to this day.

You might think that, being an adult now and in charge of my own destiny, I could have finally up and gone to all those places. You'd think I could have gazed at lakes and oceans to my heart's content.

Well, it turns out being an adult sucks.

I have no idea how our parents swung a two-week vacation every year, though I could finally understand, if not necessarily appreciate, the "oh that'd be much too expensive" reply.

There's also time off to consider, not to mention various hassles and logistics. There are spouses afraid of flying and kids with allergies, and what about the dogs, we'll have to kennel the dogs. Besides, the garage needs cleaning out . . . there's yardwork to be done . . . and we've been talking about fixing the porch roof . . .

And this and that and the other thing, until it really is easier to just stay the hell home.

My job does keep me on the road a lot, though not in any romantic rambling cross-country kind of way. It's back and forth and here and there around the metro area. Traffic and tolls. Coffee in a travel mug. Lunch usually drive-thru scarfed behind the wheel.

But, we have a lot of rivers. Waterfront parks and riverfront drives. Bridges, a multitude of bridges ranging from eight-lane concrete interstate to delicate-looking suspension. A lot of rivers, a lot of water. A fair amount of shipping in the industrial district. A fair amount of recreational and pleasure crafts where it's more scenic. Some where the surface is flat and glassy-smooth, mirroring skyscrapers and clouds. Some where turbulence rushes whitewater between rocks and rock-edged pools.

Know what I do?

That's right. I fin check. Every time.

What all have I seen so far? Pretty much zilch. Occasional sea lions or otters down by the marina. Once, a giddy moment of *at last!* life-affirming excitement as water swelled up around a surfacing mass . . . that turned out to be engineering students from a local university testing their remote-operated submersible . . . I got in a damn fender-bender over that one, rear-ending the car in front of me.

I tell myself to knock it off, to just give up. There's never going to be anything, no incredible jaw-dropping sightings. No immense white whale or toothy plesiosaur is going to rise up and stun the world. No giant squid is going to snare and tear down bridges with writhing tentacles.

And yet . . . and yet . . . and yet . . .

Still. Fin check. Every time.

Even now, especially now, as I'm sitting in bumper-to-bumper rush hour complicated by construction. I cast my gaze past joggers on the lakeshore path, moms with strollers, guys with dogs, kids on bikes. A few people are out in those stupid-looking pedal-boats. Ducks and geese that had been bobbing serenely take sudden flight in quack-honk cacophony, wings beating, shedding feathers and showers of droppings–

–*because*–

I stomp the brakes. The car behind hits mine, but we'd barely been moving and the impact barely registers. I'm

FIN CHECK

unbuckled and out my door before the other driver even starts swearing at me.

–because–

Fin check, and my god there's no mistaking, that *is* a fin for sure!

Rising eight feet above the surface, maybe ten, slicing water into sluicing wakes to either side. A fin, dark greenish-grey and mottled, somehow ridged and spiny. With the swelling displacement of a huge long body . . . with a spine-crested head emerging . . . eyes the size of basketballs, in soulless evil oil-black . . . gaping jaws and monstrous teeth . . .

It chomps one of the pedal-boats into bloodied shreds of fiberglass and flesh.

And, in the screaming chaos that ensues, I can only cheer.

For Austin James

DUMPSTER DIVING

THE BEAST WATCHED from the shadows. Hunkered down. Sleek and ready. Poised. Alert. Every sense humming, keen in the darkness, alive to the night.

Hungry but waiting. Waiting for the moment, for the time to be right.

Waiting to feed.

"The Devil."

Rachel tried not to listen.

"Devil stole my cigarettes."

Tried to tune out her aunt's voice.

"Do you hear me, girl? The Devil stole my cigarettes!"

"Shut up, you old bitch! The Devil wouldn't smoke menthols!"

Damn it. She knew better than to respond. Responding didn't do any good. All it did was make people look at her funny. Look at her funny or take those sidling little quick-steps away.

Was better when they ignored her, when she could be one more part of the city, one more part of the landscape. Just another . . .

What were they now?

Bums? Bag ladies? Street people? Homeless?

Houseless, some of them said. Proud about it. Swaggering. We *have* homes, a tent city or a cardboard box

DUMPSTER DIVING

in an alley or a sleeping bag under a highway overpass can be homes, we just don't have *houses*, don't *need* houses, fuck you.

She trudged on, shoulders bent forward in her big coat, hat pulled low, sneakers mended with duct-tape slapping the cracked concrete.

"The Devil—"

"I said shut up!" Rachel shouted.

Should get rid of her, get rid of Aunt June. People at the hospital said the meds would do that, would make it so she didn't have to hear Aunt June yowling about her goddamn cigarettes all the time. But Rachel was wise to their games. They lied. They didn't know anything. They even tried to tell her Aunt June was dead, had been dead almost twenty years, how about that for stupid? All to get her to take their evil meds? The meds were poison, maybe CIA mind-control microchips or tracking devices.

Well, she wasn't falling for that. No sir, no way, no how.

If she was going to get rid of Aunt June, she'd have to do it herself. The time she'd climbed up on the bridge, hadn't she been trying to do exactly that very thing? Not jump, not commit suicide, for fuck's sake. She wasn't suicidal; she'd never been suicidal. It had just come to her, that was all. Aunt June was afraid of heights, so if Rachel climbed out on the bridge rail, it'd scare the old bitch and she'd go away.

She had *told* them that at the hospital. Not her fault nobody would believe her.

A metallic, almost musical jingle made her glance up from the sidewalk. Here came Tommy and Jay-Zee from the direction of the college. Pushing their cart, its wire basket overloaded. Cans. Beer cans, pop cans, beer cans. On their way to the recycling center over behind the used-car lot. Obviously pleased with their haul. Grinning, giving each other good-natured shit, slapping high-fives.

Rachel grimaced. Grubby, filthy hands smacking together. Disgusting. She stopped in her tracks and fished a plastic bottle of sanitizer from her coat pocket, stripped off her heavy green rubber dishwashing gloves.

Squirt. Rub, rub, rub. The tingle, the coolness, the sting when it got into the raw, chapped patches on her skin.

Better.

The beast's nose twitched, sampling the air.

So many smells . . . food smells . . .

Too soon. Too early. The time wasn't right. Still too much activity, too much noise, too much chance of being seen.

Oh, but the hunger.

Oh, but the tempting smells . . .

"Devil came right in my room and stole my cigarettes, pissed in my coffeepot, coffee tastes like Devil piss!"

"Nobody cares," Rachel said.

Out loud again, damn it.

And someone heard her . . . a nice-dressed woman walking by heard her, stopped, frowned a frown of pitying sadness. Approached in that tentative way they did when they didn't know if you might jump at them with a knife or start babbling about Jesus–

"Are you all right?" the woman asked.

Rachel twisted away and mumbled. Sure, this might just be some nice-dressed person out to be kind, but it might also be one of those CIA operatives scanning for microchips. Or a clone. The government did that, replaced people with clones.

"Here," the woman said, holding out something.

A folded bill. A dollar?

A five!

A trick, probably. The government also coated money

DUMPSTER DIVING

with drugs that would seep in through your skin, get into your head, make you crazy. But Rachel had them on that one! Rubber gloves, so as long as she didn't touch the paper with her bare hands . . .

She pinched it from the woman's outstretched hand, hunching her head low, muttering thanks. Five dollars, that would be a hot breakfast. Or, even better, a canister of those Lysol wipes.

Once the kindly woman—or maybe government clone dispensing drugged money—had gone on her way and wasn't looking back, or following, or reporting into a walkie-talkie so that the agents could swoop in and grab her, Rachel continued down the street.

Feeding. Finally, finally, feeding!

The moist ripping, the sinking in of sharp teeth and the tearing off of ragged, greedy hungry mouthfuls. Claws piercing and pulling.

Gnash and gulp, chew and swallow.

Juices gushing, fluids oozing.

Feeding!

The apartment complex was around the corner. She paused, looking up at the bright squares of light behind the balconies. Some had curtains drawn, some did not. Some weren't bright at all, dark squares catching the reflective red-white glimmer of traffic on the highway.

Were apartment-dwellers technically houseless?

Rachel snorted. Not these ones, that was for sure. Houseless or homeless or bag ladies or bums, *they* all knew how to save. How to conserve and recycle. How to be thrifty and clever. How not to waste. Hadn't she seen Pete just yesterday at the mission soup kitchen, with his scavenged cigarette butts laid out neatly before him on a sheet of newspaper? He'd go around gathering them from ashtrays and gutters, outside of restaurants, by taxi stands, at bus stops. Then pick them apart to roll his own with the leftover tobacco and a fresh pack of papers.

"Devil stole *my—*" began Aunt June, indignant.

"Shut *up*!" Rachel emphasized it by whapping the heel of her hand against her temple, and that startled the old bitch into silence for a change.

No, these apartment-dwellers didn't know anything about that. Just as well, though, just as well for Rachel. If they had, she wouldn't find such an amazing assortment here each week.

The secret was to show up the night before trash day.

And oh, the things that just got thrown away!

Not just food, though food was the most of it. How anybody could toss a half-finished sandwich in the garbage . . . or chicken carcasses with that much meat still clinging to the bones . . . blocks of cheese only spotted a few places with mold . . . bread and rolls that were stale and hard but edible . . . peanut butter jars with tablespoons' worth of scrapings on the sides . . . pizza boxes full of crusts . . . fruits and vegetables only gone a little bit spongy-soft in places . . .

True, it did mean digging through mounds of dirty diapers, used tissues and Band-Aids and feminine hygiene products, cat food cans and stinking cat litter, salad bags that had turned to slimy green glop, rancid bacon and lunchmeat packagings, cartons of spoiled milk, eggshells, and worse.

But sometimes, there were prizes even beyond food. She often found magazines and books, video and music tapes, busted appliances, discarded clothes, shoes, cracked dishes . . . a purse with a busted handle, a broken hairbrush, a torn sofa cushion . . . all kinds of things!

Once, she'd found a gold-foil gift box with three pieces of chocolate left inside, and while it was true coconut crème was never going to be Rachel's favorite, who in their right mind would throw out chocolates?

DUMPSTER DIVING

A sound, and the beast froze. Tensed. Crouched low.
Listened.
Someone near. Someone coming.
A shrill creak, a wafting of fresher air and a spill of dim light. Movement. Noises of exertion. Panting and grunts.
The someone was *there*!
A thrust from heavy hindquarters launched the beast to attack.

Rachel jerked back as the snarling monster lunged.
"The Devil!" shrieked Aunt June. "Gonna steal *your* cigarettes! See how *you* like it! Steal your cigarettes and rape you and stab you in the urethra!"
She saw bristling fur, flat hateful glowing-yellow eyes, shreds of meat and gristle dangling from savage jaws, vicious black claws raking. She smelled its vile breath and musty, musky, loathsome animal stench. Felt the heavy impact of its hot, hairy body slamming against her, knocking Rachel back, off-balance, her feet skidding in an inch-deep layer of sour sludge.
The scream that had stuck in her throat on the inhale came out in a coughing grunt. She landed hard on lumpy garbage bags. Some burst, showering her with coffee grounds, potato peelings, long cold clammy gluey strands of overcooked pasta.
It went for her face, black lips skinning back from wicked teeth.
Her gloved hands flew out in a desperate defensive gesture.
A snag, a rubbery stretching pulling snag, and then puncture.
And then pain.
Furious, burning, boiling pain.

"Just the way I wanted to start my day."

Tony Vadin glanced over at his partner, who was grimacing and shaking her head. "At least you get to start your day, Alex," he said. "Our D-B here isn't so lucky."

She snorted, the worldly-to-the-point-of-jaded snort of someone with twice his years on the force. "Anybody who'd end up naked and strangled in a pile of garbage was never gonna be all that lucky to begin with."

A small crowd had gathered on the other side of the yellow crime-scene tape they'd strung up. More onlookers had taken to their balconies, all rubbernecking for a view. Tony and Alex had covered the corpse with a tarp while waiting for the forensic team to arrive, but there were still plenty of people taking pictures.

Including, Tony noticed, the grandmother of the teen who'd called in his grisly early-morning discovery. Poor kid was still green and shaky, but was he getting a word of comfort from anyone?

"We don't know for sure it was strangulation," Tony said. "There's blood—"

"Look at the neck. Discoloration, bruising. We're talking big hands here. Big, powerful hands, brute strength and a lotta anger to crush someone's windpipe like a damn drinking straw."

He shrugged. "We'll see."

Alex sneered a glare at him.

Just then, the forensics van pulled into the lot, threading between the garbage truck and their car. Alex shifted the glare in that direction.

"And I'll tell you," she went on, "if any of them feels like he's gotta be a CSI smartass, do the Caruso, slip on the ole sunglasses, say something like *time to take out the trash* . . . I'm gonna shoot him in the foot."

DUMPSTER DIVING

Teeth snapping, snagging her gloves, piercing them, piercing through, gouging deep into skin and flesh.

Blood running down her wrists in hot wet rivulets, spattering her cheeks and lips as she struggled to hold the beast back. It wanted her face, wanted her vulnerable eyes, her tender throat.

Claws scrabbling, digging into her upper arms and chest, raking and ripping. Tearing long gashes in the threadbare old coat, only to be stopped by the sweater under that, and the men's flannel shirt under the sweater. Layers were where it was at for warmth, and layers were saving her from being flayed wide open . . . if she could keep the beast away from her face—

Rachel jolted awake, shuddering all over. She thrashed to a sitting position before she fully knew where she was. Things around her slid and clattered, dislodged by the sudden movement.

She clutched at her chest, felt it rising and falling with panicked breaths, felt the hammering thunder of her heart beneath all those life-saving layers. Her other hand flew to her neck, then her face.

Not hurt. Not torn and bleeding.

She was in a crude lean-to, some half-assed construction of slats, pallets, and scraps of plywood. Now she could dimly remember crawling into it, onto a layer of flattened cardboard boxes and newspapers. Somebody's place; it smelled of cheap wine and B.O. and piss. But no one had shown up in the middle of the night to claim it or roust her, so now here it was morning. She'd slept; she'd dreamed that awful dream . . .

God, it had seemed so real! Real enough that when she lowered her hands to inspect them in the weak daylight, she still almost expected to see them mangled and covered with—

Blood?

Her gloves were gone. Her sturdy green rubber dishwasher gloves were gone, and her hands were caked in red-brown smears of what could only be dried blood.

"What . . . no," Rachel said.

Blood! On her hands! All over her hands! But she wasn't hurt, she didn't seem to be injured anywhere. Unless she'd suffered a nosebleed in her sleep?

A tentative snuffling inhale told her that her nose seemed clear enough.

Maybe it wasn't hers? Maybe it was someone else's blood?

That thought—someone else's blood on her, bodily fluids, filthy and disgusting, like shit, like spit, like semen—made her gag. She dumped her coat pockets in a frantic search for the little plastic bottle of sanitizer, found it, and squeezed a dollop into each palm.

The blood went from red-brown to watery scarlet. Rachel sobbed as she pulled up wads of newspaper, scrubbed her hands with them, applied more sanitizer, scrubbed again. Over and over. Over and over. Until the plastic bottle was empty. Her hands tingled with cool, clean relief. Didn't even sting at her cuticles, let alone in any scrapes or scratches she might have missed.

Better.

Then she noticed what else she'd dumped from her pockets. Her gloves. Crumpled rubber. Green streaked with more dried red-brown. Ragged with holes. Tattered into flaps. They looked like a dog had used them for a chew-toy. And clotted with tufts of what might have been . . . fur?

The dream, the nightmare, rushed back at her. Again, she felt the sharp teeth, the feverish weight of that bestial body. The gush of blood running down her wrists.

Rachel lowered her gaze to her chest. Her coat was torn in thin slashes. Claw marks. A missing button that hadn't been missing the day before. The front of her sweater was a straggle of loose yarn loops. There was fur on her clothes too. Dark, coarse.

DUMPSTER DIVING

Nightmare . . . dream . . . or memory?

She stared at her hands. Clean. Unmarked.

She remembered those same hands wrapping around a furry neck. Gripping. Squeezing. Her thumbs pushing hard against corded tendons, against cartilage that crackled and then gave with a sickening crunch.

The forensics unit had managed to refrain from doing the Caruso and instead went about their tasks with matter-of-fact efficiency. For Tony and Alex, it was business as usual: taking statements, deflecting questions, arguing with the sanitation workers and the apartment manager about how long this was all going to take and when trash pick-up service could resume.

The body was hauled out, bagged, and loaded into the back of the van. Once that part was done, most of the onlookers began to disperse. Show's over, folks, no more naked corpses to gawk at.

"As if anybody wants to look at some dead hobo's junk flopping in the breeze," Alex said, giving another sneer and shake of her head. "Makes you want to reach for the brain-bleach, huh?"

Tony nodded and moved on to continue getting statements . . . which turned out to be a whole lot of not much. Nobody here seemed to recognize the vic, know what had happened to him, or how he'd gotten in the dumpster. Not that they were willing to own up to, at any rate.

When he spotted the shabby old woman lurking furtively at the end of the parking lot, muttering to herself, he wondered if Alex had been onto something with the hobo thing. If so, if their vic was one of the city's teeming population of homeless, maybe someone else from the city's teeming population of homeless might know him.

He approached with the same kind of caution he might

use on a skittish animal, well aware from past experience that cops weren't often greeted with open arms by these folks. The cops were the ones who moved them along from park benches and doorways, the ones who slammed them in the drunk tank or the shelter or rehab.

Her hands twisted and rubbed, twisted and rubbed, moving around each other. Tony suppressed a shiver as he suddenly couldn't help thinking of a college production of *Macbeth* he'd seen, dragged to it by a drama major girlfriend. This woman was like the witches and Lady Macbeth rolled into one.

As he got closer, he realized that she wasn't as old as she'd appeared at first. She was short, stocky, wide-hipped and bottom-heavy. The masses of hair spilling from beneath her knitted cap were unkempt but fairly clean, and more black than grey. Her eyes darted this way and that, nervous, in a round and weathered face that hadn't been on the receiving end of makeup or moisturizer in a long time.

The layers of mismatched second-hand clothes . . . the sneakers with half-detached soles wrapped in duct tape . . . the scuffed satchel worn with its strap across her body and its bag clutched tight under one elbow . . . yes, definitely homeless . . . but she didn't reek of alcohol or the acrid tang of drugs, and when those darting eyes flicked up to meet his gaze, they seemed relatively clear.

"Ma'am," Tony said in his gentle-but-firm cop voice. "I'm Detective Vadin; do you mind if I ask you a few questions?"

He seemed nice. But then, they always did when they wanted to. They could seem nice as pie when they wanted to.

Rachel looked at him. He'd asked for her name, and she figured that was all right. She'd tell him her name, and then it would be her turn to ask him a question.

DUMPSTER DIVING

"Rachel," she said. "Rachel Jarvis. Are you the real you, or the clone you?"

The moment she said it, the moment it came out of her own mouth and she heard it with her own ears, she could hardly believe it. How crazy it sounded. She flinched, waiting for Aunt June's hectoring voice to start in . . . what was she doing asking about clones when she should be reporting how the Devil stole . . .

. . . only Aunt June, for a miracle, didn't have anything to say.

"Far as I know, I'm the real me," the policeman said. Watching her in that speculative, not-quite-frowning way, the way that they would when they were trying to figure out whether they should cart you off to the psych unit or the jail. "You live around here, Ms. Jarvis?"

She shook her head.

"Homeless?" he inquired, not in any kind of mean way.

"Houseless," her mouth said, for no good reason.

God, was she losing her marbles? Houseless? Really?

"Do you know what happened here, Ms. Jarvis? Rachel? Do you know anything about the man that was found in the dumpster this morning?"

Again, she shook her head. If anything was crazy around here, *that* was the crazy part. She had left the lean-to and come back here with the idea she'd look around and figure out once and for all whether she'd dreamed or imagined or what.

"There wasn't a man," she said. "There was a monster. An animal. It bit me."

"Bit you?" he asked, in a kind of prodding echo.

Rachel stripped off her replacement set of gloves and held out both hands. Small, neat, clean, unmarked. Even the spots normally so red, so raw, so chapped from washing them as often as she could, from dousing them with sanitizer, from scouring them with Lysol wipes, even those spots were smooth.

"Bit my hands," she said.

What she really wanted, needed, right now, was a sink. A good bathroom sink with hot water and plenty of soap. Lather and scrub. Scrub and lather. Rinse and rinse and rinse. Until her skin was bright pink and clean as could be.

"Okay," the policeman said with a tone of resignation, like he knew he wasn't going to get anything useful from her, but he hadn't totally closed the book yet.

"I'm not—" Rachel began, and stopped. She blinked. Not what? Not lying? Not making it up? Not delusional? Not crazy?

"Were you here last night, ma'am? Rachel?"

"My aunt is dead," she said, blinking some more, the words coming slow and stunned. "Aunt June, she's dead, she's been dead for *years*."

"All right then."

"I was hearing her. In my head."

"Okay. Sure."

"I don't hear her anymore!"

"Whatever you say, ma'am." And she could almost feel the mental snap as he did close the book. Dismissing her as just another loony.

"No, wait, please, wait!" Rachel said, and reached out to pluck at his cuff.

He drew his arm away and gave her a tight little smile. "Thanks for your help."

"But there was!" she cried as he started to ease back from her. "There was an animal, it bit me, it bit me so I choked it, I choked it!"

At that, he threw her a sharper look. "Choked it?"

She held up her hands again, remembering how she had squeezed with blood trickling out from under her shredded gloves, remembering the seething toxic agony in her mauled flesh. Remembering how her thumbs had dug into the beast's furry neck, how its eyes had bugged at her from their dark masklike markings, how foamy spit had sprayed from its jaws, how its bushy ringed grey-and-black tail whipped back and forth as its claws scrabbled against

DUMPSTER DIVING

her coat and its body thrashed like a sack of hot, damp, horribly alive laundry. Remembering how she had choked the life from it, crushed its throat, shoved it off of her, and clambered slipping in the garbage, in that rancid sludge and slime, pulling herself over the side, falling to the pavement, the hollow bang of the dumpster's lid slamming shut . . .

Rachel shrieked, flung her crossed arms over her face, and fled.

"The hell was that all about?" Alex asked. "With the Hatter, back at the scene?"

"Not sure," Tony said. Hatter, he knew, was Alex-ese for crazy person, from "mad as a hatter" and "tin-foil hat brigade."

Not sure, but it had been on his mind ever since. Nagging there in the corners.

Choked it, she'd said. The way the vic in the dumpster had been choked . . . but Alex was right in that it would have taken someone strong and powerful, someone with big hands, to throttle a person like that . . . the Jarvis woman's hands were small, though, and while she was stocky, she couldn't have overpowered a man that size.

Besides, Rachel Jarvis had also claimed she'd been attacked and bitten by some kind of animal. Or monster. And that her dead aunt talked to her. Didn't exactly make for the most credible story all around.

It preyed on him just the same.

Rachel wandered her usual haunts most of the day, feeling out of sorts wherever she ended up. Impossible as it seemed, she almost missed having Aunt June complaining about her Devil-stolen cigarettes. Her head felt emptier, lonelier, somehow.

CHRISTINE MORGAN

The shelter on Bryson Street was women only, and she got there before the evening rush. Early enough for a good hot shower and one of the beds that was a real bed, not a cot or a pallet on the floor. Dinner was going to be ham, green beans, cornbread, milk.

She sat on the lumpy mattress, fully dressed, rocking back and forth, watching the other women as the place slowly filled. Listening to their talk, their deals, their sob stories, their delusional ramblings. Crack whores, battered wives, schizos, drunks. Some had hollow-eyed kids in tow, and crying babies.

"I'm not crazy," Rachel said to the tubby, sullen girl doing her nails on the next bed over. "I was, but now I'm not."

"Whatev." With a bored eyeroll.

"It was an animal. A raccoon. In the dumpster. It attacked me. So I choked it. Killed it. But then it turned into a man. It was a . . . a . . . were-raccoon."

"Yeah."

"It bit me." Rachel looked at her hands. "The bites healed. *I* healed. My hands, my head, the mental illness. Cured me."

"Right," said the girl. "You got bit by a were-raccoon and it cured your crazy so now you're totally sane. Sure."

"I know how it sounds."

"Whatev," she said again. "Hey, got a smoke?"

Tony Vadin frowned as he looked over the ME's report.

Cause of death was strangulation. Alex had called it. Crushed larynx and asphyxiation. The bruises left by the killer's hands were oddly blurred and unclear.

Undigested stomach contents suggested he'd been eating out of the garbage shortly before he died.

Lab work showed that the blood on the vic wasn't his own . . . it came from an unidentified female.

DUMPSTER DIVING

In the vic's mouth, caught between his teeth, were several scraps of thin green rubbery material. As if from dish gloves.

Like the green dish gloves Rachel Jarvis had been wearing?

Damn it, but it didn't add up. For one thing, she hadn't been wounded despite her claims of being bitten. For another, her hands couldn't have throttled the life out of anything much bigger than a kid or a small dog.

He was technically off the clock, Alex long since gone. Tony should have been out of here himself by now.

Instead, he decided to swing by some of the homeless shelters on the way.

Ham for dinner, baked beans, cornbread, milk . . . pudding for dessert . . . and hungry though she was, Rachel left before the meal was served.

Something was going to happen. She didn't want it to happen at the shelter, didn't want it to happen in front of all those strangers.

Random pieces of thought flickered through her head. Old movies . . . gypsies . . . the full moon . . . wolfsbane . . . silver bullets . . .

And this was her *not* being crazy?

Maybe the sullen girl from the next bed had been right.

But she could feel it. Could feel the something about to happen. Feel it in her bones like there was a heat inside of them, the way a log smoldering in a fire might crack and reveal flaring, glowing embers under its coating of ash-covered bark.

She walked with her head down beneath a purplish twilight sky clouded with the murky orange reflections of city lights on smog. Her rubber-gloved hands made faint but persistent squeaky noises as she rubbed them together, rubbed them, rubbed them.

"Ms. Jarvis? Rachel?"

Her head snapped up. She found that she could see perfectly well, surprisingly well, despite the sprawling shadows of encroaching night.

"We met earlier," the man said. "I'm Detective Vadin. Do you remember?"

As if she was stupid, not crazy. When she was neither. Or was she?

A last reddish smudge slid down the windows of a skyscraper, the sun sinking below the horizon.

Pain clenched in her midsection like a hot meaty fist. Rachel cried out, bent double. Inside the rubber gloves, her hands itched, itched, bristled and itched. Her whole body, every inch of her skin, went bristly and itchy.

"Ms. Jarvis?" Sounding concerned but wary.

She had to get away from him. Off the street. Out of sight. To someplace dark, secure, safe.

"Whatever it is, I can help," he said.

Rachel shoved past him and stumbled in a clumsy run toward the nearest alleyway. It was lined with trash cans and dumpsters, strewn with garbage, but it was her haven, her only chance.

The Jarvis woman blundered down the alley, ignoring his shouts. Her voice trailed back to him in strange, guttural cries.

Tony swore, drew his gun in one hand and flashlight in the other, and followed. "Ms. Jarvis!"

She fell sprawling. Her satchel tumbled and came open, scattering her meager belongings. Tony thought he glimpsed another green rubber dish glove, this one bloodstained and chewed up like it had been run over with a lawn mower.

"Don't move," he told her.

Rachel Jarvis huddled facedown. Her body trembled

DUMPSTER DIVING

in the old oversized coat. Her limbs jerked. She drew herself in, tucking into the fetal position, curling up smaller than he would have thought possible.

He stopped a few paces away. "Rachel?"

All he could see was a shuddering fitful hump lost in layers of secondhand clothes. He inched closer. When she still refused to answer, Tony reached down with the flashlight and used it to flip up the edge of the coat.

A raccoon burst from the tangle of clothing, thrashing its way free. Tony yelled with surprise. Reflexively, he kicked out, felt the solid impact of connection, felt a quick sharp sizzle across his ankle. An involuntary step back brought his heel down on something slippery, and then he was on his ass in a pile of garbage bags.

He held on to the gun but dropped the flashlight. In its rolling, unsteady beam, he saw the raccoon take off down the alley at a clumsy-looking but surprisingly fast waddling lope.

Then it was gone, lost to the night.

Tony Vadin sat stunned, looking from the empty tangle of clothes to the direction the raccoon had gone. Finally, he pushed himself up, hissing at the pain in his ankle. He bent to investigate. Torn pants, torn sock, torn skin.

The damn thing had bitten him.

TAGGERS

"**NOT AGAIN,**" Edgar said. "Not a-goddamn-gain."

He stopped on the cracked sidewalk, about halfway between a paper bag with empty beer cans spilling out of it and a pile of dogshit that had been there so long even the flies didn't bother with it anymore.

Morning traffic rolled by on the expressways above, the rumble of tires and the drone of engines a constant steady vibration interspersed by the occasional blat of a horn, brake-screech, siren-wail, or crunch of a fender-bender. Down here, in the part of town now known as The Gulch, few cars moved. Plenty of the ones lining the streets *couldn't* move, or hadn't in years. Rustbuckets, husks, and stripped hulks, for the most part.

Not much sunlight made it through the gloom-shadow cast by the maze of concrete, asphalt, and steel overhead. What did was thin stuff, tinged like old newspapers from the perpetual fug that hung in the exhaust-smelling air. It didn't flatter what hadn't been a nice neighborhood even before the so-called marvel of urban renewal and modern engineering had gone in.

Still, there was more than enough to show Edgar Norris in all-too-clear detail what had been done to the side of his locksmith shop.

Again.

A-goddamn-gain.

Where they *got* those colors . . . so son of a bitching

TAGGERS

bright it about made his eyes bleed . . . who would even *make* spray paint in such vivid, garish hues . . .

And what the hell were any of the designs supposed to *be*? Oh, they couldn't be contented with some hasty outline of titties, or initials in a heart, or clever witticisms about who sucked what anymore. No, it had to be this kind of crap.

Fantasyland murals, illegible letters, undecipherable symbols, images of who-knew-what . . .

Reminded him of those posters from the 60s, those psychedelic head-trip ones, Day-Glo on black velvet, the kind of thing the unwashed hippies hung on their walls as they basked in pot smoke and incense by the glimmer of lava lamps while good and decent hard-working American boys supported the war and fought and died in fetid swamp-jungles half a world away. Peace and love, man, far out, Age of Aquarius, tie-dye, and if we hold hands and sing, we can make the world a better place.

Yeah. Grow the hell up, put on some damn clothes, get a damn haircut, get a damn job.

The same could be said to kids today. To kids ever since, for that matter. Spoiled, sulky brats, the bunch of them. Everything handed to them on a plate and they still whined for more, and if you expected them to actually earn any of it? If you expected them to have any respect for others?

They all needed a good swift kick in the seat of the pants, and Edgar wished he was young and spry enough to do it. If he could just get his hands on the little bastards who'd decided they had every right to scribble their nonsense up and down the cinderblock he'd only repainted last week . . .

Street art, they called it. Or had that term, like "graffiti," been deemed socially hurtful and politically incorrect? No, this was the creative expression of inner-city youth, which ought to be fostered and encouraged as a positive outlet for energies that might otherwise be stifled or turned toward drugs and crime.

CHRISTINE MORGAN

Enough to make a grown man sick to his stomach.

Otherwise turned toward drugs and crime?

Like you didn't have to be drugged out of your mind to do something like this, or consider it "art?"

Like this wasn't a crime? Vandalism was what it was. Theft too. The theft of his time and money to have to cover over their goddamn mess, robbing him as surely as if they broke into his shop or stuck a gun in his face and demanded his wallet.

Looking at the unwelcome decorations on the wall gave him a headache. They almost seemed to float there, and glow there.

Float and glow.

Flow and gloat.

Swirls. Starbursts. Stick-figure letters. Intricate, interweaving, interlaced patterns. Circles and lines. Something that was probably meant to be one of those devil-pentagrams, only with too many angles, and in a shade of pink his mind wanted to identify as "electric bubblegum."

All the colors were like that. Electric bubblegum, acid lemonade, neon watermelon, hyper-lime, fiery creamsicle. Even the darker shades weren't dark. He didn't know how that could be—how could you have bright indigo or incandescent black?

What mattered most to Edgar was the certainty that they'd be a bitch to cover up. Probably need three or four coats. Damn it.

He trudged to the front door, up three cement steps and flanked by windows behind barred grates. The glass had dulled to a murky opacity that showed little of the interior, which was fine by him. Faded sheets of cardstock tilted on the sills announced hours and services, and the emergency number, written in plain felt-tip marker. No website. The sign mounted above the door read: ABLE LOCK AND KEY, followed by the motto, "If you're willing, we're ABLE."

TAGGERS

Irene's idea, the name and motto. Back then, he'd been so young and besotted-in-love that he would have named the business anything she wanted. Didn't even mind her answering the phone that way, chirping it in her sweet, cheerful voice. He would have given her the moon on a string.

Times changed. Live and learn.

Over the years, he'd come to hate it so much he got heartburn every time he saw the motto, but never badly enough that it was worth replacing the sign. He figured it would fall down eventually. Everything did in this decrepit place. The trick would be seeing if the sign fell down before or after the shop itself did.

He unlocked the metal security gate, which creaked on its hinges, and then the inner door. Before going in, he spared a last glance up at the looming network of highways, on-ramps, off-ramps, interchanges, cloverleafs, and express lanes.

A marvel of urban renewal and modern engineering, they'd called it. Something destined to revitalize the struggling central district, bringing more business while improving the commute. A boon for this and future generations.

All for a small tax hike certain to pay for itself within the first three years, yada-yada prosperity, yada-yada working families, yada-yada progress and property values and improving the schools.

So they'd said, but the improved commute sped people past the central district faster, bringing less business, and the result was this. The Gulch. Just another lump of forgotten dogshit.

Smack in the middle of it was ABLE LOCK AND KEY. It sat along a block of similarly run-down establishments, some boarded up, some struggling along; only the pawnshop on the corner could be said to be thriving. An alley split the block between ABLE and the closed bail-bondsman's. It was this alley wall where the "street artists" did their thing.

CHRISTINE MORGAN

Edgar went inside, turning the placard to *Open* with the reflexes of long habit as the door swung shut behind him. The interior wasn't much, a front room and a back room, dim and cluttered, smelling of dust, metal, and nicotine.

In the front room, display cabinets with glass almost as murky as the windows held padlocks, bike chains, lockboxes, hide-a-key containers, a gun vault, jewelry boxes, lockable diaries, and other such assorted odds and ends like those mock-safes made to look like a can of soup. Key blanks hung on a labeled pegboard, the ink on their tags old, smeared, and smudged. On the counter, beside the phone and register, were racks of keychains and novelty accessories. The key grinder squatted on a sturdy worktable, surrounded by drifts of brass shavings.

The back room, windowless, was even grungier. Shelving lined its walls, packed with cardboard boxes, spare parts, and tools. A desk of the dented battleship-grey sort Edgar remembered from his long-ago school days overflowed with files, receipts, paperwork, and bills. The trash can and bulletin board also overflowed, one with wrappers and junk mail, the other with business cards, calendars, take-out menus, and notes. A squeaky swivel chair was tucked into the desk's kneehole. A larger chair, a battered vinyl recliner mended with duct tape, faced a folding table with a TV, radio, and coffeepot on it.

Wedged into the far corner of the back room was a bathroom the size of a phone booth. The condition of it was about three inches short of a health hazard, but Edgar didn't care. It flushed. That was what mattered.

He went about the routine of settling in for another lucrative and productive day here at ABLE LOCK AND KEY, but damned if his gaze didn't keep being drawn to the wall that faced onto the alley. Damned if he was fancying he could still *see* those garish colors and symbols, as if they shined right through solid cinderblock and everything else.

The knowledge of them was like an itch he couldn't

reach, a scent he couldn't quite identify, the title of a song he could almost remember, a persistent sound just annoying enough to be impossible to tune out. Switching on the radio didn't help, neither did making coffee.

After puttering around for a while, Edgar gave up, knowing he wasn't going to be able to get his mind off the mess until he'd gotten rid of it. He had some paint left over from last time, probably not enough, but a start. He took the can, tray, and roller back outside.

The alley wasn't as squalid as usual, which he supposed was a silver lining of sorts. Come to think, it hadn't been that bad lately. The bums had moved on, or *been* moved on, including the space-case who used to mumble about little tiny aliens and their flying saucers all lit up like Christmas. It didn't stink of piss anymore, there wasn't much of a roach or rat problem, and he couldn't remember the last time he'd seen bloodstains or busted vials.

Edgar's grudging gratitude toward whichever gang might be responsible for that did not, however, extend to forgiving them leaving their goddamn Day-Glo scribbles all over his goddamn wall.

Only *his* wall too, he noticed. The opposite wall, the closed bail-bondsman's, was far from pristine, of course. It sported layers upon decrepit layers of events posters, fliers, band logo decals, bumper stickers, and such a tangled scrawl of the ordinary kind of graffiti–titties, dicks, for-a-good-time-calls, so-and-so RULZ, so-and-so SUX– that the original color could barely be discerned. But there was none of the eye-bleeding, needles-to-the-brain neon psychedelic fol-de-rol on *that* side.

Lucky him.

Grumbling, he got to work. He painted over something that looked like a woven wreath of willow branches with stars or jewels twinkling in it. He painted over a bunch of swoops and dots that might have resembled script to someone into those hippie head-trip hobbit movies. He painted over a dark circle that gave the effect of peering down into a deep well, where ripples tried to suggest a face framed in flowing hair. He painted over what he thought was a speckled mushroom with arms and legs and a diminishing inward spiral of tiny shapes like hummingbirds or butterflies . . . or tiny airplanes, how the hell should he know?

Then he was out of paint, and he'd only managed one coat over about two-thirds of the wall. The vivid hues were muted but visible. The largest piece of "street art" left was an oval border of sharp gold interlocked triangles with a pair of ultra-turquoise handprints in the middle . . . not normal handprints, but stylized ones, very thin and with elongated fingers. Under those, in a blinding yellow-blue, were words that Edgar could at least read, even if they still made little sense.

Umbriel was here.

Whatever or whoever the hell *that* was. Good for Umbriel. If Edgar ever caught Umbriel out here again, Umbriel better be ready to run.

He got out-called for some lock changes—landlords and bitter breakups made for his main source of business—and stopped by the hardware store on the way back for another couple cans of paint. He also stopped by Dave's to pick up a pastrami-on-rye, reasoning that if he was going to have heartburn anyway, he might as well earn it.

The activist nutballs across the street had set up one of their petition booths again. Edgar surprised them sometimes by signing his name to whatever their cause-of-the-day might be. He knew he was regarded in the Gulch as a grouchy old fart, which was true enough, but on some matters, his beliefs were apparently downright progressive.

Legalize marijuana? Sure, why not? Everybody else had to pay taxes on their smokes and booze, so why should the hippies get a free pass?

Birth control and abortion? Damn right, and the more

of it the better. Someone wanted to slut around, that was their concern, and why burden the world with the perpetual cycle of their mistakes?

Women in combat? Absolutely; they wanted to fight, let them fight. Whoever thought they were too frail and sensitive must never have gotten into it with the missus. All Edgar hoped was that once they were allowed to shoot terrorists, they'd start squishing their own damn spiders.

Gay marriage? Only fair. Let them suffer same as anybody else. Let them get nagged at day and night. Let them be screwed over for alimony too. Let them shell out child support for a bunch of mouthy, ungrateful little shits who thought the world owed them whatever the hell they wanted.

Let them find out decades after the fact that it was no coincidence after all the middle brat looked more like the manager at the Stop-n-Shop where Irene had worked part-time as a checker . . .

He shoved that thought away and trudged across the street to see what the current crusade was. Some of them, naturally, he wouldn't touch with a ten-foot pole. Who gave a crap about animal testing or chemicals in food? No cell phones while driving, sure, to keep everybody else safe . . . but if someone didn't want to wear a bike helmet, well, it was their skull and their neck. More gun laws would keep people safe from criminals? That was a joke; since when were *criminals* impressed with *laws* in the first place? Illegal immigration, same deal, otherwise it wouldn't be *illegal*, would it?

Last time, it had been a "Save the Rave" rally, when a nearby warehouse converted to a dance club got shut down after a raid and drug bust. Edgar hadn't cared either way, so he signed with the idea that if the kids were going to be drinking and drugging up anyway, it would be better to have them all in one place to keep the damage localized. So far, nothing had come of it; the warehouse was still boarded over and locked up tight.

This time, it turned out they were over there now collecting signatures protesting the slap-on-the-wrist sentencing of a city official who'd been caught not just with a hand in the cookie jar but with both arms elbow deep. Edgar was glad to sign that one. If a cushy salary and expense account still wasn't enough, good riddance. Not like *he'd* voted for the greedy idiot anyway.

After lunch, he went back to the alley and finished the paint job. Three coats should have done it, seemed to have done it, but damned if he didn't think he could still see some of the colors bleeding through. Probably a trick of his tired eyes, the lingering effect of having had to look at them, having them practically seared into his retinas.

Tomorrow, if necessary, he'd do another coat. For now, he ached from the exertion. All that bending and stretching and reaching played hell on the old back.

Now, if they had a petition for health care reform, that was another he'd be glad to sign. Used to be that a person could go to the doctor without having to about take out a loan. Edgar knew he was lucky enough to have escaped many of the ailments of age thus far, but even so, keeping up with his regular prescriptions was a big enough bite out of the dwindling budget. He'd make do with aspirin.

A couple of customers came by in the afternoon to get keys duplicated, but the rest of the day was quiet. Edgar didn't mind. Channel Four was running a *Judge Janice* marathon—he enjoyed watching her rip the deadbeats a new one—and after that was the news, then game shows.

Between *Wheel of Fortune* and *Jeopardy*, he ordered in a pizza because the heartburn still hadn't abated. He crunched some token antacids while waiting for the delivery kid and washed down more aspirin with a warm leftover soda.

At some point, he must have dozed off because he woke in the recliner with the television showing one of those medical dramas where the doctors spent more time having

TAGGERS

sex than treating patients. He burped pepperoni, coughed, checked the clock, and discovered it was almost nine.

Well, not like anybody was waiting for him at home. No one had come in to loot the register while he slept either, not that they'd have gotten much for their troubles.

His back felt better, that was what mattered. Also, he had to piss like Old Faithful.

The bulb over the bathroom sink, a yellowed and flyspecked thing on its last legs, had finally given up. Edgar pissed in the flickering light from the television screen, then noticed that the water in the stained porcelain bowl had a weird silvery shimmer, as if reflecting moonlight through a window.

Ridiculous, since there was a.) precious little moonlight down in the Gulch and b.) no window in the bathroom.

He realized then that it was coming from the wall, just behind his left shoulder.

Edgar finished up with a squirt and a dribble, put the pipeworks away, and turned his head.

Irene had chosen the wallpaper when they first opened the business all those years ago, and it had never been changed since. Originally robin's egg blue with cream-colored pinstripes, it had gone to musty grey, split and peeling to reveal cheap, splintering wallboard beneath.

Shifting spots of multi-colored brightness wavered on the wallpaper.

No.

Wavered *through* the wallpaper. Coming from behind it. Where it encountered one of those peeling splits, it spilled into a slanted ray of microscopic twinkling motes, the way dust looked in a sunbeam.

Through the wallpaper and the wallboard . . . as if flashlights were being played across holes from outside.

But there were no goddamn holes through to his bathroom from the cinderblock alley wall. Hadn't he spent half the damn day out there, painting over? Wouldn't he have noticed?

It came to him then—the "street artists" were back! They were out there right now, thinking he'd gone home for the night, thinking the block deserted so they could beam their flashlights and shake their spray cans with impunity.

His hours of hard work . . . the cost of the paint . . . the last coat probably wasn't even goddamn *dry* yet . . .

The nerve!

No point calling the police. They had crack houses and raves and gang fights and domestic violence to deal with— *real* crimes. They'd only laugh at one of the neighborhood old farts bitching about kids doing graffiti.

Unless, of course, he stormed out there to confront them and the kids proved to be gang members after all and *shot* him . . .

He stormed out there to confront them anyway. If they wanted to risk gunshots, that was their problem, and if they tried coming at him with switchblades, that was why he paused long enough to grab a hammer from the worktable.

The sidewalk was empty. Overhead, on the expressways, commuters had been replaced by truckers, semis and long-haulers crossing the city. A souped-up car stereo whumped and thumped bass thunder from blocks away.

Edgar went to the corner of the building, saw nothing, took another step, and the alley was suddenly awash in glimmering lights and colors. Bright neon blurs went swooping and sweeping and swirling around, leaving streaky after-images. He thought of kaleidoscopes and prisms, rainbows, mirrored disco balls, those glowstick things kids cracked and shook, laser light shows.

Strange sounds filled the air too . . . a whirring-humming-twittering-chiming-tinkling-buzzing . . . something like tiny bells, and something like the fluid trill

TAGGERS

of harp strings . . . high girlish giggles and pure choirboy notes . . .

Whiffs of scent and taste, quick and fleeting, teased his senses and vanished. Sweet ones like cotton candy, lemon drops, roses, cake frosting, a kind of berryblue taffy he hadn't found since he was a child. Warm ones like toasted marshmallows, lit candles, cinnamon, laundry fresh from the dryer, buttered popcorn.

He felt the tingle of a brisk sea breeze, and the crisp crunch of autumn leaves, and the invigorating chill of winter air, and green grass in the sun.

Reeling, Edgar squinted and blinked. He shaded his eyes with his free hand, peering into the dazzle in hopes of finding the source.

Shapes . . .

Indistinct shapes in a sudden flurry.

Shrill cries of alarm.

Panic and confusion rushing at him, whirling around him, and Edgar couldn't see, couldn't hear.

Something whizzed past his ear like a wasp and maybe someone had thrown a rock or maybe someone had taken a shot at him and something else smacked into his shirtfront and clung there whapping and flapping like a piece of windblown paper and he slapped it away and another piece flew into his face, a whirlwind of tatters and scraps whipping around him.

He shouted, shielding his head with one arm and taking wild hammer-swings with the other, connecting with nothing more substantial than a styrofoam cup, until it struck the wall and was painfully jarred from his grip. He hunkered down, both arms over his head now, and wondered if he was going crazy, or if he'd walked into a cloud of drug fumes, interrupted an Alice in Wonderland hallucinogenic party.

Then it was over.

Darkness and calm silence descended. Edgar crouched, gasping, heart walloping in his chest, pulse doing drumbeats in his neck and ears, not sure if he was having a goddamn heart attack or not.

When he decided he wasn't, and that he hadn't been shot either, he cautiously looked around. The alley was empty except for him.

But even in the shadows, he saw the unfinished markings on the painted cinderblock. Jigsaw scribbles and designs, crosses and stars and curved triangles. They weren't as vivid as before, not luminous with that floating glow or flowing gloat.

He straightened up and touched one of the images. It smeared. A pale green residue came away on his fingertip. It did not seem like paint at all but some kind of glittery, oily chalk. Didn't smell like paint either, but like a . . . ghost, or echo . . . of the scents that had teased at him before.

The hammer lay where it had fallen. Edgar picked it up and saw residue on its flattened round head as well, though this was much brighter, and red instead of green. Not red like blood but red like the artificial color of maraschino cherries or strawberry syrup.

More red caught his eye, a brilliant shine that reminded him of brake lights on the back of a car or the red of a traffic signal. But even if a broken chunk of the plastic covering of one had been left in the alley, without a bulb behind it . . . even if it caught some random beam of light, it shouldn't have gleamed with such intensity . . .

It wasn't a chunk of red plastic.

It was . . .

A doll?

About five inches high, thin as a twig, its skin and clothes and hair reddish, its translucent glassy-looking butterfly wings patterned with veins and traceries of ruby light.

Edgar bent closer and curled his fingers around the tiny figure crumpled at the base of the alley wall. It weighed next to nothing in his hand, a soap bubble or twist of tissue paper. It draped limply across his palm, slender legs dangling.

TAGGERS

He remembered the sensation of the hammer striking something no more substantial than a styrofoam cup.

Was this what he had hit?

What was it?

Was it a doll? A fairy doll, a character from a Disney cartoon?

The body thrummed as if with a barely-perceptible vibration. A wind-up thing, one of those new remote-controlled gadgets?

He had no idea toys had gotten so intricate–

The fairy-doll twitched. The ruby shine of its wings strengthened.

It . . . felt . . . not like a toy at all.

Alive?

Was that what he was thinking?

It felt alive in his hand, inert but tingling with vitality. Weightless as a hummingbird, moth, or mouse . . . so delicate and fragile . . . yet he'd whacked it with a hammer . . .

The thought occurred to him again that he was going crazy, or had been drugged, or this was somebody's idea of a smartass practical joke. Maybe he was dreaming, still sound asleep in the recliner, and this whole bizarre scene was the result of acid indigestion.

Whichever it was, he decided he'd rather deal with it inside than out here in the alley. He went back in, shut and locked the door, switched the placard to *Closed*, and indifferently shoved papers off the desk until he'd made a clear space. He put the . . .

. . . fairy . . .

. . . in the clear space, then trained the gooseneck desk lamp full on it, a concentrated spotlight like an interrogation or autopsy scene from a movie.

The tiny red face squinched up in unconscious but reflexive reaction to the glare.

Edgar considered.

Okay, say it *was* real, say it *was* a living thing. Never mind the how or why or they didn't exist. Just go with it.

Fine. A fairy. A real live fairy.

He couldn't let it get away until he had some answers.

The thinnest length of chain and smallest padlocks he had in the shop were big and clunky by comparison, but he fashioned a manacle around the fairy's ankle and looped the other end of the chain through a ringbolt in the desktop.

Only then, when it was secured, did he let himself thoroughly scrutinize his captive.

Five inches tall . . . skin an opalescent pinkish-red . . . upswept spiky-feathery hair like a cardinal's crest . . . a teardrop-shaped face with lash-fringed large eyes, the barest nub of a nose, ears flat to the head and tapering to a point, the mouth a lipless slit. The body was long-legged and slim, the chest flat and the hips narrow.

He thought again of Disney cartoons, not Tinkerbell but that other one, the fantasy one set to classical music, with Mickey and the brooms. That was what this reminded him of.

Edgar couldn't tell if it was a boy or a girl. Maybe it was neither, or both, or something weirdly in-between. Its clothes weren't much help. The shiny red pants were so tight it might have been dunked in latex paint. The knee-high high-heeled boots fastened up the sides with intricate rows of the smallest buckles he had ever seen. Its shirt was a red halterneck-style garment of lacy mesh finer than medical gauze.

The wings were like soft glass, or hard clear jelly, resilient but slightly giving when poked with a fingertip. The glowing ruby lines ran through them like the branching veins of a leaf or thread-thin tubes of neon gas.

Nothing about it seemed damaged or injured, despite what had happened. It was obviously much tougher than it looked.

Not to mention impossible.

Edgar wondered again if he was dreaming or drugged but reluctantly concluded this was all too detailed and precise for such an easy explanation.

TAGGERS

That left crazy . . . or real.

The fairy's eyes opened. They were scintillating shades of red, faceted like jewels, without whites or pupils . . . glittering crimson orbs like beaded drops of crystallized blood.

His face must have been looming over it like a giant moon, and probably not the prettiest one either. With a darting whirr, the fairy tried to take off but was brought up short at the end of the chain.

It went nuts.

Fluttering and spinning, buzzing in all directions, yanking to the end of the chain, snapping back, it went utterly nuts.

Edgar had seen someone put a cat on a leash once. The result had been similar to this, only noisier, with more fur and claws. And without ambulance-flasher wings giving off such bright bursts of emergency red that they lit up the whole room.

Finally, it stopped its frenzied flight. It landed on the desk, as far from Edgar as the chain would permit, and tugged with both hands at the manacle. No use. It glared up at him.

Despite his distinct size advantage, Edgar leaned back, unnerved by what he saw in those glittering red eyes.

"Settle down," he said. "I'm not going to hurt you."

The glare continued, piercing. In a high piping-clear voice, the fairy said, "You hit me with a hammer, you big fuckhead."

He sat back further, jaw dropping, not sure if he was more surprised by its speech or its language.

So much for Disney.

The fairy tugged at the chain again, fixing its gaze on the links. Twin hair-fine beams of red light shot from its eyes. Edgar thought of gun-sights and laser pointers, and security grids in heist movies. He winced in anticipation of melt-sizzling metal and acrid smoke, the plink of a link breaking, the fairy's rapid escape.

But the chain held. The red light gleamed harmlessly along it.

"Shit!" The fairy looked back at Edgar.

His wince worsened, now with the anticipation of those beams searing his skin. Or blinding him; hadn't he read somewhere that shining a laser pointer into your eye was worse than staring directly at the sun? He raised his hands protectively in front of his face as if that would do any good.

"Settle down," said the fairy, mimicking his voice in unflattering caricature. "I'm not going to hurt you."

They studied at each other. An uneasy feeling of détente crept in as their speculative pause extended.

"You called me a fuckhead," Edgar said.

"*You* hit me with a hammer, and chained me up."

"Hitting you was an accident. I was defending myself."

"We were just trying to get away! You surprised us. You weren't supposed to be here. You weren't supposed to see."

"We?" Edgar remembered the kaleidoscope blurs of motion, the colors dancing and whirling. "Us? How many of you are there? And what are you, anyway? What were you doing in the alley? You're the ones who've been doing all that damn psychedelic graffiti, aren't you?"

"We're taggers," the fairy said, as if Edgar was the stupidest thing he'd ever met. "It's what we do!"

"It's vandalism, painting all that nonsense on people's walls."

"It isn't paint; where would we get paint, why would we need paint?" The fairy crouched and swiped a hand in a smooth stroke across the desktop, leaving an arc of vivid red on the scarred surface. It was just like the stuff on the wall outside, both oily and chalky, iridescent.

"Fine, so it isn't paint, it's still *my* wall you scribble all over!"

Its little shoulders hitched in a shrug, shifting its glassy ruby-marbled wings. "Well, yeah, where else? And it'd help if you'd leave it alone, you know. Think that's easy? Think

TAGGERS

we like having to keep coming back to redo it?"

Edgar sputtered. "Leave it alone? It's on *my* wall! What, are you going to give me a lecture next about not appreciating street art and the creative expression of inner-city youth?"

"You don't have to appreciate it," the fairy said. "You shouldn't even be seeing it, really, but I guess since you've *been* here so long, it's seeped in over the years."

"What's seeped in?"

"Magic, what else?"

"Magic," Edgar said.

"Dude. I'm a fairy."

"Right. And a tagger. And you tag my wall, *my* wall, with pixie dust."

A tiny hand flicked up in warning. "Fairy dust. We don't mix with pixies, and you don't want to either, old man. We're non-violent. Pixies? Pixies will fuck your shit right up."

"This is insane," Edgar said. "I'm getting a goddamn headache."

"Look, tell you what . . . unlock this chain, let me go . . . you can forget this whole thing ever happened."

"You'll go tag someplace else?"

The tiny red face twisted uncertainly. "Welllll . . . that might be a problem."

"Oh, come on, I'm not asking for three wishes or a damn pot of gold—"

"Dude, that's . . . never mind." Evidently, fairies could get headaches too, judging by the way this one pressed its fingertips to its temples.

"I just want you and your . . . your little fairy-friends to . . . to *tag* off and leave me alone."

"I told you," the fairy said, "you shouldn't even be seeing the tags. It's nothing personal. Ignore them."

"Ignore them? Those . . . colors? Those designs like . . . like I don't know what? Letters nobody can read, or if they can, don't make any sense? You want me to ignore them, there on my wall, damn near glowing in the dark, for all the world to see?"

"Not all the world. Only us."

"What?"

Tiny fingertips massaged harder at tiny temples. "Why me? Why'd he have to catch *me*?" muttered the fairy. "Why not Strobe, or Neon? They'd be able to explain. Or Glowstix. Shit, even Emo."

"Those are your names?" Edgar asked, eyebrows lifting.

"Not our real names. You couldn't pronounce our real names even if you wanted to, which you wouldn't."

"Strobe? Emo? What's yours?"

"Laser."

"Pff. I should have guessed."

"Yeah, well, in the olden days, it was shit like Cowslip, Cobweb, Moth, and Mustardseed," Laser said. "Times change."

Edgar took a deep breath. "If you say so. Just tell me how come, if only fairies are supposed to be able to see your scribbles, I can."

"Because, like I said, some of the magic here must have seeped in since you've been here so long. This place, this shop of yours, it's at a Thinning."

"At a what?"

"Like those fuck-ugly highways up there," Laser said, pointing past the roof. "A junction, an interchange, a merge. For the commute. For the rush-hour traffic flow. You know."

"Here? My shop sits on a gate to Fairyland?"

"Don't flatter yourself. It's a Thinning, yeah, a shortcut to the Low Road, but it's not a great one. We had one of those, but now that we can't use it anymore, we have to make do. This is the best we've turned up so far. We tag it so the others can find it and cross over."

"Because they, these 'others,' they can see your scribbles. Like me."

TAGGERS

Laser nodded, that feathery cardinal's crest waving. "Exactly. It's been here long enough, and so have you, and enough magic's come through from our side, that you've gotten used to it."

"The hell I have!"

"You could see our tags. You saw us when you came into the alley. Dude, you're talking to a fairy right now."

"Or maybe I've gone crazy, like that bum who used to camp out there, the one who was always going on about . . . " His words trailed off.

Little tiny aliens, their flying saucers all lit up like Christmas . . .

"Look," said Laser, "I'm sorry I called you a fuckhead, okay? Just let me go. Maybe we'll find a better Thinning soon, and you'll never have to deal with us again. Sound good? Sounds good. Deal? Deal."

"Hold on, not so fast!"

"Aw, c'mon, you said you wanted to get rid of us."

"But what *you* said makes it sound like I'm stuck with this until you find a better option. What happened to your old path?"

Though Laser's mouth was only that tiny, lipless slit, it turned down in a disgruntled scowl. "They shut us down! Closed the club, boarded it up, and now we're S-O-L!"

"S-O-L?"

"Shit-outta-luck!"

"Wait . . . club? Boarded up? You don't mean that rave warehouse, do you?"

Again, the red crest waved with the fairy's vigorous nod. "It was the greatest! The lights, the music—"

"The drugs?"

"Fuck yeah! Couple hundred or so kids blissed out on E? That kind of uninhibited energy, we used to only be able to get with a dance in a full-on fairy-ring. We took care of them too. Nobody died, nobody messed with anybody else. Umbriel made sure of that. He ran a safe place."

"Umbriel," Edgar said. "I remember that one from the

wall. About the only damn thing out there I could read, not that I knew what it meant."

"Our DJ. Best spinner ever to cross over from Underhill. The trolls always had it in for him, though. The raid? The bust? It was total trollshit, dude! Total trollshit."

"The hell's a troll?"

"Mean-ass fairy haters. A lot of them become cops, and nothing gets them off like ruining our fun."

The idea that there were trolls on the police force somehow didn't seem as surprising as it probably should have.

He was about to ask—though he was sure he'd regret it—how much *else* of this hidden world of trolls, fairies, and magic there was, especially down here in the Gulch, but before he could, there was a sharp knock at the door.

It was followed by a brief but bright pulse of ultra-turquoise light flooding in through the grimy front windows. The interior of the shop lit up with a wavering, eerie shimmer like an illuminated swimming pool at night.

"And what the hell's *that*?" Edgar said instead.

"That," said Laser, grinning, "is Umbriel. You didn't think my friends would ditch me, did you? They went for help."

"Oh . . . "

He went to the door and opened it, and found himself face to face with Umbriel. Or, at least, with a tall, pale, slim, elfin-featured pretty-boy he could only assume was Umbriel.

Certainly *looked* like someone who'd have a name like that . . .

Shock-platinum hair in a spiky mane fell over one of his heavily-eyelinered gold-flecked blue eyes. He wore skinny jeans and high-top sneakers, a thin jewel-studded belt that looped three times around his narrow hips, and a form-fitting black tee shirt with a logo on it of stylized turquoise handprints inside an oval border of interlocking gold triangles.

TAGGERS

"Mr. Norris."

Umbriel did not, however, *sound* like someone who'd have a name like that. His voice was deep, low, resonant, and husky. Not the voice of a person to screw with. Nor were those gold-flecked, eyelinered eyes the *eyes* of a person to screw with. They were . . . old . . . old and wise and filled with a kind of terrible, powerful knowledge that made Edgar instantly accept as truth everything Laser had told him.

He wasn't sure how any of this worked, so, took a guess. "Uh . . . come in?"

With a slight chin-dip of acknowledgment, Umbriel stepped into the shop.

"You've captured one of our own," he said in that deep don't-screw-with-me voice. "Will you relinquish what is ours and show yourself a friend, or keep fairy bound by mortal hand and make yourself our foe?"

Edgar gazed a moment longer into those terrible gold-flecked eyes.

We're non-violent, Laser had said . . . and whether that meant just the little taggers or whether that meant all of them, Edgar decided he'd rather not find out. Besides, skinny and girly though Umbriel might appear, there were probably plenty of magic tricks in his arsenal that could make Edgar's life miserable even without resorting to violence.

He indicated the other room, doing a shuffling backward walk through the cluttered shop to avoid taking his attention off his visitor as much as possible. Umbriel followed, moving with a poised, lithe, gliding silence.

Once at the desk, Edgar had to turn away to focus on unlocking the minuscule manacle. The nape of his neck prickled. His usually-deft fingers felt huge, thick, and clumsy, bumbling logs of dumb meat compared to the fairies' grace.

He got it, though, finally. The chain hissed into a pile on the desktop. Laser took off with a gleeful trill, zipping around Edgar's head in a streaky red blur of motion.

"Ah," said Umbriel, smiling in satisfaction.

No sooner had he than an entire host of small, glassy-winged bodies swept past him. "Laser!" cried a shrill, piping multitude in ecstatic chorus.

They were all the glowing colors Edgar had seen in the alley, vivid green and electric bubblegum, acid lemonade, neon violet and nuclear tangerine, incandescent black, a silver-white like magnesium, rainbows and prisms in a flickering-fluttering dance of lights. Some were dressed similar to Laser, some wore tight vinyl miniskirts and fishnets, some skimpy shorts and tank-tops or went bare-chested in loose saggy-baggy pants.

Laser joined the kaleidoscope dazzle of fairies. They swirled giddily, joyful, darting back and forth, weaving intricate patterns in the air, chattering, laughing their effervescent champagne-fizz laughs.

"Glowstix! Binkie! Blinkie! Jitter!"

"Laser, yay! You're okay!"

"When he caught you—"

"Me and Neon wanted to come after you but Strobe said—"

"—so worried!"

"Emo thought you were a goner!"

" . . . well duh, hammer-whack to the face . . . "

"—it hurt?"

"—he hurt you?"

"All good, he's cool, we worked it out," Laser said. "He's not so bad for a cranky old grouch."

This brought the others swarming around Edgar, engulfing him once more in that cyclone of scents, tastes, and sensations as they jostled to inspect him up close. Some, he noticed, sported nearly microscopic tattoos and piercings. Others had fuzzy moth-antennae. One buzzed right into his face on dragonfly wings like fans of radioactive Mountain Dew, the little inquisitive head topped by some kind of Dr. Seuss crazy hairdo. It patted him on the end of the nose, leaving a green fairy dust smudge.

TAGGERS

Edgar recoiled, peripherally aware of Umbriel watching with a pretty-boy smirk that was half insolent, half indulgent.

"We should help him, then!" the patter chirped, not at all put off by his recoiling.

Another, bright indigo and twinkling like a skyful of stars, agreed. "The shoemaker-and-the-elves thing, only with keys!"

"This could be our new hangout!" added a pink-and-yellow one wearing a frilly tutu and ballet slippers, clapping tiny hands.

"What a great idea!"

"We can come here all the time!"

Laser laughed, and Umbriel smirked, and Edgar's mouth went dry.

Early the next morning, to the immense surprise of his neighbors in the Gulch, a folding table stacked with flyers had been set up on the sidewalk outside ABLE LOCK AND KEY. Posters decorated with brilliantly-colored designs had been taped to the grimy windows.

By the end of the week, Edgar had collected over five hundred signatures in support of "Save the Rave."

THE NAUGHTY LIST

THEY GOT SENT in after supper, the other kids.

The other bad kids.

Sent to the basement.

No party for them.

No Christmas party with crafts and games, songs, cocoa, cookies, and a visit from Santa with presents.

Not for them. Not the bad kids, the kids on the naughty list.

Parties were a privilege. A special reward.

They hadn't earned it. They didn't have enough points.

Minda sat in the corner and watched them come in.

She never got points.

Like Derp. Derp never got points either, though Derp tried. He really did. He tried really hard to play nice and be helpful, turn in assignments, pass tests, keep his room clean, and all that good-kid point-getting stuff. He just couldn't do it right.

Minda didn't try. Minda didn't care.

Derp meant well, that's what her granny would say. He meant well, but he just couldn't do it right. Derp was big and dumb, kind of clumsy, and he scared people. He didn't mean to do that either, but he did. Even grownups, even teachers, were scared of Derp sometimes. They wouldn't say so, but they were. Minda knew. Minda could tell.

They thought because Derp got frustrated, because he yelled and waved his arms when he was upset, that he must have super-Derp powers. Retard strength, one of the big

THE NAUGHTY LIST

boys had called it. Derp would snap and start hitting, and be strong as ten wrestlers or a wild animal.

But Derp hardly ever hit anybody except for himself. He didn't want to be scary. It made him sad.

Being sent to the basement now made him sad too, Minda saw. He came in with his head down and his feet dragging. His froggy mouth turned down in a crumpled wet fold. He snuffled a sigh as he went to a table and plopped onto a chair. There were some crayons and colorbooks on the table. Derp opened a colorbook to a page with trains and started scribbling.

Tess, Jimmy, and Spencer were next, clomp-tromping down the stairs in a noisy arguing group. They'd had extra chores for being in trouble. They usually were. Jimmy for stealing and lying, Spencer for being a dirty-messy pottymouth, Tess for starting fires.

After them was Lamont, who was new to the school. Smart too. Or too smart. Or maybe both. Minda had heard that his mom was a doctor, the rich kind, the kind that gave ladies new noses. He earned lots of points by getting the best grades on all his tests and assignments. It seemed kind of strange Lamont would be here.

He looked mad about it too. He glared at Miz Parker like he wished she'd be run over by a truck.

Miz Parker didn't notice. She just sat at the desk, drinking coffee and playing on the computer. That was pretty much all she did. Solitaire, Mahjong, Minesweeper, Angry Birds. Unless somebody pitched a total fit, she'd ignore them.

Lamont moved his glare around the room like he'd never seen it before. Maybe he hadn't. Maybe this was his first time to the basement, to the detention hall.

Minda idly wondered what he did. A smart kid with a rich mom losing enough points to miss out on the Christmas party? Must have been something extra bad.

His lip curled up in a disgusted kind of sneer at the sight of the cruddy old furniture, the low bookshelves crammed with cruddy old books, the cruddy old toys. He glanced at Derp, still scribbling loops in the train colorbook. He glanced at Spencer, who was picking his nose, then at Jimmy and Tess, bickering over what to do first.

He glanced last at Minda, sitting in her corner. She kept finger-combing her long straight dark hair down over her face, and avoided his gaze. Lamont sneered the other side of his lip and went to a chair by the stack of puzzles. He sulked into it with his arms crossed over his chest.

"This isn't fair," he said in a grumbling mutter.

"Yeah, dude," said Spencer, digging deeper with a corkscrew motion. "Sucks to be us."

"I didn't want to go to any stupid baby Christmas party anyways," Tess said.

"But there's treats." Derp sighed again, a doleful-soulful sound.

"We'll have snacks," said Jimmy. "They have to give us snacks, they can't starve us in here all night."

"Snacks, right." Tess made a rude noise. "Graham crackers and juice, same as always. Not *good* snacks."

"They get good snacks at the party," said Derp. "Hot cocoa with marshmallows. Frosted snowman cookies. Candy canes."

They all fell silent, thinking about that. In the hush, from beyond the basement, came muffled but cheery holiday music. The party was starting. Footsteps thudded their vibrations as excited kids rushed along the halls and stairways.

Everybody had seen the preparations underway, of course. The school's gymnasium, auditorium, dining room, and courtyard being all decorated . . . twinkly lights and glittery garlands, wreaths, ribbons, cardboard reindeer and penguins, construction paper snowflakes, a real Christmas tree covered in ornaments, a big red chair where Santa would sit to give out presents . . .

"And we're stuck here." Lamont blew out his breath with what was almost a snort.

THE NAUGHTY LIST

"Why're *you* here anyway?" Tess asked the question that had been on Minda's mind.

Lamont scowled and re-crossed his arms.

"I know why." Jimmy flashed a sly grin. "He cut Mikey Nelson."

"No shit?" Spencer perked up. "That was you? Dude!"

"He had to get, like, ten stitches," Jimmy added.

"What'd you cut him with?" Spencer continued, regarding Lamont with interest. "A switchblade? A boxcutter?"

"Should've shot him," Tess said. "Mikey Nelson is a turd."

"A scalpel," said Jimmy when Lamont didn't seem to want to answer.

Derp's forehead creased. "A what?"

"A doctor knife, doofus. You know. Like on the shows. Nurse! Scalpel! Forkseps!"

"Forceps," Lamont said.

"Forksex," snickered Spencer.

"Should've shot him," Tess said again. She made a gun-hand and mimed aiming a headshot at Miz Parker, whose oblivious attention remained fixed on the computer. "Pow."

"She always wants to shoot people," Jimmy told Lamont.

"Or set them on fire," Spencer said. "She's a firebug."

"I am not! You're a litterbug and a bug-killer! But I'm not a firebug!"

"You set shit on fire!"

"That's not why! Jeez! I don't like *fires*, I like *explosions*!" She clenched her fists in front of her face and sprang them open. "Ka-boom!"

"You're Lamont, right? I'm Jimmy. That's Tess. He's Spencer."

"I'm Derp," said Derp. "My real name's Walter, but everybody calls me Derp."

Lamont glanced at Minda again, or at the curtain of

hair concealing her face. He lowered his voice. "Who's she?"

"That's Minda." Jimmy paused, his freckled face twisting in thought. "She's . . . uh . . . "

"Weird," said Tess.

"Effin'-A," Spencer said, not without a note of approval. "Minda's one weird-ass *chica*."

Tess nodded. "Even since before her brother died."

Lamont took yet another look. Before he could decide whether or not to say anything else, the detention hall door opened to admit a shrill, complaining whine.

"You can't do this, I'm telling, I'm gonna tell! My mommy's gonna be sooooooo mad at you!"

Miz Parker leaned over from the computer, saw who it was, and pinched the bridge of her nose like she had a sudden ice cream headache.

"You can't *dooooo* this! I'm the Christmas princess!"

"That's enough, Jolene," said Mr. Gregson, the vice principal. "You had plenty of chances and plenty of warning."

Then he marched in Jolene Sinclair, all sprayed blond curls, chubby pink cheeks, and eyeshadow. She wore a poofy green satin holiday dress trimmed in shiny gold lace, gold tights, and green velvet shoes with golden buckles. Wedged under one arm was a stuffed rabbit almost as big as she was, a fluffy white rabbit wearing a curly blond wig and a green satin dress identical to Jolene's.

"Now you stay here and behave—"

"But I'll miss the paaaaaaarty!"

"Yes," Mr. Gregson said. There might have been a grim glint of satisfaction in his barest hint of a smile. "You should have thought of that before you pushed Kayla off the stage."

"She was in *my* spot! She's a bratty-bratty-bratty-brat and she was in *my* spot!"

The vice principal turned away from her to have an annoyed-sounding conversation with Miz Parker, leaving Jolene to huff in indignation.

THE NAUGHTY LIST

The rest of them watched as she flounced her way to the middle of the room and stood there, pouting.

"What are *you* staring at?" she demanded.

Nobody said anything.

Then Derp spoke up. "That's a really pretty dress."

At once, the pout became a dazzling toothpaste-commercial smile. "Thank you!" She skipped to his table. "I'm Jolene, and this is Bunny-Hoo-Hoo."

"Bunny what?" asked Jimmy, eyebrows raised.

"Bunny-Hoo-Hoo," repeated Jolene. She did a giggle that sounded like metal screeching on glass. "Because she's a bunny, and . . . " She flipped the rabbit over so that its dress fell up around its head. " . . . and here's her hoo-hoo!"

Underneath the skirt were no tights or panties, just furry bunny butt and a puff of white tail, and the kids all laughed like maniacs.

All but Minda, of course, who stayed where she was, quiet in her corner, running her fingers through her hair.

Mr. Gregson's phone beeped. He unclipped it from his belt to check the text.

"And, of course, to top it all off, the damn Santa's not only late but lost," he told Miz Parker. "I need to talk him through the directions."

"Oh, great."

"Then figure out what's going on with the choir microphones . . . " He pressed his temples. "Just make sure this bunch stays out of trouble."

"Sure," she said.

He dialed and left with the phone to his ear. Miz Parker went right back to the computer, clicking away.

"Did you hear that?" said Derp. "Santa's lost."

"So?" Spencer, having worked a fat yellow booger from his nose, squish-wiped it under his chair.

"So, Santa!"

"Not like we were gonna get presents anyways," Tess said.

"*I* am," proclaimed Jolene. "*Lots* of presents. The *best* presents. For me and for Bunny-Hoo-Hoo."

"Are not," Jimmy said.

"Am so!"

"Are not, not now. You're stuck here with *us* now."

"You get squat," Spencer said. "Jack-shit-diddly-squat."

Her lipsticked mouth made a wounded O-shape. "But . . . "

"They're right," Lamont said.

"But that's not *fair*!"

"Tell me about it."

Spencer shrugged and started picking pieces of rubber from the tattered soles of his sneakers. "We're screwed. Effed in the A. Or in the hoo-hoo."

"While everybody else gets Christmas." Derp drew a sad face in the colorbook.

"I didn't do anything wrong!" Jolene fussed with her rabbit's wig.

"Did you really push Kayla off the stage?" asked Tess.

"She was in my *spot*! She's a show-offy bratty-brat, and she thinks she's prettier than me!"

"And she gets Christmas and you don't," said Derp.

"The *good* kids do," Lamont said. "The mama's boys and daddy's girls."

"The goodie-goodies." Tess made a face. "The teachers' pets."

"The kissbutts," said Spencer.

"The tattle-tales," Jimmy chimed in.

Another grumpy silence fell as they pondered the ginormous cruel injustice of it all. Outside, the music was the Rudolph song, bright and bouncy. There were laughs and shouts. Vague whiffs of yummy smells–popcorn, gingerbread, cocoa–wafted on the air.

Lamont looked around at the rest of them again. "We should do something."

"Color?" suggested Derp. "Or puzzles, there's puzzles—"

Spencer flicked a speck of shoe-rubber at him. "No, derp-for-brains!"

THE NAUGHTY LIST

"He means do something about being stuck here," said Tess.

"While *they* have fun at the party!" Jolene added.

"Do something like what?" Jimmy asked.

"Bust out?" Tess did gun-hands again. "Never take us alive, coppers?"

"Jailbreak!" crowed Spencer.

Jolene smacked him. "Shut up! Gawd! Tell the world!"

Miz Parker, without looking over, raised her voice in a bored not-listening way. "Quiet, keep it down."

"She's not gonna let us go," said Jimmy. "And even if she did, then what?"

"Then we go to the party, duh!" Jolene said.

"We'd get in trouble," Derp said. "They'd put us in detention."

"We already are!"

"Oh yeah."

"What else could they do?" Lamont spread his hands. "And at least we'd be able to grab some cookies before they threw us back in here."

"Let's do it!" Tess hopped up from her seat.

"What about her?" Jolene pointed at Miz Parker.

"I got an idea." Jimmy grinned his sly grin again. With his freckles and his red hair, it made him look like a crazy wooden puppet devil-clown doll. He beckoned, and the others leaned close to hear him whisper.

Minda, from her corner, didn't move. Her ears were good but not that good, good enough to only catch snippets of what they said.

" . . . know how she always . . . "

" . . . yeah, in the janitor's closet . . . "

" . . . thinks nobody will . . . "

" . . . won't she . . . "

" . . . how do we get . . . "

" . . . take care of that, trust me . . . "

" . . . let her out, right?"

" . . . worry about it later . . . "

"... I dunno, guys ... "
"... want cookies, don't you?"
"... well yeah ... "
"... everyone agreed?"
"... what about ... ?"

Minda felt six pairs of eyes focus on her then. She ducked her head, hunched her shoulders, and hid behind her hair.

"She's okay," Tess finally said.

"She wants cookies too," said Derp.

"She's with us," Jimmy said to Lamont.

"Can she even talk?" asked Jolene. "Can you even talk?"

"She can talk," said Tess. "She just ... uh ... "

"Doesn't," Jimmy finished. "But she's cool. Right, Minda?"

Minda did a quick nod, still averting her gaze.

"So, we just wait until ... ?" Lamont sort of jerked his chin at Miz Parker.

"Yeah. Act regular."

Jimmy's advice was easier said than done; they tried not only to act regular but act innocent, sitting quietly, coloring, doing puzzles. Miz Parker swept them a few suspicious, uneasy looks. Then she went back to ignoring them in favor of Angry Birds or whatever.

Eventually, more or less on schedule, Miz Parker pushed back from the desk. She made a show of cricking her neck side to side. "I'm going to stretch my legs," she said. "I'll be back in a minute, so, no nonsense."

What she really meant was sneak into the janitor's closet for a cigarette, though the whole school was supposed to be no-smoking. "A Proudly Smoke-Free Zone" the signs said.

Miz Parker stepped out into the corridor. Her shoes clacked on the cement floor. Jimmy, fast like a fox, darted to catch the door before it latched shut. He held it open just a crack, enough for them to peep through.

THE NAUGHTY LIST

Light bulbs in wire ceiling cages cast Miz Parker shadows on the painted-cinderblock walls. The janitor's closet was at the far end, past the stairs, the bathrooms, and the ancient drippy drinking fountain.

Jolene tried to elbow her way between Spencer and Lamont for a better view, or to make sure Bunny-Hoo-Hoo could also see. Derp started to say something, too loud, and Tess elbowed him.

Jimmy gave Miz Parker enough time to get settled and light up. Then, still fox-fast, and quiet as a ninja, he zipped down there, pulled a key from his jeans-pocket, and locked her in. Then he spun and did a big beaming "ta-da!" gesture.

"Hello?" came Miz Parker's startled but muffled voice.

She tried the door, but Jimmy had left the key half-turned and half-stuck from the lock so she couldn't open it from her side.

"Hey! Hello? Is someone out there? Hey!"

Rattle-rattle-rattle. Knock. Thump thump.

It stayed shut. The other kids crept into the hall, tentative and amazed, like mice surprised at being let out of their cage. Freedom, but wariness, because what if it was a trick, a trap? What if the cat was ready to pounce?

Minda trailed after them.

"Hey! Open this door! Did you little shits lock me in?"

"She said shits," said Derp, eyes agog.

"Potty-mouth! That's detention for you!" Spencer whooped at the door. He high-fived Jimmy. "You da man, you slick effin' bastard!"

The rattles, knocks, and thumps, joined by some hammering bangs, resumed loud and angry, but the door continued staying shut.

"Oh, you're going to be in *so* much trouble!" raged Miz Parker.

"Wow, it worked," Lamont said. "Awesome!"

"Bunny-Hoo-Hoo wants to know what if someone hears her?" Jolene danced the rabbit back and forth.

"Nobody will," Jimmy said. "Not for a while, not with the party and the music and the choir and everything."

"Where'd you get a key?" Lamont asked.

"My dad. He works in the cafeteria, that's why they let me go to school here. He's always losing stuff, forgetting where he puts it, when he's drunk. Sometimes he gets mad and blames me." Jimmy winked. "Sometimes he's right."

"So let's go already!" Tess headed for the stairs.

They went up, reminding each other to avoid the teachers, avoid the prefects and tattle-tales, not make a big deal of it, blend in, and–

"Eat *all* the treats!" Spencer cried, thrusting a fist in the air.

Then Lamont stopped them at the top of the stairs. "You guys . . . " he said. "Look!"

The stairwell came up into a lobby, with the infirmary and nurse's office one way, the school mail room another way, glass double doors opening onto the courtyard, and a glass side door opening onto a parking lot. It was the parking-lot door where Lamont pointed, and when they looked, they saw three people out there by a van with a light-up wreath hung on its front and cartoon reindeer decals along its side.

One of the people was a curvy girl, and another was a short midget guy. It was the third person, the jolly fat man with the white beard and the red suit, that riveted the kids where they stood.

"Santa!" Derp gasped.

Santa.

And two of his elves.

The short midget guy wore green pants with triangle hems, shoes with jingle bells on their curled-up toes, a red jacket, and a pointy hat with more jingle bells. The curvy girl had on candy-cane-striped tights, a short red skirt with a white fuzzy hem, a ruffled white top, candy-cane earrings, and a cute little cap.

Jolene, clutching Bunny-Hoo-Hoo, uttered a high-pitched greedy squeak as the two elves began unloading boxes from the back of the van.

Presents! The boxes were full of presents! Gift bags with tissue paper blooming out the tops! Packages wrapped in shiny foil or fancy paper, tied with ribbons or topped with bows! So many presents!

"You guys," Lamont repeated. "You guys, I got a better idea."

"Yeah," Jimmy and Tess said together.

"Fuck yeah," said Spencer.

Moments of hasty, hurried planning later, Jolene pranced out the side door. She pirouetted, made pretty-feet, waved, and chirped, "Santa! Hi! Santa, over here!"

Santa, in the process of poking his white-gloved thumbs at his phone, jumped and looked around. He seemed confused for a second, then put the phone in his coat pocket and went, "Ho, ho, ho, hello there, little girl, Merry Christmas!" in a full, jolly voice. "Aren't you a pretty darling?"

"I'm Jolene," she said. "I'm our school Christmas princess!"

"I can see that you are, ho, ho, ho."

"And this is Bunny-Hoo-Hoo!"

"Mr. Gregson said we should meet you out here," said Jimmy, moving up beside Jolene. "In case you got lost again."

"How come you got lost?" asked Derp. "Santa shouldn't get lost."

"Ho, ho, ho," laughed Santa, patting his belly. "Santa's elves are still getting used to our new GPS."

"The reindeer never got lost?" Tess asked.

"That's right, not my sleigh team!"

"C'mon in," Lamont said, holding the side door wide open.

"Mr. Gregson said we could help you while everyone else is at the choir concert," Jimmy added, as just then from the auditorium there drifted the sounds of a bunch of kids warbling their way through the first part of "Away in a Manger."

"Well, isn't that nice of you!" He chortled and mussed Jimmy's hair. "And what's your name, little boy?"

"Jimmy."

"Jimmy! That's a nice name. These are my helpers, Candy and Jingle."

"Merry Christmas, kids!" Candy did a perky bounce that made Jolene's eyes go all squinty and mean.

"Yeah," said Jingle, lots less perky. He slammed the van's back doors. "Merry Christmas."

As they shuffled into the lobby, carrying boxes of presents, Santa went ho-ho-ho some more and asked the others' names, asked if they'd been good little boys and girls. They all introduced themselves and said yes they had. When it was Minda's turn, she just murmured, so Tess explained she was shy.

"It's this way," Lamont said. "Downstairs."

"Downstairs?" asked Jingle. "You mean, like, in the basement?"

"In the rec room," Jimmy said. "It's all set up."

"Santa's workshop, and a tree, and everything!" said Tess.

"Why, that'll be wonderful," Santa said.

"What's that banging noise?" the candy-cane elf girl asked.

"Uh, er, um," said Derp.

Jimmy nudged him. "The pipes. Boiler room and stuff."

"You sure?" Jingle looked around. "Sounds like someone pounding."

"They make weird noises. Some kids think the place is haunted."

"Hrm." He didn't seem convinced.

They started down the stairs. Behind Jingle's back, Lamont and Jimmy shared an anxious grimace. If Miz Parker started hollering again, ooh they were gonna get it.

THE NAUGHTY LIST

Then she did holler, and things happened fast.

"Hello? Is anybody out there? Help! I'm locked in!"

Santa, already most of the way to the detention hall door, paused and turned.

"What the—?" Jingle began.

Spencer tripped him at the same time as Lamont gave the short midget elf guy a great big hard push. His words turned into a startled squawk. He pitched headfirst down the steps. His box tumbled.

"Steve!" screamed Candy, dropping her box too.

Presents went flying, scattering everywhere in the hall. Jingle's jingle bells jingled like crazy. There were some thick snapping sounds as he cartwheeled, and a meaty whump sound when he hit the cement.

"Oh, jeez, Steve, are you okay?"

"Get them in there!" Lamont jumped the rest of the way down.

"Ste—"

Jolene smacked Candy in the face with Bunny-Hoo-Hoo. "Shut up!"

Miz Parker banged on the door and hollered some more.

"*This* way, Santa!" Derp yanked at the back of Santa's broad black belt.

Caught off-balance, Santa wobbled and fell on his butt. "Oof!"

It took four of them to sort of drag Santa the rest of the way into the room. Some super-Derp-strength would have been really useful.

Santa, dazed, seemed to think they were helping him. He blinked, perplexed, when he saw no special Santa's workshop or anything. "Wait, didn't you say . . . ?"

They heaved him into a chair.

"What is this?" asked Santa. "What's going on?"

Tess dashed over from Miz Parker's desk with a roll of masking tape. It made long rippy-farty noises as she wound it around and around, taping Santa's arms to the chair arms and legs to the chair legs.

CHRISTINE MORGAN

"Now just a—" Santa said, blustering, puffing himself up. "What . . . "

"It was a trick, stupid," Jimmy said.

"Good little children shouldn't play tricks on Santa. You'll end up on the naughty list for sure."

"We already are!" Lamont said. "We already are on your damn naughty list!"

"See here—"

"Ow!" Candy cried. "Ow, my hair, let go of my—ow!" Jolene had her by a fistful of it, towing her along all bent over and flailing. "Let go of my hair, you brat!"

"I'm not a brat! Kayla's a brat! Kayla's a bratty-bratty-bratty-brat and so are you!"

"This is not funny!" Santa said. "Whatever you think you're doing—"

His phone rang in his pocket. Everybody froze like they were playing statue-tag. When Lamont went to fish the phone out, Santa tried to twist away and almost knocked his chair over.

"It's the school," Lamont said, looking at the screen. "Probably Mr. Gregson wondering where Santa is."

He tossed the phone to Tess, who caught it with a gleeful whoop. In the same drawer where she'd found the tape, she'd also found a lighter and a bunch of stuff confiscated from earlier detentions, including one of her own old cap-guns, some firecrackers, and a few packets of those snap-pop things. She untwisted the tiny knots of paper and poured until she had a gritty mound of gunpowder or whatever was in them.

In the hall, Spencer cackled. "I think the elf's broken. Watch." He poked.

Jingle twitched and groaned, scrabbling at the floor. Blood oozed from his leg, where a jagged part of bone stuck out through his sock.

"Hey!" Santa wasn't jolly anymore. "Knock it off, kid!"

Spencer kept poking and laughing like he did when he caught a spider or a beetle. Jingle kept twitching and groaning. Each twitch made the bells on his shoes jingle–his hat had fallen off and lay crumpled over by the drinking fountain.

Jolene tugged Candy to her knees. By now, the curvy candy-cane elf girl was blubbering, still trying to talk but crying as she did.

"Steve's hurt, ow quit it, we have to call 9-1-1, let go of me owwwww!"

"I said shut up!" Jolene hauled off and smacked her again, not with Bunny-Hoo-Hoo but with a loud slap that left a vivid red mark on Candy's cheek.

"That's enough!" roared Santa. "You kids cut the crap, right now!"

He strained at the masking tape. A few strips popped. Lamont grabbed a pair of scissors from the desk drawer.

"Cut what crap?" he asked, making the scissors go *k-snip, k-snip* at the air.

Santa gaped. Santa sputtered.

Candy, who Jolene and Jimmy were taping to another chair, went on blubbering.

"She's crying," Minda said quietly.

Nobody listened.

"Ready?" said Tess, who'd wedged Santa's phone into the pile of gritty powder and surrounded it with a crisscross of firecrackers.

"What are you–hey! Don't! That's my—" Santa said.

Derp covered his ears.

Tess lit it up.

Ka-pang-ga-pow-ka-popopop! Flashes and sparks, the phone flip-jittering until it flip-jittered off the edge of the desk and landed on the floor with grey smoke-streamers drifting up from it.

"Yee-haw!" Tess cheered, doing a victory fist-pump.

Jolene stood in front of Candy, hands on her hips, bottom lip pouted. "Thinks she's so pretty, look at her, thinks she's so pretty, do *you* think she's pretty?"

"Huh?" said Derp, taking his hands down from his ears.

CHRISTINE MORGAN

"Stop this, you all just stop this—" Santa said.

"So she's pretty, so what?" Jimmy said.

"Bet you want to *kiss* her too!"

"Kiss her? What?"

"Dooooo you?"

"No! Gross!"

"Bouncing around with her big boopiedoops . . . " Jolene hooked her fingers into the front of Candy's ruffled top and tore it open. Candy recoiled so hard her chair almost went over backward, screeching.

"Leave her alone!" Santa yelled. "You kids are going to be in so much trouble—"

Lamont stabbed the scissors into Santa's fat belly.

Everybody gasped.

No blood came out when Lamont pulled out the scissors. Only some puffs of white stuff.

"The heck?" Tess asked.

"Hey . . . " Lamont said. His teeth ground together. "Hey! It's a *pillow*! He's got a *pillow* under his coat!"

"What the hell's wrong with you?!?" Santa thrashed in the chair. "Are you insane?"

Derp reached for Santa's beard and it came right off. Derp held it, looked at it, and dropped it on the floor. He sniffled.

"Aw, crap!" said Jimmy. "All this and he's not even the real Santa?"

"What?" Spencer came back in. "You're shitting me! You're effin' shitting me! Not the real Santa?"

"Hey, look . . . " Santa, or whoever he was, some pudgy man with no chin and brown stubble under the fake beard, tried to smile at them. "Let's not do this, huh? Let's find a way to—"

"You dirty liar!" Jimmy punched him in the nose. It didn't go crunch and bleed, but the phony liar Santa yelped and his eyes watered.

Lamont taped his mouth shut and turned to the others. "*Now* what do we do?"

THE NAUGHTY LIST

"He'll tell on us," Tess said.

"He better not," said Jolene. "Or we'll tell on *him*."

"Tell on him what?" asked Derp.

"We'll say he showed us his wee-wee."

Santa choked. "Mmm-hrrgh-hmm!"

"He showed us his wee-wee," she continued, "and said if we wanted presents, we had to touch it."

Tess grimaced. "Eew! No way!"

"Yeah, no way, I'm not touching anybody's dick," said Spencer.

"Wee-wee," said Jolene.

"Not touching that either!"

"You don't have to really touch it! We just *say* that! We say he told us we had to touch it if we wanted presents. Or kiss it."

"Eew!" Tess said again, louder.

"Omigod they're crazy they're all crazy oh God," sobbed Candy. Her head hung down, her hair all messy in her face, her top torn open so they could all see her bra.

"She's still crying," Minda said. "She should stop. She shouldn't cry."

From the hall, there was a struggling, jingling kind of sound. They looked. The short midget broken elf guy was trying to drag himself up the stairs by his arms. His legs, bowlegged to start with and all bent and crooked now, didn't seem to want to move right. They left smears of blood like red snail-trails.

"Wuh-oh," said Spencer. "Some buttwipe thinks he's getting away. Bad Jingle!"

He ran over, climbed past the crawling green-suited figure, let him get halfway, then kicked him back down. Jingle bleated. His body went splinter-crunch splinter crunch on the steps. His shoes clinked and dinged. His head clonked on the floor like a bowling ball. He made a long juicy tootling fart.

"Dude!" Jimmy said, impressed. "Did you *hear* that?"

"Whew!" Spencer waved a hand in front of his face. "Did you *smell* that? Think he shit himself!"

Miz Parker wasn't pounding and hollering anymore. Maybe she was afraid to. Maybe she hoped they forgot she was in the janitor's closet.

Santa's eyes bulged. His pudgy cheeks did too. Snot bubbled in and out of his nose.

"And pissed himself," Spencer added, using his foot to roll Jingle over so they could all see the wet splotch on the front of his pants.

"Ste-e-e-eve . . . " Candy kept blubbering.

"Make her stop," Minda said. "She's crying, make her stop."

"So she's crying." Jolene primped her hair and adjusted Bunny-Hoo-Hoo's dress. "So she's a crying-crying-crybaby, so what?"

"My brother cried a lot."

"So?"

She glanced at Jingle. Tess and Jimmy had joined Spencer in the hall, all three laughing as they pushed the crippled elf around with their feet, playing soccer.

"He was stinky too," she said. "But the crying was worse. He cried all the time. *All* the time."

Lamont, who'd been listening, raised his eyebrows. "What'd you *do* about it?"

Minda brushed her hair aside and let her gaze slide across them. "I made him stop."

"How?" asked Jolene.

"Yeah, how?" asked Derp.

"I'll show you."

She got one of the gift bags. The tag said "BOY" on it but Minda didn't care. Inside was a pack of rubber dinosaurs, which she didn't care about either and indifferently tossed away. Derp picked it up.

"Dinosaurs! Can I have them?"

"Sure," said Lamont when Minda didn't reply.

Minda took the tissue paper that had been in the bag. It was holiday tissue paper, white stamped with green tree-shapes. She wadded it up and pressed the wad to Candy's mouth.

THE NAUGHTY LIST

Candy shook her head. Her lips were tight-shut now, tight-shut in a line. Minda twisted her dangly candy-cane earring.

"Ow!"

As soon as she opened her mouth to go *ow*, Minda stuffed in the wad of tissue paper. Candy tried to spit it out, but Minda wouldn't let her.

"Get more," she told the others.

"Open the presents?" asked Derp, with a wide dopey-happy smile. "Really?"

"I'm next, I'm next, I pick next!" Jolene snatched up one marked "GIRL," found a plastic tiara-ring-necklace set, and squealed. She gave the tissue paper to Minda.

Seeing what they were doing, Jimmy, Tess, and Spencer abandoned their soccer game to come help. Jingle had stopped moving anyway, just lay there all limp, so they were bored.

Gift bags and wrapping paper and ribbon and tags shredded in a greedy frenzy, revealing toy cars, fashion dolls, picture books, army guys, paint-by-numbers, bean-bag animals, sidewalk chalks, clay-dough, and more. Some of the gifts contained goodies–tins of cookies, chocolate, spicy Christmas gumdrops, caramel corn, peppermints.

And there was tissue paper.

Lots and lots of holiday tissue paper. Red and green and white, plain and patterned, some with trees and some with stars or snowflakes, some with silver and gold speckles.

Piece by piece, wad by wad, Minda forced the tissue papers into Candy's mouth.

At first, when she couldn't spit, Candy tried to swallow them down, but there were too many and Minda was too fast. Candy started to choke and gag. She threw up but the throw-up clogged with the papers. Some trickled out her nose. She lurched her whole body, and the chair fell over with her still taped to it. Her face turned purple.

Meanwhile, Santa did a huge Hulk-out effort that

popped most of the tape holding him. He lunged partway to his feet, strips of tape flapping at his wrists, the chair scraping across the floor where one chair leg stayed stuck to his ankle.

Lamont lunged to his feet too, with the scissors gripped tight in both hands. This time, he didn't stab the steel blades into Santa's fat pillow-belly. This time, he stabbed them into Santa's neck.

This time, there was blood.

Lots and lots of blood.

Santa went, "Glurk!"

He tottered around in a circle, pawing at the scissor-ends. His legs tangled on the chair. He crashed down. He shuddered. He kicked. He gurgled. Then he didn't do anything at all.

No one spoke for a minute.

They looked at Candy. They looked at Santa. They looked at Jingle, out in the hall.

They looked at each other. Cookie crumbs on their chins, chocolate on their lips, sticky gumdrops in their teeth.

Eventually, Mr. Gregson or somebody would come. Miz Parker would get let out of the janitor's closet. Teachers would be mad, and parents would be called.

But that was eventually. That was later.

For now, the kids on the naughty list still had plenty of presents to open.

DON'T LOOK BACK

THE CONCERT WAS going fine until Johnny Harlowe saw his dead girlfriend in the third row.

He faltered, fingers skidding on guitar strings just as the rest of the band went into the instrumental bridge. If anybody noticed his lapse, he couldn't tell. Didn't care. He blinked, looked again.

She was gone.

If she'd ever even been there.

Third row and to the left of center. Where Edie had always preferred to be when she came to one of the shows. He remembered asking her once, why there, and she'd considered it for a long time before tilting her huge dark eyes to his and saying, softly but impishly, that it was close enough to see but not close enough to get spit on.

A fist of panic seized Johnny. He was on the verge of losing it right in front of several thousand fans and a film crew. His hands were shaking, his mouth had gone dry, and a wild screaming sensation was rising in his throat. When it reached the top, he would either shriek or throw up.

There she was again. Edie. Waves of long black hair framing her face. Looking up at him solemnly. Pale beneath her olive complexion. A space around her despite the way that the audience was on its feet, dancing in place or crowding the stage. As if those nearest Edie, not noticing her, were still somehow aware of her presence. And shying away from it.

Gone. Like she'd never been there.
Snuffed out.
Dead.
Lost to him forever.

A low, strangled cry issued from Johnny. He fled the stage, feeling the shocked eyes of the rest of the band on him, catching a brief glimpse of Carlotta's face, carmine lips mouthing questions at him as she kept on with the drumsticks, kept on with the rock.

He ignored them all and ran, avoiding loops and bundles of electrical cords, veering around a startled roadie, plunging down a dark passage that led to the backstage area. He didn't slow until he had slammed through the door into his own dressing room and swept it shut behind him.

Edie.

"Edie." He said her name into the numbing silence, barely hearing it with his ears still throbbing from the music. Didn't need to hear it. *Felt* it, stabbing him, as sharp as any knife.

A flood of hot tears surprised him. He'd thought he had cried himself out after the funeral. Cried and then done his best to move on, though one tragedy after another had made it seem like his career was over. Surely his career with Scarlet Angel was, once Nick got himself killed. Not that Johnny had shed any tears over Nick's death. If anything, he'd been gladdened by it. If anyone deserved to die that way, that horribly, it was Nick. The only shame was that it had been over so quick.

In the months immediately following Edie, he had done his best to go through the motions. The tour must go on. Music videos weren't going to make themselves. Scarlet Angel was poised for stardom. Then Nick was rudely erased from the picture, and Scarlet Angel fell apart.

Johnny had gone home after that. Not home to the apartment where he'd lived between shows; he'd gotten out of there fast because memories of Edie were everywhere.

DON'T LOOK BACK

Not home to the studio he'd rented after that either. Home to the mansion high in the Hollywood Hills, home to his family.

He'd thought he was doing better. Healing. Getting back on track. He couldn't imagine a life without music. It was as much a part of him as his cobalt-blue eyes, and similarly inherited, going back generations. Probably as far as some minstrel in the Middle Ages, or the first caveman who ever clapped two rocks together or blew into a bone whistle.

"We can't live without music, Johnny-boy," his mother had told him. She still wore her hair as long and kinked as she had during her days as a folksinger in the sixties, still favored loose granny dresses and Red Zinger tea. "It's in our blood."

His father, a classical violinist, agreed. So did his grandmother, who'd sung torch songs and gone to entertain the troops in WWII.

In his blood. Maybe so . . . but how could he go on when it only brought him pain? Edie had loved his music, loved him for his music, and without her, it was all meaningless.

Edie . . . not beautiful in the California sense. On the short side, slim, small-breasted, dusky. He wouldn't have given her a second look except that she kept turning up. Whenever he played, she'd be there. Third row, left of center, most of the time. Those eyes, her best feature, fixed on him. Looking into him so intently that he finally realized he had to get to know her.

Maybe if he hadn't gotten interested, she would still be alive. Maybe, if not for him, Nick never would have noticed her either.

He choked up as he saw, all unbidden in memory's relentless recall, the party. Opening for Attraction at the Civic Center. Edie hadn't wanted to go. She would rather keep to herself, didn't like those big noisy scenes. But so many important people were going to be there, people who could make a difference for Johnny. So they'd gone, and she had encouraged him to go around and mingle, talk, make those vital connections.

And like a circling shark, that was when Nick made his move. Maybe because she was just the type he liked—an innocent to defile and abandon. Maybe because he was stung by a recent review that called his singing "incoherent screeching" and said good things about Johnny. Calculated or spur of the moment, it hadn't mattered.

When Johnny couldn't immediately find Edie, he first assumed she must have left, quietly, so as not to draw attention. Then someone mentioned having seen her leave with Nick and said that she hadn't looked well. Sick, almost fainting.

White-hot rage blasted through Johnny, obliterating all the good feelings he had about the party, the evening, the band. He knew in a flash what Nick was up to. Had witnessed it countless times before. When his blond bad-boy good looks and arrogant charm didn't do the trick, a surreptitious dose of whatever new drug was on the market usually did.

He had gone charging after, to Nick's hotel room, knowing what he would find and feeling his soul flayed alive at the vision. How many girls had it been? Ten, a dozen? They'd wake up the next day, alone and naked and sore and sticky, with one of Nick's autographed photos propped on the other pillow as a remembrance of what they couldn't remember.

Not Edie. Not his Edie.

They had been going out for six months, taking it slow, not rushing things, and Johnny was starting to think he'd finally found The One. She was so sweet. He knew she would have if he pressed her because she had loved him from the beginning, but knowing that made him not want to press her. Made him want to wait until *she* was ready. Better that way. Special.

Then along came Nick to take all that away.

DON'T LOOK BACK

He'd reached the door and kicked it open, fueled by adrenaline. Too late. Not too late to save her virtue . . . too late to save her life.

The medical examiner blamed it on the date-rape cocktail that Nick had given her. A bad reaction. Like snakebite. Her respiratory system had shut down, her circulation moments later. Nick had gotten her unconscious form half-undressed before she stopped breathing. He had been dithering uselessly, debating whether or not to call the hotel desk, when Johnny burst in and knocked out two teeth, dislocated his jaw, and split his lips.

That had been the functional end of Scarlet Angel, though the band had limped on for another couple of months. Nick, out on bail and awaiting trial on charges of manslaughter and attempted rape, offered a casual apology to Johnny and seemed to think that made everything all right. Johnny, too stunned and hurt to know what he was doing, continued with the tour until the night that Nick got torn to pieces. The police tried to connect Johnny to that one but couldn't.

And so here he was. Wishing that there was something, anything else he could do with his life and knowing there wasn't. He was born to be a musician. It was all he had ever known, and now that Edie was gone, it was all he had left.

Gradually, it occurred to Johnny that he wasn't alone in his dressing room. He had been so lost in the past that he couldn't recall hearing the door open or close, yet there was a man sitting on the long black faux-leather couch, regarding him evenly with cool, dispassionate eyes.

"Huh!" The sound was jerked out of Johnny, wet, almost a sob. His face was drenched with tears. He swiped his sleeve across it and straightened up, searching for righteous indignation. "Hey, who the hell are you?"

Even as he said it, he recognized his unexpected visitor. It was the guy Carlotta had been seeing, some New Age mystic who made his living as a "psychic advisor" and told well-to-do older women that they could expect romantic visits from tall dark strangers. It seemed an oddball choice for a girl who'd teethed on the music of Sheila E.

Johnny groped and found the guy's name. His real name, not the hokey "Alastair Cayce" moniker he put on his business cards.

"Jeez, Ferryman, what are you doing here?" he asked. "Waiting for Carlotta?"

Charles Ferryman smiled at him, which only unsettled Johnny's nerves further. He was tall and thin, abhorring the famous California sun in favor of a chalky pallor, and when on the job, he wore black contacts that gave the impression he had no eyes at all.

"Carlotta tells me you've been having problems," he said. "She thought I might be able to help."

"What are you talking about?"

"Edie."

"I'm not having problems, and even if I was, there's no way you could help," snapped Johnny. "So go peddle your Tarot cards somewhere else, okay? I'm not in the mood to be manipulated."

"Is that what you think it is?"

"Ouija boards, palm reading, astrology, past life regressions . . . what else am I supposed to think it is? I suppose you want to invite me to a séance and you're going to shoot ectoplasm out your nose and conjure Edie's spirit." His tension and grief morphed eagerly into anger, because in anger, he didn't have to think, or hurt.

A tight smile flitted across Ferryman's thin, bloodless lips. "Not quite what I had in mind. I know what you're experiencing, John. I can help. I want to help."

"Get out of here."

"You're seeing her. She comes to you but not all the way. She wants to come back."

"I said get out!" Johnny lacked four or five inches but had plenty of mass and muscle on Ferryman, and stepped toward him with the intention of throwing his bony ass bodily out the door. Without opening it if necessary.

He halted abruptly as Ferryman leaned close, black eyes glinting like orbs of volcanic glass. His hair was so blond it was almost white, cropped close so the shape of his skull was clearly defined, and he favored the kind of voluminous trench coats that made cops stop him on the street thinking he might be on his way to shoot up a school, post office, or fast-food joint.

"Do you want her back or don't you?"

Something in the question chilled Johnny. "Of course I do. I loved her. But she's *dead*."

"There's a chance, if you're brave enough. Let me help you."

"Knock it off," Johnny said, but weakly. Those black eyes were draining the anger out of him. He could almost believe Ferryman was serious.

But of course, he was putting Johnny on. Had to be.

"Come with me," Ferryman said. The compulsion was so strong that Johnny was halfway across the room before his wits collected.

"Wait. What is this? I told you, I'm not going to any séance."

"No, you're not. If you really want her, you'll have to go much farther than that." Ferryman's coat flared like a cape as he went to the door.

Johnny followed helplessly. "This isn't funny."

"Do I seem like I'm joking?"

"I don't know what you seem like. Besides damn spooky and weird."

Ferryman's chuckle was the sound of bones rolling in a tomb. He probably practiced it as diligently as Johnny practiced guitar chords.

Speaking of which . . .

"You'll need that," Ferryman said, pointing to a guitar case in the corner.

Johnny picked it up. Inside was his battered but well-loved old Gibson, given to him by his parents when he was fourteen. He rarely played it anymore but took it everywhere with him for luck. "What's this for?"

"What do you think?"

He strode down the hall, Johnny trailing along behind with the guitar case. The muffled din from above, from the arena, told Johnny that Carlotta and the others had kept right on playing. The show must go on. He hadn't been with them that long anyway, and probably wouldn't be missed.

They emerged into the private parking garage. Ferryman led Johnny to a jet-black car on the far side of the tour bus. It had windows tinted dark as its paint job, and light seemed to soak into it rather than shine on it. The car was of no make Johnny could recognize, though the plate was a standard California vanity plate. He saw CHAR and that was all before Ferryman stood in front of him with one pallid hand outstretched.

"You play piano?" Johnny reflexively asked, his family's automatic question upon seeing anyone with fingers of such length and grace.

"You'll have to pay me," Ferryman said, ignoring him.

"What?"

"Before we go. I don't do this for free, you know."

"For one, *you* came to *me*," Johnny argued. "For two, I don't have any cash. You didn't tell me to bring my goddamn wallet. This is crazy. I don't know what I'm doing out here."

The doors of the black car sprang silently open of their own accord.

"Get in," said Ferryman. "You can play me a song while we drive."

"No way."

"For Edie. Or you'll never see her again."

A thousand protests bubbled up, and Johnny bit them all back. Yes, this was crazy. Yes, she was dead and he understood the irrevocability of that. But something in

DON'T LOOK BACK

Ferryman's tone, or manner, was so eerily persuasive that he walked around and got in on the passenger side, unlatching his guitar case.

"Any requests?"

"Your discretion," Ferryman said, taking his place behind the wheel.

So Johnny played a variety, somehow finding in the strings of the old guitar the comfort that had previously eluded him. He saw the scenery rolling by, Los Angeles streets dark as a river, armies of vagrants and hookers and other lost souls of the night wandering by.

The guitar resting across his lap, he strummed idly. The entire episode had taken on an air of unreality. What was he doing here, tooling the city with Carlotta's weird boyfriend when he was supposed to be on stage?

Ferryman pulled up in front of a club, all pulsing neon and pounding bass. A line of hopefuls stretched to the corner, and the sunken stairs leading to the entrance were guarded by the biggest man Johnny had ever seen. He was shirtless in tight leather pants, wearing a choke-chain around his bull neck, and his bare, broad chest boasted an intricate tattoo of some hellish mutant wolf with three fanged heads and foaming jaws.

Above the bouncer's head, red neon spelled out the word "Erebus." Johnny thought he was pretty well-versed in the local clubs but had never heard of this one.

"This is as far as I go," Ferryman said.

"What, you want me to go in there?"

"And talk to my boss. He's the only one who can give you what you want. If you can convince him."

"I don't know about this."

"Go on. He's a sucker for good music."

Somehow, Johnny found himself on the sidewalk with the line of wanna-be club hoppers looking at him. In the fey, flickering light, they were waxen and ghoulish. And utterly silent.

Johnny descended the steps and was blocked by the

bouncer with the three-headed dog snarling eternally on his pecs. "Yeah?" the man growled, sounding rabid himself.

An instinct that he couldn't understand—*music and the savage beast*, some corner of his mind misquoted—led him to strum a few chords. The bouncer's eyes narrowed, then he shrugged and a wistful grin lit his face, turning it almost handsome.

"Okay," he said. "You can go in."

The door, like those of Ferryman's car, swung open untouched. The music swelled, and rotating beams of light splashed out. Johnny, nodding his thanks to the bouncer, proceeded into Erebus.

The club was all pitch-black walls and floor and ceiling, with chrome table edges and barstools turned lurid shades by the neon and multicolored lights. He paused in the entryway, sizing it up.

The interior was divided not by rooms but by vaguely discernible groups. The beautiful people were off to one side, laughing and dancing and partying like there was no tomorrow. The majority, on the main dance floor, shuffled dolefully to the beat.

And some, here and there, were wretched. Johnny saw a scrawny guy straining to reach a tray on a table just beyond his stretching fingers. The tray was loaded with little dishes of pretzels and bottles of beer, and whenever the guy scooted his chair forward, the table somehow got knocked a few inches away. Beyond him was another man, this one far older than the usual club-goer, trying single-handedly to wrestle a piano up a flight of stairs. He was within a riser of making it when the piano shifted and tumbled with an awful jarring of keys to the bottom. Groaning, the old man trudged down and started again.

Holding his guitar close to him now, feeling obscurely threatened and out of place, Johnny struck out across the dance floor. He was making for the raised, glassed-in platform where a deejay in a black suit was dividing his attention between the sound system and a sleek woman

DON'T LOOK BACK

picking plump, juicy seeds from a pomegranate and sliding them, savoringly, between her lips.

As his foot touched the step at the bottom of the platform, the music cut off and the resulting silence was loud enough to hurt his ears. Everyone was looking at him, and in none too friendly a manner either. A trio of waitresses in scanty outfits, but with wild hair and harridan faces, swooped down on him out of nowhere and surrounded him. Each, bizarrely, had a short scourge tied to her belt, a bundle of braided lashes hanging from a stout handle.

The deejay, who boasted a deep widow's peak and backswept ink-dark hair, fixed burning, hooded eyes on Johnny. The woman beside him licked pomegranate juice from her fingers and raised one intrigued eyebrow.

"Who are you, and what brings you to Erebus?" intoned the deejay in a voice that would have made James Earl Jones green with envy.

"I was told you could help me," Johnny replied, knowing somehow that this had to be Ferryman's boss. "It's about my girlfriend, Edie."

"Only the dead know Erebus," the woman with the pomegranate said. "You do not belong here."

"I'm not planning to stay," Johnny assured her.

At this, the waitresses hissed and drew the scourges from their belts. "Let us flay the skin from his living flesh, my lord," one of them beseeched.

The deejay held up a staying hand. His demeanor seemed more amused than angry. "Let us hear him out."

Not having the faintest clue what to say, Johnny lifted his guitar. "I understand you like music."

Flickers of interest made the rounds of the room, and the beldam waitresses backed off a few steps. The deejay gave Johnny the nod.

"All right. Show us what you can do, and maybe we can deal."

He played. Later, he would never be sure exactly *what*

he played, but he put his entire being into the music. For a while, he lost track of the club around him, lost track of everything except the melody he was producing. Every love song he'd written with Edie in mind poured from him and blended into something he knew he could never repeat. Emotion sobbed in every note.

As he brought it to an end, he blinked and came back to himself with a shudder like waking, unashamed and unsurprised to find he was crying, and Edie was there.

Johnny sucked in a breath. It was her, just as he'd seen her at the concert. Not a girl who bore a resemblance. Not a trick of the light. Edie. A tentative smile of love and hope on her face. Saying nothing but *there*, only arm's reach away. He extended a hand.

"Stop," said the deejay. His deep voice had gone husky, though he struggled to keep a severe expression. Beside him, his woman was surreptitiously wiping away a tear. "You play pretty good, kid," the deejay added. "What is it that you want?"

"Her," Johnny said. "Edie. I want her back. Loving her was the best thing that ever happened to me, and losing her was the worst. I want another chance."

"A chance . . . very well. You'll have your chance if you can handle it. Think you can?"

"What do I have to do?"

"Go," the deejay said. "Go and don't look back. She'll follow, but only as long as you have trust. The moment you give in to doubt and look back, she'll be gone. Mine. Forever."

"Okay." Johnny, trembling but resolute, turned from the control booth and faced the gathered crowd of onlookers.

They parted to let him pass. As he moved between them, the music started up in a clash and a roar, drowning out the soft steps that had been trailing after him. The activity and dancing resumed with its frantic yet oddly empty energy.

DON'T LOOK BACK

He kept his gaze on the exit, the fine hairs on the back of his neck prickling. Was it her breath? He remembered evenings they'd spent on the couch, her breath a faint breeze on him as they cuddled. Never so cold, like the exhalation of a grave.

Awful thoughts popped unbidden into his mind. *The Monkey's Paw*, for instance. Beware of what you wish for. What if he got to the street and found Edie with him all right, Edie as she'd be all these months after her death? Shrunken and rotting but horribly alive and bound to him.

If she was even there at all. If this was even happening at all.

The waving, sweeping lights threw his shadow all around his feet, a capering, leaping thing. Terror whispered into him as he saw no others, only his. No one else cast one.

Except . . . was that a feminine shadow, thrown briefly by a rotating beam? Edie's shadow?

And had that been a step he heard in the lull between tunes?

Or were they watching him, the deejay and his woman and the rest, sneering at his gullibility? Nothing was back there. No one was following him. Ferryman had pulled some nutty joke, and Johnny had fallen for it.

She *was* there. She had to be.

The doors were dead ahead. His guitar was slick in his grasp from the nervous sweat sheathing his palms. He listened intently, agonizing to hear something. Why didn't she speak up? Why didn't she say his name?

He couldn't stand it. Was she really there?

The deejay's words echoed in his ears. *Don't look back.*

But he had to know.

The doors, so close, so close now.

A soft gasp. Surely not his imagination.

Edie was with him.

Unless it was a trick.

What if he turned and it was the woman with the

pomegranate, or one of the waitresses? How they'd laugh! Laugh at him for being a fool. Maybe, since in a place like this violence was never far beneath the surface, strike him with one of those scourges.

No. It *was* Edie. Otherwise, it had all been for nothing.

He walked on, almost to the doors, almost to the bouncer. The big man's eyes were flat, non-reflective, and devoid of humanity. Not so much as a hint. It wouldn't have taken much to assure Johnny that all was well. Just a hint. Was she there, or wasn't she?

If he left, dark certainty told him that he would never find this place again. He had one shot and one shot only. Blow it, and that was all.

But if they were tricking him . . .

He had to know. Nothing else mattered. Had to look, and see, and *know*. His eyes would find truth. Seeing is believing. Everything else was stardust and fancy.

He *had* to know.

Johnny surfaced from blackness with a sick and queasy groan. He rolled, meaning to go from his side to his back, and succeeded in falling from the couch to the floor. He groaned again. Sat up, felt a swaying turbulence in his head, and rested it on his knees, eyes shut.

The cliché words came to him and he uttered them, thickly, hoarsely. "It was only a dream."

Rather than relief, it brought a stab of inner pain. Only a dream. Or some bizarre drug thing. He stayed clean, always had and always would, but Ferryman might have slipped him something. The man was a walking, talking freakshow.

Someone rapped at the door, and Johnny, without raising his head, mumbled, "Come in."

The door opened. He heard the distinctive click-clack of Carlotta's spike-heeled boots. She may have modeled her performances after Sheila E., but her legs were pure Tina Turner.

"Johnny?"

"Tell your boyfriend to stay the hell away from me," he said, eyes still shut.

"What?" Distracted, mentally thrown off-stride, and only then did Johnny hear the near-hysteria in her voice. "I haven't seen him in a week, what?"

"Never mind."

"Johnny . . . I don't know how to tell you this . . . God!"

He winced. This was where she fired him, kicked him out of the band. His last shot, and he'd screwed it up. "It's all right, Carlotta. I understand."

"You mean you knew? And you're okay with it? If I were you, I'd sue somebody!"

"What?" He wasn't tracking and lifted his head from his knees with considerable effort. "What are you talking about? Who'm I going to sue?"

"I wish you'd told me. God, Johnny, she about scared the crap out of me. I thought I was seeing a ghost."

A slow, creeping awe tinged with horror spread through him. He tried to speak, but only a raspy noise came out. He cleared his throat. "What?"

Then he heard the footsteps. Soft footsteps. And a shadow on the floor of the hallway. Coming closer. Closer.

"Edie," he whispered.

"This time, you didn't look back," she said.

And she was *there*.

WITH BLACKEST MOSS

MAUDE PROMISED HERSELF that if it turned out to be wall-to-wall spiders in her mother's old gardening shed, she'd take up some different hobby.

Scrapbooking, maybe. Crocheting. Something, anything, some way to fill the waiting hours.

Let go. Downsized. Fired. Taking involuntary advantage of the early retirement program. No matter what you called it, out of work was out of work.

She wasn't sure when anybody had last been inside the shed, but she ought to at least see what there was before she went spending a bunch of money on tools.

The door stuck. Maude pulled. She heard and felt a soft ripping giving-way, like muffled Velcro, as it opened. She backed up in case those anticipated wall-to-wall spiders came out in a swarming flood.

Nothing came out, no spiders, swarming or otherwise. Only a draft of air, cool, heavy, and musty-smelling. Not stuffy and sweltering like she would have expected, but a basementy smell, a subterranean cellar-like smell.

The doorway showed only a rectangle of shadow in the hazy, sepia-toned smoglight of yet another southern California summer. Maude squinted through her sunglasses, waiting for her vision to adjust.

This wasn't the way things were supposed to be. This wasn't how her life should have turned out.

All those things she'd wanted to do, meant to do . . . but kept putting off . . . until the time was right, until the

WITH BLACKEST MOSS

money was better, until the divorce was final, until the kids were out of the house . . .

Maude sighed.

Too late now.

At her age? In this economy? What, go back to college, get her degree? Start her own business? Begin a new career? Travel? Date? Remarry?

Have a life?

Yeah. Yeah, that'd happen.

"Oh, but, Maude," everyone told her, "you're always *so* good about putting your family first."

Married right out of high school, and divorced fifteen years and three kids later. Custody battles and child-support hassles. Working full-time to keep their heads above water and stay a step ahead of the expenses both expected and unexpected.

Putting your family first.

Telling yourself that once they were grown, once they were settled and on their own, once the nest was empty, there'd be the chance for something else.

Maude sighed again.

Instead, here she was. Back home right where she'd started. Pushing sixty and already washed up. A dead end with nothing to look forward to but getting older, maybe with the hereditary dementia into the bargain, like a bad bonus prize.

She noticed a black, fuzzy smudge along the shed door's edge. Thready in fine straggling wisps, like a torn piece of linen or a skein of brushed wool, it ran all the way down, as well as along the top and bottom . . . in fact, the entire inside of the door was covered.

Maude touched the stuff. It felt fibrous, a little crumbly, a little springy, a little furry, and a little . . . moist? No, not moist, not quite, but not dry.

She thought of dust, the greasy but fluffy dust that accumulated in range hood fans and under stoves. Or soot, ash, the waxy char-black residue that came off a burnt candle wick. Those were close, but not quite right.

Weird, not unpleasant, but odd and foreign and . . . strange.

She poked a fingertip into it, made a divot, pulled her finger back, and watched as the whatever-it-was filled the depression slowly back out. Like one of those fancy foam mattresses, the kind that, on the commercials, suggested you could jump on the bed without spilling your wineglass.

Spongy, sort of. And thick. An inch-thick layer, coating the inside of the door. Top to bottom and side to side. With a rounded hump where the inner half of the doorknob mechanism was, and longer, narrower humps over the hinges.

When she looked at the jamb and saw it there too, all the way around, the Velcro sensation made sense. She'd pulled until the stuff had . . . had just torn along the seam like an old pair of pants.

She scraped at it with her nail, scratched at it. She pinched a tuft, plucked it off the way she'd pluck a lint puff off a sweater, and rolled it between her forefinger and thumb. The texture made her think of oily strands of hair wadding into a ball . . . or the clumps of fur that used to be left in the comb after she groomed the dog.

Rubbing her palm back and forth over the strange black layer was almost like petting Woozles again . . . the woolly feel of his coat . . . smoothish one way, nappier the other.

A tickle on her cheek startled her, and only when she wiped away a tear did Maude realize she was crying. Standing here in the hot midday smoglight, crying over a dumb, sweet goof of a dog who'd gotten out one day and run off when the gate had been left unlatched. Hadn't she been wondering just a few minutes ago when that hereditary dementia would catch up with her?

Maude snapped herself out of it and took a closer look, as well as an experimental sniff. The scent of the stuff was the same as she'd smelled on that cool draft . . . musty, heavy . . . an earthy plant smell . . .

WITH BLACKEST MOSS

It was some kind of moss, or mildew, or mold.

Her nose wrinkled. She thought of the nasty brownish slimy spots that appeared in the bathroom corners, no matter how often she sprayed and scrubbed.

Only this stuff wasn't nasty, wasn't slimy.

It reminded her of the ground-covers people might choose for their gardens, something that would spread in a nice low pad. Hardy, durable, not needing a lot of fuss and maintenance.

The moss, or whatever it was, had overtaken the whole interior–door, walls, floor, ceiling–in carpets and cascades. Here and there, it bunched up in hummocks dotted with little shiny-black domes like mushroom caps. It was so thick over the windows that not a single pencil-thin ray made it through the shutter-slats. Long, feathery-fine tendrils dangled from the ceiling, stirring in the desultory breeze.

The shed was much cooler than the yard outside . . . cooler than it'd be in the house, for that matter. The old house had no air conditioning, just fans that made a constant stuffy whirr all summer.

Out here it was cool, and quiet. Muffled-quiet, padded-quiet. No whirring fans. No unsynchronized ticking of clocks. No yellowish-miasma nicotine buildup on the wallpaper. The musty, earthy smell was . . . pleasant. Comforting.

If she closed the door behind her, she'd be isolated in this cool, quiet, comforting, fragrant darkness. The way the moss sank under her feet told her that it really would be as soft as one of those foam mattresses.

What a wonderful thing it would be to sleep, to sink into a full, real, restful sleep for a change. For the first time in a long time. For the first time since she'd come home again. Sleep without the subliminal anxiety of listening for her brother . . . without being on alert for the next outburst or disturbance . . . how nice that would be!

"Oh, but, Maude, you were always *so* good about putting your family first."

Yes, it would be nice, but she couldn't. Sleep? Out here? That was crazy.

She pushed the door closed.

Besides, it was Friday; Friday was grocery day. She went into the house for her purse, list, and keys.

"I'm going shopping now," she called.

No answer from the den down the hall.

Two hours later, Maude pulled into the driveway, turned off the ignition, and listened to the engine clunk-chug-wheeze its way to silence. She got out, popped the trunk, and hauled in the groceries in one trip by laddering the plastic bag handles up her arms. They dug into the flesh and left sweaty red marks.

"I'm home!"

"Did you bring chicken?"

"Chicken's for Monday!"

"It isn't Monday?"

"No."

"Didn't you go to work?"

"I don't go to work anymore, remember?"

Fred's reply was a disinterested snort, signaling the end of the conversation.

The groceries got put where they belonged, a place for everything and everything in its place, where they'd gone for as long as Maude could remember.

Clocks ticked. Fans whirred. Pipes gurgled. The house was as stuffy and sweltering as ever. Furniture sat and pictures hung where furniture had sat and pictures had hung for over half a century. The same knickknacks gathered the same dust. Each year, the rug got a little more worn, the wallpaper a little more yellowed.

She set frozen fish fillets onto a baking sheet because it was Friday; chicken was for Monday, take-out rotisserie chicken; frozen fish fillets were for Friday. Saturday, their big day, they'd go out to the smoke shop and beer barn to stock up, then have an early dinner at the Heartland Buffet.

WITH BLACKEST MOSS

As the oven pre-heated, she poured herself a soda and went to check messages.

Nothing from any of the kids. She wasn't surprised, had no reason to be–they never called; they'd write sometimes, but they *never* called because Fred might answer.

"He's dead to us," they'd told her. "As far as we're concerned, he's your brother, not our uncle. He's no relation of ours. He's not welcome in our homes, and we don't want him anywhere near *our* children."

Maude thought they were being a little extreme. Okay, they didn't like him, he gave them the creeps, but he'd never *done* anything to them.

"He beat up Grandma," they'd said.

"He didn't beat her up," Maude tried to explain. "He slapped her once, and you know how she was toward the end, she was out of control."

"She was eighty years old and about eighty pounds total, and he *hit* her, and now you're defending him just like *she* always used to do! Like you *promised* you wouldn't!"

Maude's hand had been *on* the telephone, ready to pick up and dial–elder abuse, domestic violence, assault!–when her mother, already bruising, said, "Maudie-don't-you-*dare*!"

Couldn't anybody understand she didn't have any choice? What else was she supposed to do? Later, her mother had begged, from her very deathbed, that Maude "look after my Freddie." How could she refuse?

"He can't live by himself," she'd said, trying to reason with her kids. "Without me, he'd end up—"

"In prison? Dead? Rehab? In a loony bin? On the streets?"

"That, or some kind of adult care home—"

"So what? Let him!"

"He's your uncle—"

"He's a shitbag alcoholic racist sexist homophobic asshole parasite waste of space!"

They insisted duty and obligation only went so far. They said they wished Fred would need a transplant and one of them the only donor match so they could refuse and watch him die.

"What about you, Mom?" they'd asked. "What if something happens to you? He's in for one hell of a rude awakening if he thinks any of *us* are going to take care of him!"

Furthermore, if it fell to any of them to make Fred's final arrangements? They'd donate him to one of those cadaver farms like you saw on *CSI* or *Dirty Jobs*, and the only pity was a place like that would expect him to be dead first.

"He knew Grandma was getting worse," they'd said. "He didn't do a goddamn thing."

"He didn't want to worry me," replied Maude.

"He didn't give a shit."

Her mother had eventually been pulled over by the Highway Patrol for erratic driving, halfway to San Diego when she'd only been going to the beauty parlor. When she'd been too confused to answer their questions, they called the house and got Fred, whose main concern had been that "the dumb old biddy" was supposed to bring rotisserie chicken and asked if the cops would stop and pick some up when they brought her back.

Hiring someone, that was out of the question. So were nursing homes, retirement facilities, assisted living, anything of the sort was met with mulish stubbornness.

So, Maude, always *so* good about putting her family first, went to stay with them for a while to help out.

For a while. That had been the plan. Her mother deteriorated rapidly after the highway incident, and Maude told herself it'd be a matter of months, maybe a year at the most.

On that count, she'd been right.

Those final words, though, that deathbed plea . . .

"Maudie, you have to take care of him, you have to look after my Freddie."

WITH BLACKEST MOSS

"He cost us our grandmother," her children said. "Now he's costing *our* kids *theirs*!"

They wouldn't visit her, and she couldn't visit them. They kept inviting her for Thanksgivings and Christmases, but was she going to leave him alone on the *holidays*? What would her mother have thought of *that*?

She was stuck, and why was that so hard for her kids to understand? Why did they think she could throw Fred to the wolves, let him sink or swim, fend for himself? Sure, he largely ignored her when she was around, but he didn't like it when she was gone. He'd accepted her going to work out of necessity. Anything else was abandonment.

Why should she put her selfish wishes against his legitimate needs?

"Why not?" they'd say.

So, she needed something to keep her busy, a hobby, but one that would also be homebound, keep her near at hand. Something like gardening.

Their mother had gardened. The roses, the geraniums, the flower beds and rows of terra-cotta flower pots she'd set along the porch rail . . . Maude didn't know if she had inherited the green thumb, but she didn't think Fred would object the way he objected to other proposed changes.

The way he'd object to another pet, for instance. Neither he nor their mother had warmed to Woozles—"that damn dog," was how they'd peevishly referred to him.

And, of course, any suggestion of selling, moving, remodeling, even clearing out the garage or attic of a half century's worth of clutter was out of the question.

The smell of baking fish fillets and boxed Parmesan noodles drew him from his lair in the den. He shuffled into the kitchen, filled his plate without a word, grabbed the hot sauce from the cupboard—he doused everything in hot sauce, pepper, or both—and went to the fridge.

"Where's the beer?"

"Right where it belongs?"

"I finished the last one earlier."

"Then we're out."

"We can't be out!"

"If you finished the last one, then we're out."

"Why didn't you get more?"

"We'll go to the smoke shop and beer barn tomorrow."

"But we're out!"

"Can't you drink something else?"

"I don't want something else!"

"It's only until tomorrow—"

He flung his plate against the wall. It smashed beside one of the cuckoo clocks and fell in pieces to the brick-tiled floor. Fish fillets and noodles went everywhere. The clock let out a surprised chirp.

"*There*, look! Are you happy *now*?"

"Fred—"

"What good are you, can't even keep enough beer in the house?" He stormed out, stomping down the hall hard enough to make the floor shake.

Maude looked at the mess. Her appetite was gone. She just felt so damn tired, so damn used up. All she wanted to do was crawl into some cool, dark, quiet place and let the world go away.

She knew just where.

Okay, maybe it *was* crazy, but so what? She didn't care anymore.

The sky had the color of an old penny beginning to corrode and go green. The air hung flat, limp, and humid. Planes droned overhead. Traffic made its steady snarl.

The shed door peeled open not with a Velcro sound but a barely-sticky-tape sound from where the tattered mossy threads had already started knitting back together. The cool, musty draft washed over Maude.

She stepped inside, feet sinking into that spongy cushion. She closed the door. Blackness enveloped her. Soft, silent blackness. Wispy tendrils whispered against her face as she moved. The layer of moss at the shed's center was deep, thick, a plush upholstery.

WITH BLACKEST MOSS

The tiny mushroom-cap things pop-pop-pippety-popped with a delightful bubble-wrap sensation when touched, and gave off whiffs of that mild, earthy fragrance.

Maude sat down, then reclined and stretched out. The moss supported and conformed, it molded itself around her in marvelous comfort. It was goose down and fleece, clouds and cashmere.

Eventually, she noticed that the darkness wasn't as total as she'd thought. No light seeped in from outside, but faint speckles of some sort seemed to float, to drift, to waft effortlessly above her. Faint, pale speckles . . . like dust motes . . . spores that eddied on the currents of her breath, swept toward her in whorls when she inhaled, billowed spiraling upward when she exhaled.

She was breathing the stuff, and that might not be so good, but this was too peaceful, too restful, too relaxing for her to worry about possible adverse effects.

Her fingers sank into the moss, combing through it, the substance parting and closing back in to fill the channels. Soothing . . . it was so soothing . . . it would make everything all right again. Shouldn't she be the one taken care of for a change?

This sweet, simple, undemanding, unconditional welcome . . . affection, almost . . . no judging, no anger . . .

Then, her slowly dredging fingers snagged on something not-moss, and Maude brought it up with a vague dreamlike sense that she should have known, or that deep down she'd known all along. The collar's imitation leather was moss-caked now, the encrusted tag dangling.

More tears slipped from the corners of her eyes. Gotten out, they'd told her. Must have gotten out and run off. The gate left unlatched, an accident, such a shame.

That damn dog. Her Woozles.

Not even when she felt the moss creeping over her could she dredge up the energy to be concerned. It not-quite-tickled on her skin, a gentle spreading embrace as it enfolded her limbs. It wove through her hair like a million filament fingers massaging her scalp, and made fluffy earplugs. It blanketed her body.

So quiet. So private. So cool and dark and comfortable.

The moss crept to her cheeks, her forehead, her chin. Tendrils followed the tracks of her tears. Maude closed her eyes to what felt like the delicate brushing of an eyeshadow applicator. She suppressed a slight urge to sneeze as the moss tickled into her nose.

It reached her lips. Her mouth. It cocooned her completely.

The silence held.

The cool air in the shed grew cooler still as the sun finally descended and the sky turned the murky purple-orange of a Los Angeles dusk, heading for the muddy denim that was the closest it ever got to full dark. In the bushes, crickets commenced their chorus.

Later still, as a famous nearby theme park set off its nightly fireworks extravaganza, the vibrations of their thum-*thud* echoing explosive concussion blasts penetrated into the shed, causing the mossy mass at the center to quiver, and rustle, and stir, and rise.

Maude crossed the backyard and patio. The crickets hushed as she passed. The bugs flitting and flicking against the porch light dispersed in a panicky scatter.

She went into the stuffy house. Fans whirred, clocks ticked. Fish fillets sat room temperature on the baking sheet; the pot of noodles had congealed into a Parmesan clump. Pieces of plate and spilled food still littered the floor.

Her footsteps were as muffled and silent as if she wore thick wool slippers, but that didn't stop the old floorboards from creaking as she went down the hall. The den's door stood ajar, the television tuned to a right-wing rant-a-thon about gay marriage and immigration.

The smoke-filled room smelled of alcohol . . . not beer, but the harder stuff he swore he'd given up on and she thought she'd gotten out of the house. Fred, slumped in his

WITH BLACKEST MOSS

recliner with the remote in one hand and bottle in the other, didn't turn as she came in. A full ashtray rested on the arm of the chair, a butt smoldering in the ashy heap.

"*There* you are, about damn time," he said. "Did you want me to sit here and starve all night while you sulked?"

When he didn't get the expected contrite reply, he turned; but by then, Maude was to the recliner. He saw her and gaped.

She grasped him by the head.

Moss rippled along her arms and hands . . . moldy, fuzzy, living black gloves. It rushed over his face with surging, rapid, hideous eagerness. It seethed up his nose and into his mouth, choking off his scream. Fibrous, expanding like a dark fungal form of spray insulation, it clogged his throat and filled his lungs.

Fred thrashed in the chair. Always florid, he went maroon. His bloodshot eyes bulged. His body heaved and lurched. His chest swelled up like that of an enraged bull. One flailing arm hit the recliner's lever, pitching him backwards, kicking his feet up on the footrest. With the other hand, he clutched at Maude and only came away with an oily, fetid fistful.

His spine stiffened, arching him up from the seat. His heels drummed. Then he collapsed, loose and slack, limp deadweight. He shuddered. His fingers twitched.

Then . . . nothing.

Maude waited.

The moss plugging his nostrils and windpipe dissolved with a foamy-hissing-bubbling sizzle like hydrogen peroxide. The wad clenched in his fist withered, going brittle and white, disintegrating into powder. Fred's swollen chest deflated, expelling a sickly gas of alcohol fumes, cigarette smoke, and decay.

Soon, no traces remained, no residue.

Heart failure, they'd decide. Stroke or embolism. Unsurprising in a man of his habits, who hadn't been to the doctor in years because he knew what they'd tell him to do and had no intention of doing it. A pity poor Maude had to find her brother this way, but at least it had been quick.

She'd taken care of Freddie right up until the very end, and isn't that what their mother would have wanted?

The moss prickled and tickled as it crept down her body, the hairlike little rootlets withdrawing from her skin. It flowed onto the den rug, forming a fuzzy lump that grew and coalesced into the semblance of a little black dog. Maude picked it up, stroking the woolly coat. It wiggled with happiness, wagging its stub of a tail.

There'd be so much to do . . . selling the house, starting over . . . but before beginning any of that, she'd call the kids to chat and catch up and apologize.

After all, as people liked to tell her, she'd always been *so* good about putting her family first . . .

FOR BOBBY

THE GUY LOOKED totally normal, and totally out of place because of it.

Maybe that was why Chase's gaze kept twitching back to him during each brief lull as the wranglers moved the line along. They were brisk about it, brisk and efficient. Greet, gush, sign, pic, off you go. Next, please. Lather, rinse, repeat.

He was an older guy, for one. Hardly so strange, there were plenty of aging fanboys in the crowd, as well as plenty of dads. But, the fanboys, you could spot a mile away, regardless of their age, and this guy wasn't one. Nor was he riding herd on a pack of squealing kids or mortifying his teens or tweens by his mere presence.

Nor, for that matter, was he checking out the cosplayers. Not even the scantily-clad ones . . . including a body-paint Queen Moondark probably borderline illegal. Or the dude who'd built an entire replica of Solar Knight's battle armor, complete with lights and sound effects.

Instead, the guy was largely oblivious to the noisy, lively, colorful chaos all around him. As the line advanced, he shuffled forward. Waited. Shuffled forward. Waited. Didn't talk to anyone. Didn't fiddle with his phone.

His expression was somehow both resigned and resolute. A DMV expression. A jury duty expression. A dentist's office expression. Enduring a tedious but necessary evil. It must be done. This, too, shall pass.

The more Chase glanced at him, the odder the guy's

attitude and appearance seemed. Dressed like an off-duty bus driver, no logo- or character-emblazoned tee shirt, no geek-slogan buttons, no tatts. He wore a yellow single-day admission wristband but carried no swag bag or program.

Weird. Weird in a different way from the way the rest of the con-goers were weird. Theirs was a known weird, an understandable and reliable weird.

Take the girl talking to Ammy right now, for instance, eyes alight as she put forth her pet theory about Starglow's true origins and omigod wouldn't it be awesome if Starglow had a long-lost secret little sister? To which Ammy smiled and said gosh and wow and what a great idea. While, at the next table over, a sweaty neckbeard argued with Daniel about how particle accelerators *really* worked; and two spots down from them, security was ushering away an aspiring artist who'd only wanted an honest critique of his portfolio and it was *not* furry porn it was adult anthropomorphaphilia.

You know, ordinary weird.

Chase's gaze twitched to the guy in line again. Closer now. Directly behind a trio of giggly middle-schoolers in iridescent Nebula cloaks and an about-to-lose-it mom telling her toddler to stop that whining or they could just go home right now and he'd never get to meet Space Dog.

Why they'd had to add that stupid goddamn Space Dog... "to appeal to the younger demographic" yeah right whatever. Oh, and "to add a touch of bumbling comic relief." Ugh. To sell stuffed animals, more likely.

Then someone untubed and unrolled a first season promo poster on Chase's table, pushing disgruntled thoughts of Space Dog right out of his head. A collector? No, worse. A resaler. Didn't want it personalized. Only signed. The better to eBay you with, my dear. Couldn't give half a shit about the characters or the show.

Suppressing a sigh, he took up a metallic marker and scrawled his name beside the image of his younger self. Back when Kid Cosmic really *had* been a kid. That uniform.

FOR BOBBY

That haircut. Okay, maybe it hadn't been *that* long ago, but still.

After the resaler was an earnest nerdboy who asked if Kid Cosmic ever got bullied at school, which drew a sympathetic wince from Ammy. Chase never knew how to handle these types of questions. The MCU bunch made it look so easy. He did his best to reassure the nerdboy without advocating either wimpiness or violence, slid him a Cosmic Courage sticker, and shook his hand.

Lather, rinse, repeat. Next!

A pair of MILFy cougars posing with him for a rather uncomfortable let's-make-a-Chase-sandwich pic . . . parents coaxing a shy-struck kindergartner in last year's Halloween costume . . . a pretty girl with a boyfriend glaring jealous daggers Chase's way the entire time she told him how totes dreamy he was . . . some twelve-year-olds wanting to know who'd win in a fight, Kid Cosmic or Spider-Man . . .

Sign this, sign that. Headshots. Programs. An action figure still in the packaging. Sign my boobs (j/k lolz . . . unless he actually wanted to, in which case . . . ahem, moving on!). Did Kid Cosmic know Umbra killed his father? How come the Shriekers' sonic blasts worked in open space? Were Kid Cosmic and Starglow *ever* gonna, y'know–?

Next, please!

A somber, silent presence stepped up to Chase's table. A rough-weathered, callused hand–wrist girded with a yellow single-day admission band–placed a small, scuffed, faux-snakeskin-covered red book beside the stack of glossy 8x10s. Square but thick, like a journal or album, it had clearly seen better days. He left his hand resting atop it as if holding it shut.

Chase raised his gaze. And there, of course, stood the guy he'd noticed earlier. The normal guy, too normal for this scene, so normal he was weird.

Up close, he looked less like a dad and more like a

granddad, or great-uncle. Grey of hair, lined of face, bent of posture. Less like an off-duty bus driver and more like a farmer made to put on his going-to-town clothes when he would've rather stayed at home in biballs and work boots.

He, also, had clearly seen better days.

And his eyes . . .

A legit chill ran down Chase's spine.

At cons, you saw all kinds of crazy fan eyes, from the giddy and overenthusiastic to the pervy-creepy to the scary-stalkery. You saw all kinds of indifferent, annoyed, and even hostile eyes, from unimpressed event staff to hotel guests who didn't know what the fuss was about but sure hated room parties.

This guy, though . . . *this* guy . . .

Legit chill.

His eyes weren't crazy, indifferent, or hostile. His eyes weren't even hollow or empty. His eyes were *dead.*

Chase shivered despite himself.

The old guy slowly drew his hand back from the book. His trailing fingertips rasped against its texture in a really unpleasant way. It was some cheap scale-patterned vinyl or plastic, creased and cracked, stained, even looking scorched in places. The corners had worn down to expose patches of pressboard. Across its front, embossed remnants of gold-tone calligraphy must have once read, "Autographs," though some of the letters had peeled or been all but completely eroded away.

"It ain't mine," the old guy said by way of introduction. Dry. Gruff. "Belongs to my boy." His scarred thumb—clean, but the laborer's grime crusted under the nail was the sort that'd never wash out—rubbed at the fake snakeskin (fakeskin?).

"Your boy," Chase said.

"Bobby." Those dead eyes—faded-denim-blue irises, yellowed and vaguely bloodshot whites, sunken in nests of wrinkles—held his. "He likes your show, my Bobby does."

"That's, uh, great." Any of his usual easygoing charm

FOR BOBBY

and patter seemed to have flown the coop; Chase felt like a dope.

"And you, your fella that you play, you're his favorite."

"Kid Cosmic."

The guy gave a curt nod.

"Is . . . uh . . . your boy . . . is he here with you today?"

The headshake was as curt as the nod. "Bobby, he ain't well."

"Oh . . . I'm, uh, sorry to hear that." Floundering, fumbling, he threw a silent appeal Ammy's way to overhear and step in to help. She was good with these situations.

But Ammy was currently listening—with a familiar pained but polite smile—to some 'shippers earnestly explain how Eclipse wasn't a *villain* deep-down, only misunder*stood*, and if Starglow gave him a *chance*, she could totes save and redeem him!

Which meant Chase was on his own. "Is he . . . uh . . . in the hospital or something?"

"Home. We look after him, me and his ma."

"Wow. That . . . uh . . . must be rough on you both."

The curt shrug matched the headshake and the nod. "Had a nurse what would come in couple times a week, until the insurance run out. For the best, I reckon. Bobby, he don't like people to see him the way he is."

Chase sat feeling awkward, not knowing what to say beyond another round of "sorry to hear" and "must be rough."

He thought of the MCU bunch again, Evans and Downey and Reynolds and Holland and them, going around to hospitals to visit injured fans and sick kids. Cancer wards. Burn units. The Make-a-Wish thing. Doing it in costume. Being kind. Being heroes. Making it look easy. Maybe it *did* come easy to them.

The old guy, meanwhile, seemed to have thawed or warmed to his topic, not that it showed in those dead eyes. "Even us, me and his ma, though G'd knows we're used to it. Ain't so bad, really, not that there's any convincing him that. He's got it in his head folks'd run screaming. Makes us keep the lights down when we come in to bring him his supper or give him his bath."

"Jeez," Chase murmured without intending to, then winced.

If he'd given offense, it went without reaction. "Spends all his time in his room nowadays," the old guy went on. "By himself, mostly, though sometimes he'll let us sit with him, watch a movie or some of his shows, them Netflixes and YouTubes on the computer. Folks what film themselves playing video games and the like. Or lets us read to him if he's too tired to read on his own. Comics, though he's also a bear for a good adventure book, is my Bobby."

"Yeah, reading is great." Jeez, could he sound any lamer?

"The ones about the kids with the time machine, he loves those." His roughened hand touched the worn cover again. "Fella what wrote them, his signature's in here. Last appearance he was ever at, turns out. Right before he, well . . . "

"Yeah." Chase recalled the headlines well enough, and the follow-up spates of PSAs about depression and opioid addiction. "My cousin was a big fan of the Timeskip books too," he added, relieved to have something to say that didn't sound as inane. "And Harry Potter."

"Bobby didn't care for the boy-wizard ones so much," mused the old guy, continuing to stroke the scuffed and peeling faux-snakeskin. "Fine by me, I reckon; no way we ever could've landed *her* autograph. Still, we do by him what we can, his ma and me. I don't mind me a long drive, or a long wait, coming to a place like this. Worth it for Bobby. Sometimes, though, it's too far, or too 'spensive, and we have to let him down. Breaks our hearts, it does."

"I know what you mean," Chase said, once again thinking of the MCU bunch and how Hemsworth could charge a hundred bucks a pop for autographs, let alone posing for photos. His own agent—Ammy's and Daniel's as

FOR BOBBY

well–tried now and then to push for raising their appearance rates, but thus far, despite the show's success and thriving fandom, they were nowhere near raking in that kind of cash.

The old guy patted the book. "Used to be, we could take him around in person. And did he love that? Did he ever! First one was a fella who hosted this TV program all with singing and puppets. About made my ears bleed, you know how it is with those songs, but Bobby, he was over the moon. Got the fella to sign his book, brought it to school next day for show-and-tell. Never seen him so proud and so happy. Sometimes it was just the police chief or department store Santa, or the lady what did our local weather reports, but that didn't matter none to Bobby. Each was special."

"And now, since he . . . can't, uh, go out anymore . . . you do it for him. That's . . . really . . . " Had he already said "great?" He had, hadn't he?

"We do by him what we can," the old guy repeated. "His ma and me. Some ball players in here, an astronaut, couple of them video-game YouTubers, a singer who was on America's Next something-or-other, that little gal from the SnackPack commercials—"

"Oh wow, yeah, I remember her. Do you think they'll ever find out what happened?"

The headshake this time was slower, solemn. "Gone for good, I reckon. Shame."

One of the wranglers approached to indicate they'd used up their allotted time–or exceeded, which was how it felt from where Chase was sitting; he'd been trapped under those dead eyes for what must've been an hour already.

Noticing this, the old guy seemed to gather himself, and even made an effort to muster a smile. "Wouldja mind?" he asked, nudging the book closer to Chase. "Signing, that is. For Bobby. Mean the world to him, it would. Like I said, you're his favorite."

"Sure." Chase reached for a pen. "I'd be glad to."

CHRISTINE MORGAN

An elastic band, stretched thin and frayed, was attached at the top and the bottom of the front cover, serving as a bookmark as well as sectioning off and securing the first clump of pages. The coarse-grained paper had an aged newsprinty tinge to it, and the ripple-warp effect from having been gotten wet and allowed to air-dry. The page edges were slightly ragged. There were more smears and splotches and stains along them. Maybe ink, maybe pencil or charcoal. Maybe tea. Coffee. Chocolate. Blood.

Chase shook himself. Blood? What the hell? Okay, the guy had maybe thrown him off his stride, even spooked him. The fun facts about the author of the Timeskip series and the poor little SnackPack girl hadn't helped. But, blood? Get a grip! Next, he'd be wondering if the aforementioned YouTubers were the same gaming livestreamers who'd gone missing after a convention appearance, or the singer among those killed when a sore loser shot up a reunion show.

"Ain't the prettiest, I know," the old guy said. "Been through a lot. Bobby had it with him when he and his sis, well, when they had the accident. Was on their way to this big kids' channel live-on-stage holiday thing up the city. TV magician who Bobby just adored was set to be there; oh, he wanted to meet that top-hat magic-man more than anything. Been talking about it for months. But then I got called away for work, and the weather turned so's his ma didn't feel safe driving that far."

The pen in Chase's hand felt slick with his own clammy palm-sweat. He wanted to just scribble his signature in the damn book and be done with this unfolding tragedy, but the old guy's dead eyes and low, matter-of-fact tone held him spellbound. Even with the wrangler's signaling growing more urgent, even with the backed-up line of fans in Kid Cosmic t-shirts.

"She meant well, his sis, she did," the old guy went on. "Loved Bobby much as any of us. Thought sure she could

FOR BOBBY

handle it. She were only sixteen, though, and just had her license, and with the roads and the dark and the ice and the pouring-down rain . . . " He trailed off into a sigh, a sigh-of-the-ages type sigh so heavy it even weighed Chase's bones.

"She, uh . . . was she . . . I mean, did they . . . " he fumbled.

"Lost her. Near lost Bobby too. Would've, but a couple fellas coming along behind was able to get his door open and pull him out a'fore the fire went full-on. Whole time? He never let go of his autograph book."

It drew Chase's unwilling gaze again–the dried-waterlogged ripple to the pages, those blistered, half-melted scorch marks, those stains. Blood, he'd thought, and then chided himself. But what if it was? Bobby's or his sister's?

The old guy sighed again. "We hoped someone from the show might hear about it–was on the news and all–and they might offer to come visit Bobby in the hospital. They do that, sometimes, y'know. Celebrity types."

"Yeah," Chase said. "Like the Marvel superheroes. We've, uh, we've done that too."

"Right good of you. Better than the magic-man. Couldn't be bothered to so much as send a card."

He winced, peripherally aware that Ammy was listening in from her table with a stricken sob-story expression. Say the word, and she would've been out of her chair like a shot, ready to costume up the whole cast and go visit Bobby, no matter how he looked. Was that where the old guy was leading?

No, all he did was tap the book again. "Since then, like I said, we do by him what we can. Couldn't hardly pass by the chance to add you to his collection, now, could we? Him loving your show, you being his favorite, and all."

"I, uh . . . yeah . . . yeah, I'd be glad to . . . "

"We all would," Ammy said, leaning over. "We'll have everyone sign, and—"

"Very kind, miss, but that'd be too much to ask. I've done taken enough of your time already. Bobby wouldn't want a fuss."

"Oh." She sat back, blinking, nonplussed. "We have special souvenir gift packs we could—"

Another curt headshake and a raised, weathered hand. "That's all right. Won't be greedy."

"Then, uh . . . " Chase reached for the book, despite not really wanting to touch it. "I should, uh, I can . . . "

"If y'would."

As the old guy went to open it, the frayed, age-stretched elastic band broke—didn't have the oomph left to snap, just kind of feebly parted—and the sectioned-off clump of pages riffled, revealing a flurry of signatures, messages, well-wishes, doodles, and dates.

Wait . . .

Had he just seen . . . that one hadn't been . . .

Couldn't be . . .

He must've misread the numbers. And some of the names.

Major Gillespie? The old guy *had* said there was an astronaut in there, but . . .

And Tornado Joe? *The* Tornado Joe, the daredevil stunt pilot?

And a smudged pink lipstick smooch above "To Bobby, XOXO Angel Leigh"?

Couldn't be. Flat-out impossible.

Sure had looked like, though . . .

"Ah, rat-drat-it," said the old guy, hastily pinching the stray pages together and turning to a blank one. Blank, but yellowed, worn, and far from pristine. He held it there, firmly pressed. "Here you go. If you please."

"How, uh, how old did you say your boy was?" Chase asked, taking two tries to uncap the pen thanks to his suddenly-worsening clammy hand sweats.

The old guy hesitated a beat. "Ten."

Might have been the ordinary let-me-do-the-math

FOR BOBBY

hesitation people sometimes had to do; Chase did it himself whenever pressed to remember anniversaries and stuff.

Still . . .

"Ten?" he asked without meaning to.

The old guy–who had to be pushing seventy, or a hardscrabble sixty at *least*–fixed him again with those dead eyes, his jaw set. "That's right. Ten."

It hung between them, a silent challenge, a dare. Go on. Go on and do it, go on and say something, go on. Go on and ask how a ten-year-old kid could have gotten Angel Leigh's autograph. How, if not for the whole 80's nostalgia craze, a ten-year-old kid would have even known who Angel Leigh *was*.

Chase drew a breath, forced a smile, and bent to the blank page with the pen gripped in a not-trembling-too-badly hand.

"For Bobby," the old guy reminded him.

"Absolutely." He scrawled, *For Bobby, keep it COSMIC and reach for the stars! Your friend, Chase Palmer.* Followed by a quick doodle of Kid Cosmic's sunburst logo and the date.

Before he could add anything else or take a closer inspection of the book, the old guy whisked it away. "Appreciated," he said, doing the curt nod again.

"Uh, yeah, sure . . . " Chase began, but by then, he'd already made a brusque turn and vanished into the crowd.

The next group of fans bustled up to his table, all whoa-dude-so-cool with bright eyes and excitement. One displayed Kid Cosmic's sunburst logo on his forearm, asking Chase to sign next to it so he could go straight from here to the tattoo parlor and have it inked over. One wanted a selfie because "my bros will be so jealous!"

Chase complied, managing to neither pass out nor puke, but it all seemed to be going on at a distance, a step or two removed from solid reality.

Ammy leaned back over, brow cutely furrowed. "You okay? You look kind of funny."

Fair enough; he felt it. As if he might, at any moment, pass out or puke. Or both. The tremors he'd mostly held off came back with a vengeance, the pen still in his hand skidding across the topmost of the stack of 8x10 headshot glossies and scoring a jagged slash through his own image's trademark Kid Cosmic dimpled grin.

"Chase?" Ammy's voice sounded faraway, fuzzed with static.

The way Major Gillespie's famous final transmission had sounded before losing all contact. No one ever knew what happened. No one ever would. Not that it'd stop Matt Damon from making the eventual movie.

Or the way Tornado Joe's historic biplane's radio might have sounded at that fateful airshow, uttering a hiss and a squelch as the storm swept in out of nowhere. Obliterating the fairgrounds. Nineteen dead, dozens more injured.

With an abrupt shove, Chase pushed back his chair and stood.

So many people, looking at him. Looking worried. Murmuring to each other. He surveyed the crowd, searching.

Seeing fans and attendees, cosplayers, moms with kids in tow, dads embarrassing teens and tweens by their mere presence. Seeing events staff, vendors, security. Seeing the wrangler in charge of his table approaching with a concerned frown. Seeing Ammy get to her feet, extending a hand.

Not seeing anyone totally normal and totally out of place because of it. Not seeing an old guy with dead eyes carrying a scuffed faux-snakeskin autograph book.

That singer, those YouTubers, the little SnackPack girl.

Angel Leigh. The sensational crime-scene photos.

Some kids' channel live-on-stage holiday thing with a magician. The accident had made the news.

FOR BOBBY

Maybe it was better not to think about it. Not to wonder.

Or maybe it was already too late. After all, he'd done it, hadn't he? Already signed it, signed his name.

For Bobby.

THE SUITCASE

Just when I'd been starting to think my suitcase had taken another flight, here it came, appearing at the top of the ramp and sliding down onto the baggage claim conveyor belt.

No mistaking it; I'd chosen a neon-yellow glossy hardshell partly because I was sick of playing spot-the-tag in a crowd of basic black. And partly because, well, who'd try to steal the garish, shiny thing? Even if someone did, they'd be easy to spot, easy to remember. I knew because of the looks I got whenever wheeling it around the airport.

As the belt brought it closer to where I stood with my carry-on, I frowned.

It *was* my suitcase, wasn't it? Had to be. No mistaking it, hadn't I just been thinking?

Neon-yellow glossy hardshell. With four sturdy little wheels on the bottom, an extendable handle. Easily held all I'd need for one of my frequent business trips and far less frequent weekend getaways.

Yet, as the belt carried it toward me, I still frowned. Something seemed different, something seemed wrong, but I couldn't put my finger on it. Damage? Had it been dented, scraped, and scratched up, given over to an angry gorilla handler like in those old commercials?

Not that I could see. Looked same as ever, same as when I'd checked it several hours and most of the country ago. It rode among the others—black suitcase, black suitcase, army-green military duffle, black suitcase,

THE SUITCASE

overloaded backpack, black suitcase–like a vivid yellow shout.

Mine. Of course it was. Whose else could it be? Yet there I went, squinting as it jostled along, trying to play spot-the-tag after all.

No tag.

That was the problem. That was what was different. The tag had come off. It'd been a cheap faux-leather thing with a clear plastic window, into which I'd tucked one of my travel alter-ego's cards, but now the tag was gone, card and all.

So, I noticed, was the airline's label, the long sticky-strip the attendant had affixed around the handle. I had the corresponding number slip in my pocket, not that there was now any way to match them up.

As it came within reach, a harried-looking woman elbowed me aside to snag a bag–yet another black suitcase–and the neon-yellow glossy hardshell slipped past for another rotation on the belt.

It looked wrong headed away from me too. Wrong in a way the missing tag and sticker couldn't account for. I had the strangest urge to turn and leave. Just go. Just abandon it there, riding the belt of metal wedges around and around as the others all got claimed and it was alone. Alone until the next flight landed, until the next avalanche of black suitcases came riding down the ramp and the cycle repeated. Alone until some airport employee eventually retrieved it, saw the lack of tag, and trundled it off to the lost luggage area . . . or until someone else, some random person, did decide to try strolling off with an unclaimed orphan.

Good. Let them. Better them than me. Better a TSA drone be the one to open it, to pop the latches and lift the lid and see what was inside. Better an opportunistic total stranger. They'd deserve what was coming to them. They'd deserve whatever happened.

The curving belt carried it out of my sight. As soon as

that poison hornet yellow slid from view, I shook myself. What the hell was I thinking? What was this, a weird jet-lag, a headache delirium brought on by miscalculated cabin pressure or airline food? I hadn't been drinking—never, when I was on an assignment, no drinking, no drugs, nothing to mess with my reflexes—but paranoia reared its shifty head. Had someone slipped me something?

The kid!

Flying solo, escorted on by an attendant, given a plastic flight-wings badge, ensconced across the aisle from me, almost swallowed up by the cushy first-class seat, sneakered feet not even touching the floor. The kid, who'd cheerfully offered me a stick of gum at takeoff "because it helps pop your ears." I hadn't needed it, never did, never had that trouble, but I'd taken the gum anyway. Minty-fresh.

The little brat! And who would *do* that, use a *kid*? That was low. That was dirty.

They were onto me. My cover, this cover, this alias, must be blown.

Or it *was* just jet-lag, travel fatigue, ordinary exhaustion. Had me twitchy, jumping at shadows, making something out of nothing.

Instincts, though . . . my instincts had always been good . . . sharp as a stiletto, accurate as a sniper rifle . . . and my instincts were saying—

A flash of poison hornet yellow caught my eye. The suitcase, appearing again around the belt's bend. Alone now; riding alone on the conveyor. Alone, like me in this current baggage claim lull between flights, alone with the arrivals and departures board flickering through time-gate-destination.

Alone, except for . . .

The kid. The chewing-gum kid from first-class, being escorted by another attendant toward a uniformed driver waiting by a sleek tinted-window limo. The kid, chattering a-mile-a-minute while rolling along a wheeled suitcase,

THE SUITCASE

pushing it by its extendable handle, steering it as if driving a toy racecar. I could see the cheap faux-leather tag, and the airline sticker flapping like a papery white tongue against neon-yellow hardshell.

I spun again to the baggage claim conveyor, grabbing the other suitcase. Heavy! So heavy I nearly dislocated my arm heaving it off the metal belt, so heavy I dropped it. Its latches clicked, its lid sprung ajar. Its contents spilled messily onto airport floor tiles.

People screamed.

Hadn't I been alone only a second ago? Yet now suddenly there was a crowd, a screaming crowd, pointing and panicking. Suddenly, there were security guards, shouts, sirens.

And the kid. The kid up on tip-toe peering to see. The kid, meeting my gaze with a mocking grin before ducking into the limo, vanishing behind tinted glass.

The kid, who—this thought, my only consolation—was also going to be in for one hell of a surprise when *he* opened *my* suitcase.

For Heather and Sean Seebach

EATING FOR TWO

"THE STORE BOUGHT ONES kept coming back negative," Charlene said. "But I *knew*."

White paper crackled under her. A draft tickled through the gap in the back of the flimsy gown.

"And when was your last period?" the nurse asked, pen poised.

"Three months ago."

The pen scratched. Charlene swung her feet. A third of the way there, she was a third of the way along already. After waiting so long, *wanting* so long . . . to think that her dream was finally coming true!

Martin would be thrilled. She hadn't said anything yet, harboring her happy suspicions to herself until she could say for sure. Martin, dear though he was, had a stickler streak and the first words out of his mouth after an expression of joy would be to ask what the doctor had said.

As if any doctor could know a woman's body better than the woman herself.

The nurse finished noting down Charlene's statistics. They'd weighed her on the way into the exam room. Not much gained yet. Not even enough that Martin had noticed. He had remarked on the increase in her appetite, though.

Was it any wonder? She was eating for two now.

The very thought filled her with such a warm and giddy tingle that she laughed aloud.

The nurse presented Charlene with a cup, a plastic tube

EATING FOR TWO

with a black lid, and some folded sheets of gauze. "C. Bryant" was scrawled on the tube in blue grease pencil.

"I know what to do," Charlene said before the nurse could explain the proper technique. After doing it, she washed her hands, examined her face eagerly in the mirror for the "motherly glow" that hadn't arrived yet, and hugged herself.

"A baby," she said to her reflection. "At last!"

The typical wait for the doctor was made far more bearable by contemplating names. Allison or Sarah, Michael or Jason. She flipped through magazines aimed at working mothers, storing away ideas for the nursery. A bright, sunny yellow, she decided. Good for either a girl or a boy. With a bear and honey-bee motif.

It just figured. Most of the week, there was nothing good on, but the shows he liked had to be scheduled opposite each other. He flipped back and forth between two of his favorites, catching synchronized commercials on both channels. That figured too.

"Martin?" Charlene sat down and took the remote away. "I went to see the doctor today."

"You . . . what's the matter?" He straightened up. "You've been looking pale lately, but I didn't want to say anything–"

She set her fingertips to his lips. "Everything's fine, Martin. Better than fine. We're going to have a baby."

"Oh, Charlie! Really? When?"

"Early January. A New Year's baby. I even had an ultrasound." She remembered the cold, clammy jelly and the thrill of hearing the quick watery throbbing inside her. "But it's too soon to tell if the baby's a boy or a girl. I'm not sure I even want to know until the time comes. What do you think?"

"Whatever you want is great with me," Martin said,

putting his arms around her. They leaned their heads together, brow to brow. "Just tell me what you need me to do."

"I can give you a whole list," Charlene said. "We'll need to turn the guest room into a nursery, and buy a car seat, and a million other things."

"What about *you*, though, Charlie? You've been so tired all the time."

"That's because my energy's been going to the baby. Don't you worry. Dr. Wales referred me to a specialist. Dr. Lysander. I've got an appointment with her next Tuesday."

"I'll call Stan and tell him to find coverage for me," Martin said.

"Don't be silly. I can handle it on my own."

"But I should be there."

"When the baby's born, you will be. But save the time off until then." She kissed the tip of his nose. "Someone will have to keep the house clean, do the shopping, cook all the meals, take care of the laundry . . . "

"My grandson's going to be a twelve-pounder if you keep packing it away like that," Jane Keller said.

"Eating for two," Charlene said, beaming. She patted her stomach and let her palm linger on the rounded bulge. "And it might be a granddaughter."

"Or triplets, by the look of you. But, Charlie, honey, you still don't look well. Have you been having bad morning sickness?"

"No, hardly at all."

"Sleeping all right? Is he kicking you and keeping you awake at all hours?"

"Who, Martin?"

Her mother gave her a narrow, humorless look. "The baby."

"Mom, please. Everything is fine."

EATING FOR TWO

"What does the doctor say?"

Charlene rolled her eyes. "You're as bad as Martin, I swear."

They had a window booth, and Charlene could see a ghost of herself in the glass. The maternity smock proudly showcased her six-month pregnancy, and if the scooped neckline revealed prominent collarbones, so what? Her face was thinner, but that suited Charlene fine because she'd been cursed with chubby chipmunk cheeks since she was little.

"When I was carrying you," Jane said, "I remember my hair got so thick, so lustrous. Yours looks like a dry nest."

"Thanks, Mom." She touched her hair self-consciously. It did feel on the brittle side, and more of it had been coming out in her comb, but . . . "I switched conditioners. Must have been a mistake."

Waddling back to the car made her lower back ache, and she had a time of it trying to squeeze herself behind the wheel, but she relished these minor discomforts. Emily or Christopher would make it all worthwhile.

The message light was blinking on the answering machine when she got home. As always, it sent a nervous pang through her. She played them back, saving the ones for Martin and the innocuous ones from her friends.

The ones from Dr. Wales's office and Dr. Lysander's nurse, she erased.

"What would you think about a midwife?" Charlene asked on Thanksgiving night, the soporific effects of turkey countered by the I-should-have-saids buzzing around in her mind. Her mother had brought an extra dish to the table this year: a heaping platter of nosy questions.

In the darkness of their bedroom, Martin was only a shadow outlined by the dim blue radiance of the clock radio, a man-shape looming beside her as he rose up on one elbow. "A midwife? You mean, like for a home birth?"

"That's exactly what I mean," she said. She was curled on her side with a pillow between her knees and her left arm cradling the swell of her belly. It had taken her fifteen minutes to get comfortable in this position and she didn't want to wreck it. "Natural childbirth."

"Sounds kooky to me."

"What's so kooky about it? Women have been doing it that way for thousands of years. In some parts of the world, they still do."

"In some parts of the world, they still live in mud huts," he said. "I'd feel a lot better knowing that we were in a nice sanitary hospital with plenty of doctors around. Just in case."

"You're sweet, but I keep telling you it's going to be fine," Charlene said. "Wouldn't you rather our son or daughter was born right here in our own house?"

"Frankly, no," he said. "What does Dr. Lysander say about it?"

She sighed. "We've discussed a bunch of options. She provided me with a list of qualified, certified midwives. And, you know, if something *did* go wrong, we're only five miles from the hospital."

"That can be a long way in January."

Tears sprang to her eyes. The weeping fits came at the drop of a hat, perfectly normal. Hormones. Emotions. "I want it to be special!"

"Charlie, it will be special," Martin said, touching her shoulder. "No matter where we are, it will be special, because this is our baby, our family, that we're talking about."

"So why can't it be born at home?"

"Look, I . . . Charlie . . . maybe we could talk about it together, all of us, you and me and Dr. Lysander. I'd probably feel a lot better about it then."

"You don't trust me."

"I do, I trust you!"

"You don't think I'm telling you the truth about what

EATING FOR TWO

the doctor said," she said. "You and my mother, everybody, you all think I'm hiding something!"

"No, of course we don't."

"No? So how come every time I have an appointment, you or Mom try to come with me? I'm a grown woman, Martin. I think I know what's best for my body and my baby."

"I *want* to be there, Charlie. It's my baby too. I want to hear the heartbeat and see him or her on the ultrasound. You won't even let me feel the baby kick." He moved his hand around as if to lay it on her abdomen, and Charlene angrily batted it away.

"I'm tired, Martin. I don't want you groping me."

"I'm not trying to grope—"

"Groping, prying, pestering, everyone telling me I look like hell, giving me a hard time about how much I eat; don't you people have anything better to do?"

"Look," Martin said, and she could hear the controlled irritation in his voice. "I know you're upset, you're going through all sorts of changes—"

"Thank you so much, Dr. Bryant! What a brilliant deduction!"

"But the people who care about you have a right to worry, Charlie. I love you, I love our baby, and I want to help. We should be going to the childbirth classes together."

"They're during your work hours."

"I can rearrange my schedule. I can come with you to your next appointment—"

"We've already discussed that." She sniffled and wiped her eyes, which were hot and puffy and wet. "Now, can't I *please* get some rest?"

"Fine. Fine, Charlie. Maybe I'll go sleep on the couch so I don't bother you."

"Maybe you should," she said.

With a sort of fuming snarl, he lunged out of bed. She lay there in the dark, her body rigid, feeling the pulsing throb in her crowded womb and the faint plea from her squashed bladder. Her throat tightened and a fresh spate of tears brimmed, but she held back the storm until he was out of the bedroom and the door was closed behind him.

The house had all the warmth of the tundra. Charlene wasn't speaking to him, her lips pressed into a white line. Hadn't his father advised him to never go to sleep with an unresolved quarrel? Or never start a fight before bedtime?

The office was a welcome refuge after a tense holiday weekend. Martin poked at his work, wondering what he could have done differently. There had to have been a better way to handle it.

He'd been doing everything she wanted. At first, it had been fun. He'd enjoyed the cliché of running out to the store in the dead of night to satisfy her urgent need for ice cream. They had decorated the nursery together, paint and wallpaper, furniture, toys, drawers full of tiny unisex clothes at the ready. Their list of names was updated and amended weekly, with Jeremy or Ashley being the current picks.

But Charlene . . . if she could see herself, really step outside and *see* what she looked like . . . for all the time she spent in front of the full-length mirror, Martin didn't think she ever looked at herself. Always at the rounded bulge of her stomach. Never at her pallid skin, her sunken eyes, her thinning hair that had somehow lost all of its color.

She said the sores around her lips were normal, a reaction to the prenatal vitamins. Martin hadn't found that side effect listed in any of the books and articles he'd been collecting on the sly. Charlene's feet didn't bloat from water retention either. She said that some women lucked out of that malady. Maybe so. But his unofficial poll of his co-workers, which opened him up to more new-parent war stories than he'd ever wanted to hear, didn't jibe with it.

EATING FOR TWO

And now this midwife thing . . . it sounded crackpot to Martin, conjuring mental images of the Middle Ages. He was willing to admit that he might be having a knee-jerk 21st century reaction, but if Charlene wasn't going to give him the chance to learn more, what else could he do?

He was staring blankly at his computer when Stan popped over the wall of the cubicle and beaned him in the forehead with a wadded-up piece of paper.

"Get your phone, why don't you, Marty?"

Martin shook himself and realized that his phone was emitting its polite little burr. He picked it up and identified himself.

"Mr. Bryant, this is Jim Wales. I'm sorry to bother you at work, and I realize this may be a trifle out of order–"

"Wales? Oh, right." Sudden dread sank through the center of Martin like a lead weight. "This is about Charlene, isn't it?"

Wales cleared his throat. "Do you know, has she been following up on her appointments with Dr. Lysander?"

"Yes, regularly," Martin said.

"And how's that all going?"

"Isn't that something you should be asking Charlene?" In the following pause, Martin could sense Wales's discomfort.

"Your wife hasn't returned any of our calls," Wales finally said.

"I see," said Martin, who didn't.

"I suppose it's not for me to worry about," Wales said. "Dr. Lysander is among the best in the field, and I'm confident that Mrs. Bryant is in expert hands. I'm sure this glitch in the records department will get cleared up eventually."

"What glitch?" Martin asked.

"We haven't received any copies of Dr. Lysander's notes for our file," Wales said. "They've recently switched to a new computer system at Community Central, and I'm sure you can imagine the chaos that causes. When I tried to request the copies by phone, the secretary I spoke to wasn't even able to find your wife's name in their records. But, like I said, I'm sure it will be cleared up."

"These things usually are," Martin said, barely aware of what he was saying. "I'll tell Charlene that you called and ask her to get in touch."

"I'd appreciate that, Mr. Bryant."

Wales seemed about to say more, but Martin's other line rang then, and he had to cut the doctor short. "I'm sorry, but I have another call. Thanks, Dr. Wales."

He pressed the button by the blinking light, expecting it to be a colleague and hoping for it to be Charlie, and being wrong on both counts. His mother-in-law's voice filled his ear.

"Martin, I know Charlene thinks it isn't any of my business, but I had to talk to you. I'm so worried about her lately. Can we meet?"

The mall was dazzling with holiday decorations, but this late in the season, the atmosphere was turning from cheer to scrambling desperation. The line at the gift-wrapping station stretched the length of a football field.

Charlene sat by the fountain nearest the food court, arms folded on the high shelf of her tummy, praying that Nina Foster would arrive before the gushing of the water made her have to trek to the bathroom again.

She was aware of passers-by looking at her, most of them women. Some were clearly envious of her condition. Some were scornful, paying more attention to her thin face and lifeless hair, turning to their girlfriends with whispered catty remarks. And some, particularly the new mothers pushing strollers or ambling along with their babies in their arms, looked at Charlene with warm smiles, as if they were welcoming her impending entrance into their exclusive club.

EATING FOR TWO

Beneath her hands, Jillian or Nathan stirred restlessly.

"Mrs. Bryant?"

Charlene sized her up. Admirably slim in a way that Charlene had never been even before the pregnancy. Short brown hair and an engaging grin. Not the wizened Druidess that she knew Martin was envisioning.

Charlene struggled to get up, but before she could so much as gather her legs under herself, Nina Foster dropped onto the bench beside her. Charlene saw a dubious concern in the woman's hazel eyes.

"Don't get up, Mrs. Bryant. Are you okay?"

"Fine," Charlene said. "And please, call me Charlene. You should see me try to get off the living-room couch. I know you prefer to meet clients in their homes, the environment where you'll be working and all, but I thought it'd be better if we got to know each other here first. Besides, it's less of a drive for you."

"More of one for you," Nina Foster said.

"Believe it or not, I can still reach the pedals. I just have to mind my breathing or I honk the horn with my belly button."

"And your due date is in two more weeks? I wish you had contacted me sooner. I like to work in concert with the obstetrician so we can coordinate a proper plan of care. Who's your doctor?"

"Jane Keller," Charlene said.

"I don't think I know her," Nina said.

"She only opened her practice here last year. I got your name and number from a handout they gave me." She rummaged in her purse and produced the folded photocopy listing local birth centers and midwives.

"Huh," Nina said. She studied Charlene. "Well, I really should consult with Dr. Keller. You and your husband should be there too. This is a team effort, after all."

"Martin?" Charlene laughed brightly. "I'm afraid he wouldn't be much help with the actual birth. He's scared silly by the whole thing, says he'd probably faint dead away."

"Mrs. Bryant—"

"Charlene."

"Charlene," Nina said. "Why do I have the feeling you're not telling me everything?"

"Why wouldn't I? This is the most important thing I've ever done, having this baby. I want it to be perfect." She struggled to her feet. "I'll tell you what. Let's go back to the house. I'd love to have you look over the nursery and tell me what else needs to be done. We can call my doctor from there, and when Martin gets home, you can meet him too. You can ride home with me and Martin can bring you back to pick up your car later. I'll even make dinner."

"I couldn't impose—"

"Nina," Charlene chided. "You're going to help bring my baby into the world. That makes you practically part of the family."

"Sneaking out for lunch with another woman?" Stan asked as Martin, briefcase in hand, passed his cubicle.

"Har har, very funny," Martin said. "Not that it's any of your business, but I'm meeting my mother-in-law."

"You're either the best son-in-law in the history of the world or you get mega bonus brownie points for ass-kissing."

Lacking a retort, Martin scowled and made his way to the elevator. He felt almost as sleazy as if he *were* sneaking out to have an affair. It was every bit as much a betrayal, at least from Charlie's point of view.

"Martin, we have to do something," Jane said when the pleasantries had been exchanged and their meals ordered. Meals, he knew, that both of them would pick at since they lacked Charlene's enormous appetite.

"I know, but what? What can we do? I've read that being pregnant makes a woman go through some personality changes, but this is like living with a total stranger. Every time I try to talk to her about the baby, she clams up."

"We might need to go over her head and talk to her doctor," Jane said.

"You mean behind her back."

"Whichever. You're right, Martin. She isn't herself. She hasn't been herself in months. You're her husband, and I'm her mother, and no matter what Bill says, we have a right to know what's going on."

"Bill doesn't agree, I take it." Martin wasn't surprised. His father-in-law had some old-fashioned ideas about what constituted men's business and women's business, with bread-winning falling into the former category and childbearing the latter.

"You know how he is. He says I should leave Charlene alone to make her own decisions. He says I shouldn't take over the birth of her first child for her the way I took over her wedding."

That was almost enough to make Martin smile. "Isn't that the prerogative of the mother of the bride?"

"That's what I told Bill. But never mind. I think something's wrong, Martin, seriously wrong, and Charlene's not telling us. She's always been like that. When she was a little girl, if she cut her finger or burned herself, she'd run to her room and hide from me rather than let me help."

"She wouldn't do that with something this important," Martin said.

It was wishful thinking and he knew it. Jane's description matched exactly with the way Charlene acted whenever she was hurt or sick. Under the guise of "I didn't want to worry you," she never told him when she had so much as a dentist appointment for a routine cleaning.

"We have to talk to this Dr. Lysander," Jane said. "And if she tries to give me any nonsense about doctor-patient confidentiality, I will read her the riot act, just you watch me do it."

"You don't have to convince me," Martin said. "Charlie told me that Lysander's office was at Community Central. That's not far from here. Should we call first or–"

"Oh, mercy, no," Jane said. "They'd brush us off and then contact Charlene."

"I don't like tricking her."

"It's for her own good, and the baby's too. We'll march right into that office and demand some answers."

Nina Foster held her bag on her lap, a prickle of unease at the back of her neck.

Something was wrong in this car. Something was wrong with the woman sitting in the driver's seat, which was rolled back as far as it would go to make room for her stomach behind the steering wheel.

Charlene Bryant's pale, gaunt face was intent, her glittering eyes fixed on the road as she drove through the maze of tidy upscale suburban streets. She hadn't spoken for several miles. Every now and then, she would contort and groan as if in the initial stages of labor. A rough ride like this wasn't going to do her or the baby any favors. But when Nina mentioned it, she got no reply.

"Here we are," Charlene said, stopping the car in front of a house as tidy and upscale as the rest.

This was bad. This was wrong. Nina's instincts were screaming at her. She would not have been surprised– terrified, but not surprised–to see some axe-wielding maniac come lurching out the door, as out of place in this quiet neighborhood as a circus elephant.

"It's going to be wonderful when it's–" Charlene broke off with a strangled cry, bending double. She clutched at her stomach. A gush of fluid suddenly darkened her stretch pants.

"Oh, no," Nina said. "Your water? You are in labor, aren't you?"

EATING FOR TWO

"Is it time? Is my baby coming?"

For a horrible moment, all sensible thought abandoned Nina. She gripped her bag and looked wildly around for help. Then, with a deep shaking breath, she got control of herself.

"Come on, Charlene. Let's get you inside, out of the cold. Here, lean on me." She was alarmed by the feverish heat of Charlene's skin and how bone-thin Charlene's arms were.

"Keys . . . in my purse," Charlene gasped out. "Oh, God, it hurts. Help me, Nina. My baby's coming."

The hospital lobby was clean and bright enough to allay some of Martin's fears. The staff seemed respectful and professional as they went about their duties. Nothing bad could happen to Charlene if a place like this was involved.

"Over there," Jane Keller said, pointing to a large board on which the names of the doctors were listed by department.

Martin looked under O, spotted a listing for H. Lysander on the fourth floor, and started toward the elevators. Jane's fingernails dug into his arm.

"What?" he asked as he jabbed the *up* button.

"Martin . . . " Jane said in a small, faint voice.

He looked at her and thought she was about to pass out. Her skin had gone the color of cottage cheese, and her eyes were swimming with shock. Heart attack? There were worse places for one than the lobby of a major metropolitan hospital, but . . .

"Jane, what's the matter?"

"Didn't you see it? What it said?"

"Sure. Fourth floor. Obstecology, or whatever they call it."

"No, Martin." She swallowed and crushed his hand in hers. "Dr. Lysander wasn't listed under Obstetrics. Her name was under Oncology."

"Oncology? No, that can't be right. That's for—"
"Cancer," Jane said. "It's for cancer."

Charlene's body strained, muscles locked and quivering. She pushed until starbursts filled her vision. When the spasm passed, she fell back onto the makeshift bed of sofa cushions that Nina had hastily arranged on the floor.

"That's good," Nina said, but she looked sick with worry. "Hold on just a second so I can call someone. An ambulance—"

"No," Charlene said. Puffing in short, sharp breaths, she pushed again. She thought that was what they recommended in the childbirth classes. Maybe she should have attended one after all. "I want it to be born here at home. No doctors. I don't trust them anymore."

"But, Charlene, you have to think of the baby's health. It's a couple of weeks early, and—"

"My doctor," she said, "my own family doctor, tried to tell me that I would never have a baby. Can you believe it?"

"Charlene," Nina interrupted, peering between Charlene's legs. "I don't want to frighten you, but I've never seen discharge this color before."

"He wanted me to go into the hospital," Charlene said, ignoring her. "He wanted them to cut me, operate on me, give me radiation treatments."

Another clenching contraction seized her. She gritted her teeth and pushed with all her might, feeling inner tissues stretch as Jillian or Nathan inched closer to birth.

"I see the . . . " Nina's voice trailed off as her eyes widened.

"The head?" Charlene craned her upper torso, trying to see, but the bulk of her body prevented her.

"Uh . . . uh . . . " Nina said. She had gone waxy-white, and her mouth worked as the glottal sounds came from her throat.

EATING FOR TWO

"He said," she panted when the contraction passed, "that I had a uterine tumor. Growing out of control. He said they should take it out before it became inoperable. That I'd probably have to have a complete hysterectomy. What kind of a doctor is that, I ask you?"

Another one struck, the most intense yet, wringing a cry of pain from Charlene as she bore down hard as she could. This time, she felt movement, a slippery-sliding-evacuating sensation.

Rather than moving to catch the newborn, Nina tottered back and collided with the edge of the mantle.

A mewling wail rose from between Charlene's knees.

"Is it a boy or a girl?" she asked. She heaved herself into a sitting position and looked down at the lumpy, mottled thing that had exited her womb. It was moving clumsily, as if searching, and making that reedy, plaintive cry.

"Oh, there, there," cooed Charlene, gathering it into her arms. She held it to her breast, feeling its warm pulse of life. She rocked back and forth. "Mama's got you, and everything's going to be just fine."

Martin breathed a sigh of relief when he saw Charlene's car in the driveway. The other vehicles pulled in behind him. Jane Keller looked anxiously back at the ambulance and the police car, grimacing.

"What a spectacle for the neighbors," she murmured. "To have them see her taken away like this, like some kind of lunatic carted off by the men in the white coats."

"What the neighbors think is the last thing on my mind," Martin said. "Charlene *has* to get treatment. It might already be too late."

Helene Lysander had stepped out of the back of the ambulance and was conferring with two orderlies and a female police officer. Martin gestured for them all to stay back.

"I'll go in first," he said. "Maybe I can talk some sense into her."

He opened the front door, and a stink slapped him full in the face. It was high and meaty, a blood-smell but something else as well, something like oranges gone all soft and rotten. Gagging on it, he went inside.

Someone was singing. He could hear a sweet voice crooning from upstairs, from the nursery. Charlene's voice, singing a lullaby.

As he started for the stairs, Martin was brought up short by a trail of scarlet footprints on the carpet. He turned his head, looked into the living room, saw something by the fireplace. A woman. He thought so, anyway. Or at least, it used to be.

Martin's throat clicked as he tried to speak. He coughed, nearly vomited. "Charlene?"

Upstairs, the song broke off and she called, "Up here, darling. In the nursery."

He mounted the stairs on legs that felt like jointed wood. At the end of the hall, the door was standing ajar on a room of sunshine yellow with honey bees and bears.

Charlene turned to him and put a finger to her lips. "Shh," she said, and indicated the crib with a tilt of her head. "The baby's already eaten, such a hungry thing too! Now it's sleepy-bye time."

Something was in the crib, partly covered by a crocheted yellow blanket that rose and fell in rhythmic heaves. Martin bent over for a closer look and choked.

"Oh, you," Charlene said, smiling at him. "They all look a little funny when they're first born. Now we just need to decide on a name. What do you think of Daniel, or Diana?"

WINDOW DRESSING

A TRIO OF smirking teenage girls outside the coffee place kept glancing her way . . . in between glances at their phones, that was. They didn't actually talk to each other aloud; the conversation seemed to be being conducted via text.

Well, via text, smirks, eyerolls, and snide, knowing looks.

Marcella tried her best to ignore them, or at least not to let on that she was aware of their silent commentary. High school nonsense. She was well past that, thank you very much. She was a grown woman, a career woman with an office and a bank account and her own apartment.

True, it wasn't a private corner office, not yet, but it was in one of the shining glass-and-steel skyscrapers of Century Plaza. And true, her no-frills apartment was a bus ride and two rail transfers away from work, but its comparatively cheap rent certainly helped shore up the bank account. When she finally did get her downtown condo, she'd be able to furnish it in the style of which she'd always dreamed. Until then, she didn't mind scrimping and saving wherever she could.

Such as coffee, for instance. The contents of her travel mug had been brewed in her tiny kitchenette rather than whipped and steamed by some sullen barista for nine dollars plus tip. Nor did she need a new phone every other month, laden with pricey and frivolous apps. Those smirking teenagers probably had daddy-money, Ubered everywhere rather than stoop to (eew) public transit, and as for their clothes . . . paying a fortune to look like trashy tramps . . .

Now, to be fair, most of Marcella's budget *did* go toward her wardrobe. Clothes and shoes, accessories, hair and makeup products. But that was different. A vital and necessary business expense. Dress for the job you want and all that. Sweet promotions weren't offered to frumps. People who didn't keep up appearances didn't get executive titles and their names on the door.

Yet, it somehow seemed her outfit was the object of the teenage smirks. As if they had any idea! Them with their artfully shredded jeans or tight mini-skirts, their crop-tops and pierced navels, their slutty stack-heel strappy sandals. The nerve of them, sneering and snickering at her smart corporate attire!

Unless . . .

Paranoia gripped her with cold, intangible fingerlings of fear. Did she have a run? A stain? A split seam or errant tag sticking out like a designer tongue? Was she misbuttoned, or inside-out? Horror of horrors, had she sat in something on the bus?

From down the block, the big sleek silver-white cityrail J-line hummed toward the stop. Marcella, trying to be casual, not wanting to let the girls know they'd gotten to her, risked a quick peek at the nearest window of the old brownstone behind her.

The dull and dingy pane of warped plate glass served as a murky mirror, showing her a distorted reflection more like something from a funhouse: spindly and tall, limbs elongated, head so blurred by grime it might not even have been there. Made for a kind of creepy effect.

As far as she could tell, though, her outfit looked fine. Smart suit with slim skirt and trim blazer over silky blouse–

With a whirr and a whoosh, the railcar arrived. Its doors slid open and the usual commuter do-si-do began,

WINDOW DRESSING

people embarking and disembarking, maneuvering briefcases and laptop bags.

Marcella joined the on-board migration, swiftly finding a seat amid the jostle of newspapers, phones, and travel mugs. Nobody in the railcar sneered or smirked at her appearance.

Just bratty teenage girls being bratty teenage girls, she decided as she settled in for the ride to work. Might not have had anything to do with her after all.

The next morning, though–Wednesday–it happened again.

Not with a trio of teens but a pair of little old ladies, eating muffins and sipping coffee at one of the cafe's outdoor tables. Lacking phones with which to text, they tipped their frail blue-rinse perms together and whispered behind wizened, ring-laden hands. But a smirk was still a smirk, as a sigh was just a sigh, fundamental things of life and what the heck was their problem anyway?

Again, anxious but trying not to show it, Marcella surreptitiously checked her reflection in the brownstone's dingy window. She wore dark blue today, a demure knee-length dress with three-quarter sleeves, and a patterned scarf to add a touch of vibrant color. The goal was to come across capable and serious in the meeting but not too somber or funereal.

She'd studied herself thoroughly before leaving the apartment and been satisfied overall. Now, second-guessing: Was the scarf too much? *Too* colorful, crossing the line into gaudy? But without it, the dress was understated almost to the point of being drab; she couldn't go into that meeting resembling a nun, or an Amish woman, or something!

The reflection, wavery and distorted in the murky glass, wasn't much help. It made her look almost freakishly tall and thin, washing out her skin tone to a pallid and weirdly unnatural shade. It reminded her of those artist's depictions of UFO aliens, only without the bulbous bald head . . . because that grimy smudge erased her head into a blur . . .

The dress was fine, though! Not drab, not dowdy, not nunlike or Amish. And the scarf wasn't gaudy at all . . . her shoes were subtly elegant without being obvious, matching today's purse almost–

Wait.

Marcella looked down at the purse hanging at her side and at the travel mug in her hand. She looked up at the window again. Something was–

Right then, an errant ray of morning sun-glare beamed between buildings, splaying across the murky glass, turning it into a dull dazzle. At the same moment, she heard the hum of the J-line approaching and got nearly bumped aside by a hurrying businessman who scowled as if it was her fault for not watching where he was going.

She boarded the railcar. Having no luck finding a seat– the businessman had bulled past her to claim the last one–she stood and held on to one of the looped vinyl straps with the hand not holding her travel mug. Which of course *must* have been part of her reflection; she'd only imagined the empty curve of long thin fingers around nothing.

A trick of the eyes, thanks to dirty glass and sun-glare, that was all. Or a trick of the nerves. She'd been under a lot of stress lately, a lot of important meetings coming up. Teenage girls and little old ladies weren't really smirking at her. Why would they? She looked fine. Cool, crisp, and professional. Fine.

Nonetheless, she darted another peek over her shoulder. Silly; she was in the railcar, the heads of fellow passengers and the stop shelter itself were between her and the brownstone's window, and anyway, the angle would be all wrong . . .

But she saw, for the merest fleeting instant as the

WINDOW DRESSING

railcar accelerated, the tall slender figure in the dark blue dress and colorful scarf . . . without a travel mug in hand, without an arm raised to hold the commuter strap . . . standing perfectly poised and perfectly still . . . and perfectly headless.

Thursday dawned warm, muggy, and rain-drenched grey. The streets and sidewalks were awash, the gutters frothing and flooding. Awful traffic and awful moods went along with the awful weather. Everyone was wet, everyone was cranky, everyone was running late.

Marcella included, rushing from the bus stop to the railcar stop with her slicker and umbrella. She'd forgotten her coffee, hadn't had time for breakfast, and the man who'd sat beside her on the bus had smelled like damp dogs.

The covered shelter was packed sardine-tight with grumpy people. The cafe's outdoor seating area was deserted, chairs upturned on the round tables, water dripping steadily from the awnings. Irritable brakelights of slow-moving cars coated the asphalt with red sheens like fresh blood.

Overheard snatches of annoyed conversation informed her that the railcars were running late too. Which was good in the sense she hadn't missed the J-Line downtown, but bad in the sense that she might miss her crosstown connection, and she did not relish the prospect of trudging nine blocks in the rain.

Or being late for work; yesterday had gone badly enough. Important meetings were no place for rattled nerves and being off one's game. Her supervisor had told her later that she'd done fine, just fine, but Marcella knew better.

She edged into the slightly recessed doorway of the old brownstone rather than try to cram herself into the shelter.

CHRISTINE MORGAN

It wasn't much, but between its overhang and her umbrella, she at least wouldn't drown.

Faded gilt lettering on the glass beside her caught her attention. Hours of operation, long since flaked and peeling. The building had once been home to a department store, not one of the big-name upscale ones, now decades closed. Signs occasionally came and went—FOR SALE, FOR LEASE, RENOVATION COMING SOON, PROPOSED LAND USE ACTION—but nothing ever seemed to actually happen. Kind of peculiar, really, now that she thought about it. It was a decent location, the property worth too much to be left derelict and vacant.

As she shifted around to try and read more of the bygone lettering, partly curious and partly trying to fend off the killer combo of frustration and impatience, she jumped and nearly squeaked aloud when suddenly someone was right there. Though she managed not to squeak, she did gasp, but the steady rain and traffic covered her noise.

The someone loomed in front of her, tall and thin, a figure carrying an umbrella and wearing a sleek dolphin-grey slicker almost identical to her own.

Almost? No . . . *identical* to her own . . .

Then she realized, with a flush of embarrassment, she was only seeing her own reflection again.

Then she realized, with a little laugh and a hotter embarrassed flush, she wasn't seeing her own reflection at all.

She was seeing a mannequin. A department store mannequin on the other side of the glass. With a mannequin's stretched, sylphlike proportions . . . a mannequin's unnatural "flesh"-colored skin tone . . . a mannequin's long headless neck ending in a smooth stump.

A mannequin! Wearing a sleek dolphin-grey slicker like hers, carrying an umbrella like hers. Even wearing the same cutely buckled boots and designer slacks.

The past couple of days, instead of the window serving

WINDOW DRESSING

as a dull, dingy, distorted mirror, it had only been a silly mannequin wearing the same clothes!

Wait.

Wearing the same clothes? Each different day?

The same smart suit on Tuesday, yesterday's dark blue dress with the colorful scarf, and now this?

But . . .

But that didn't make any sense.

The department store was *closed*! Had been closed for years. For *decades*! Was someone changing the mannequin's outfit to match hers each day? How did they know what she'd wear? Was someone pulling some kind of stupid prank? Who? *Why*?

The laugh dying on her lips and the flush turning to a cold prickling chill, she stepped back from the window. She kept an eye on the mannequin, half-expecting it to mirror her movements, but, of course, it didn't. It just stood there in the same precise, stiff-limbed posture. Eyes that didn't exist seemed to stare sightlessly from where its absent head would have been.

Marcella touched her own head at that one, feeling her brow for a fever, squeezing her temples, wondering if she'd somehow been drugged. Having missed breakfast and forgotten her coffee, she doubted it was likely. Lack of caffeine? Low blood sugar? Had another person on the bus—the man beside her who'd smelled of damp dogs, maybe—been giving off fumes of illicit substances and she'd inadvertently gotten a contact high?

None of which would explain yesterday, or the day before. Or the teenage girls and old ladies smirking at the sight of some woman wearing the same clothes as a department store mannequin. Maybe they thought it was part of a marketing stunt, a bizarre ad campaign leading up to an eventual grand reopening? Maybe they thought Marcella was just an oblivious, clueless fool? Maybe there were hidden cameras, maybe she was being secretly filmed, pranked?

With another, sharper step back, she cast a shrewd gaze over every visible nook and cranny in the brownstone's weathered facade. She saw no glints of lenses or lights, no wires, nothing. Nothing but the mannequin, standing solo in its display nook, window-walls on three sides, a blank partition on the fourth. Peering through the door only showed her a dim, dusty, cavernous interior of sheet-draped counters and vintage fixtures that probably hadn't been used since before she was born. A quick test of the handle proved it solidly locked.

What would she have done if it wasn't? Gone in? Gone in there, confronted whoever was behind this . . . this . . . what even *was* this?

A deeper hum cutting through the sounds of rain and traffic, accompanied by a stirring of motion and voices, alerted her to the imminent arrival of the railcar. Still eyeing the front door and window display with narrow suspicion, Marcella sidled over to join the waiting crowd, losing herself in the merging surge of bodies.

She hardly ever called in sick, even when she *was* sick. Least of all on a Friday, when half the office tended to come down with mysterious weekend flu.

After Wednesday's lackluster performance at the meeting, though, followed by Thursday's general complete disaster, Marcella figured her supervisor wouldn't be all that surprised and probably just as glad to have her take some time off to get herself back together.

If she could. She'd spent half the night searching her apartment, which now looked like the aftermath of a drug bust police raid. To no avail; not a microphone or hidden camera anywhere to be found. However whoever knew what she chose to wear, the info wasn't obtained that way.

The hall? The street? The bus? No way she could scour her entire route! If she tried different routes, would that

WINDOW DRESSING

narrow it down? If she packed a spare outfit and changed clothes along the way? If she dressed utterly at random? If . . .

A thought struck her. In the chaotic tossing of her closet, she'd found a gift box still containing a really horrible sweater crocheted from glittery multi-colored yarn. It had been made for and given to her by a doting, doddering great-great-aunt. Although Marcella had never worn it, she'd kept it carefully just in case. People got snubbed or remembered in wills for lesser reasons.

But, the important thing was the garment was a true one-of-a-kind. No way, *no* way that some department store mannequin could *possibly* . . .

With a triumphant laugh, Marcella donned the sweater. It hung on her, as itchy and uncomfortable as it was ugly. Over a long plaid skirt in retro 70s shades of avocado, mustard, and burnt orange . . . paired with the totally wrong blouse . . . mismatched shoes and a purse that went with neither . . . a hodgepodge of accessories . . . fine, so she looked like a newly-escaped lunatic trying to disguise herself as a bag lady, so what?

No *way* that damned window display mannequin would be dressed like this!

Still laughing, she left her building by the side exit, walked three blocks over to a different bus stop, and commenced a circuitous journey to the downtown transit center. From there, she caught the J-Line in the other direction, noting at this hour so much later than her usual commute that the railcars were far less crowded, the passengers more mommies-with-strollers and senior citizens out and about.

At least now when people smirked and snickered, she expected it and knew why. She barely cared. Some temporary anonymous embarrassment would be worth getting this foolishness out of her system, putting her mind at ease.

The J-Line hummed up toward the intersection. The cafe's outdoor seating was well-occupied thanks to the nicer weather and lunch rush. The brownstone hunched in its usual corner spot, windows dulled and dingy, nothing visible from this angle except lurking gloomy shadows.

Marcella positioned herself by the doors so she could be among the first ones off. As soon as they slid open, out she sprang, and dashed over to the window. She nearly skidded to a halt before it, flung her arms wide, and voiced a wordless challenging kind of cry—*hah!*

No.

Impossible.

No!

Mismatched shoes and purse that went with neither. Retro-hued plaid skirt with totally wrong blouse. Hodgepodge accessories.

Really horrible handmade one-of-a-kind ugly crocheted sweater.

But that was plainly simply utterly *impossible*!

She stood there, posture as stiff and frozen as a mannequin herself. Unable to move, unable even to breathe or blink. In her peripheral vision, she was aware of gawking people parting around her, clearing a *very* wide berth. Dimly, rushingly, as if heard through a seashell, muted giggles and cautious mutterings reached her ears.

The mannequin also just stood there, motionless as ever. Their poses weren't the same, its slender alien-arms not outstretched, its elongated legs not braced in a combative stance, its fists not clenched as hers were. The smooth stump of its headless neck gave the impression of gazing into the distance, serene and unconcerned. If it'd had a face, the features would have been a model's: flawless, poised, impassive.

This wasn't . . . this couldn't . . .

Her mind skipped and stuttered. Her lungs felt locked.

Wasn't, couldn't, shouldn't! Impossible!

Voices murmured, dubious, inquisitive. A little girl asked her mommy if the funny-clothes lady was okay; mommy shushed her. Someone wondered aloud if they

WINDOW DRESSING

were filming a commercial or what. An elderly gent gave an exaggerated eyeroll and twirled his finger beside his head in a universally-understood gesture. Several people had their phones out, capturing the moment. Another day, another slice of big-city weirdness, another funny meme or viral video in the making.

A ragged scream burst from Marcella's throat. All at once, she *could* move, could whirl and grab a metal trashcan tethered to the railcar shelter by a short length of chain. The chain snapped like a frayed shoelace. Heavy though the can was, she heaved it above her head. Latte cups, muffin wrappers, crumpled napkins, and receipts scattered in a papery snowstorm.

The murmurs and dubious comments became cries of alarm, the crowd surging backwards to widen the berth around her—except, of course, for the ones who held their ground so as not to lose the shot. She hurled the can at the brownstone's window with another violent burst of strength. Murky glass fractured, spastic cracks racing in all directions, a dully glittering cascade of shards showering down.

They let her out on Monday, after a 48-hour hold for "observation."

She'd had to call in sick again—*well, hello, nice long weekend;* her supervisor sounding smugly knowing and amused. That was fine with Marcella. Eventually, the insurance claim would go through HR and the real truth would come out, but until then, she was fine letting everyone think she'd just been partying too hard.

When the truth did come out, though . . . kiss that sweet promotion, corner office, and executive title goodbye.

She sat hunched on the railcar, hands folded atop the cheap nylon zippered tote they'd given her at the hospital. It held the torn and disheveled clothes she'd been wearing, her purse, and other personal belongings. They'd also provided her mulberry scrubs and a pair of flimsy slip-on shoes.

Maybe she just looked like a nurse was headed home after an exhausting shift. Lank hair, no makeup, general haggard weariness. Yeah. As if she'd pulled some overtime and . . .

Maybe, if she'd remembered to remove the plastic I.D. bracelet first. Oops.

Memories flickered in her head like scenes from a movie of someone else's life. Picking up the trashcan, snapping its sturdy chain, hurling it with abnormal crazy strength. Scramble-clambering through the broken window, jagged edges snagging on her clothes, gouging her palms and knees and shins. Dismembering the mannequin, snapping off those slender arms at the shoulders, popping the elongated alien legs off at the hips, trying to crack the headless torso in half.

Her own shoulders, hips, and back still ached from the exertions. Her own limbs felt stiff and lifeless. As blurred and foggy as her head felt, it might as well have not even been there.

With its familiar deepening pitch of hum, the J-Line slowed, approaching the stop. Marcella rose from her seat without raising her gaze. She kept it downcast to the sidewalk as she disembarked. In her peripheral vision, she was aware of the afternoon crowd in the cafe's outdoor seating area and the looming dingy bulk of the brownstone on the corner.

Nearing it, despite her best efforts, she glanced up. A sheet of plywood had been placed across the gap, covering the missing pane. Any vestiges of broken glass had been swept up. Nothing else seemed to have changed. She wondered how long it'd be until the building's owners sued her, until she got summoned to court for property damage and vandalism. How would *that* go over at the office? Not to mention what it'd do to her bank account.

WINDOW DRESSING

She sighed.

All because of a mannequin! A stupid *mannequin*!

Which hadn't, when she got close, been wearing the same clothes as her after all. It'd only been draped in this bland grey smock, more like a dustcloth than a garment. The rest had only been . . .

Only been what?

Best not to think about it. Best to let it go. A passing incident, an episode. A sign she needed to take it easier at work. She'd been under a lot of stress and pressure lately. The doctors suggested a nice vacation . . . once they'd finished suggesting meds and therapy, or an inpatient stay if she thought she might be a danger to herself.

Marcella sighed again. She turned the corner toward the bus stop, glumly anticipating the mess waiting for her at her apartment. Before she could stop herself, she turned her head and peered in through the department store window's side pane, unbroken, not covered with plywood.

The mannequin stood there, lofty and aloof, headless, tall and spindly and weirdly "flesh"-colored as ever.

She stopped dead in her tracks.

She'd busted the damn thing, she was sure of it! Arms snapped from sockets, legs popped at hips, hollow torso cracked across its wisp-thin waist! She'd busted it, left a jumble of pick-up-stick limbs on the musty mildew-smelling carpet!

It wore mulberry hospital scrubs and flimsy slip-on shoes.

This wasn't right, this wasn't real, this wasn't happening.

Sinking into a crouch, she dropped the cheap nylon zippered tote and clutched her head in both hands. She squeezed her eyes shut tight, clenched her jaw. Harsh breath hissed between her teeth. People were probably staring. Probably hauling out their phones. Marcella rocked back and forth on her haunches, willing it all to go away.

CHRISTINE MORGAN

Hectic starbursts danced in the closed darkness behind her eyelids. Her ears filled with a rushing white-noise static. Tension tightened every muscle in her body. She fought not to scream.

Get a grip, get a grip, get a grip, she told herself.

The rest of the world seemed to recede. The starbursts and static sensations did too. A serene and very welcome calmness settled over her.

Okay. Okay, good.

When she felt steady again, she opened her eyes.

Or, tried to. They didn't open. Wouldn't open. Because . . . because she had no eyes.

She had no eyes, but somehow she could still see. No ears, but could still hear. No head, but still could think.

She had a body, but she couldn't move. Her posture felt strange and rigid. Her skin looked smooth . . . utterly unblemished . . . "flesh"-colored. Her limbs stretched out, stiffly poised, slender, and elongated.

Around her were windows on three sides, clean clear sparkling glass. Behind her was a decorative partition still smelling of fresh paint. Beneath her point-toed arched-soled Barbie feet was a plush swatch of brand-new carpeting. Softly flattering pale golden rays beamed down from discreetly placed spotlight fixtures.

Outside, the morning sun shone brightly. Railcars hummed along their tracks. Traffic bustled busily on the streets and sidewalks. Workmen in crisp coveralls were hanging a broad banner, and although the lettering was backward from her perspective, she read it easily enough.

GRAND REOPENING, it proclaimed.

THE HUMMING

WINGS WHIRR WINGS blur zip zip zip and sip. Dart head. Beak and tongue. Sip sip. Pulse race flutter flutter. Up down forward back sample sip sip sip. Liquid sweet. Dart and zip. This one. That one. Wings whirr whirr whirr.

Craving hunger craving need. More more. Sweet. Sip and drink. Beak poke. Tongue flick.

Need need.

More-more-hurry-faster.

Zip. Whirr. Up-down. Thiswaythatway.

Faster-faster-faster!

Whirring wings whirring wings frantic.

Hurry hurry!

Sweet need sweet need *sweetneedsweetneedneed!*

Jannie bounced out of bed and dashed to the window. She pushed aside her frilly princess curtains. Morning sunshine dazzled in, early-summer morning sunshine, as light and yellow as the scoops of whipped butter they served at Becca's.

Her stomach pinged and poinged at the idea of crisp hot waffles with syrup oozing in maple-gold rivers to puddle on the plate, and powdered sugar. And those kind of strawberries or apples that were gooey like pie filling! And chocolate milk!

CHRISTINE MORGAN

She looked out over their back fence at the golf course, which was still partly misty, especially down by the artificial lake. Dew glimmered on the bright green grass and in the treetops. A few golfers were there already, driving their little carts or towing their golf bags on wheeled frames. Most of them wore checkered pants with polo shirts and funny caps.

It made Jannie wonder if there was a special shop they went to, just for those clothes. Or maybe there were special shops just for old people. Like the old lady, Mr. Schromm's grandma or great-auntie or whoever she was, who'd just moved in with him next door.

Poor old lady. Jannie felt bad for her. She was *really* old, *old*-old, way older than the golfers. Like, ancient-old, all tiny, wrinkled, hunched frail and helpless in her wheelchair.

A nurse stayed with her while Mr. Schromm was at work. Though, as far as Jannie had been able to see, the nurse would basically just park the old lady by the birdfeeders and watch TV the rest of the day, pigging out on donuts and cookies.

She checked, but the old lady wasn't there yet. Their patio was empty, messy with stray leaves and windblown crumples of stuff that looked like tissue paper or discarded wrappers.

A golfer hit a ball that arched way high and white against the pearly blue sky. It plunked into the lake, sending circles of ripples across the smooth water. Sometimes, there were ducks paddling around. Sometimes, there were geese, which were mean, honked, chased people, and left long squiggles of slimy green-black poops.

More dew dripped from the fine mesh of net that hung between the golf course and the houses. Despite it, every week Jannie could count on finding at least a dozen golf balls. She collected them and turned them back in at the clubhouse for a quarter apiece.

THE HUMMING

Breakfast, she decided, and then the great golf ball hunt. Maybe she could say hi to the old lady in the wheelchair. Who called her "Jenny," but that was okay. She seemed nice–the frump-a-grump nurse was another story–and it was neat to see the birds visiting the feeders.

Hummingbirds, mostly, in all kinds of rainbow-jewel colors. Their wings went so fast they blurred almost invisible, and they hung in the air like magic. With their long thin beaks, she imagined fairies could ride on them and have jousts or do fencing duels.

Giggling, she dashed around her room, holding her arms straight-out and not swoop-flapping them but vibrating them up and down way-super-fast. She swung her head around and jabbed her nose at things as if it had a musketeer sword growing from the end.

Silly. But fun!

After a quick trip to the bathroom for bathroom-stuff, she got dressed in jeans, sneakers, and a sparkly unicorn shirt, and did her ponytail all by herself. She went down the stairs two and three at a jumping time and skipped into the coffee-smelling kitchen.

"Can we have waffles?" she asked.

Her mother, filling a travel mug, said, "What, sweetie?"

"Waffles?"

"I think there's still half a box in the freezer."

"Mo-o-om," said Jannie, drawing it out and rolling her eyes. "I meant *real* waffles, like at Becca's!"

"I don't have time this morning. I'm already running late."

"You always say that."

With a laugh that might have sounded like it belonged to a crazy person, her mom said, "I'm always running late. Tell you what, though. This weekend, we'll make some at home. How about that?"

Jannie gave her a dubious look. "You always say *that* too."

"I know. I know. I'm sorry. I'm just so busy." Mom

smooched Jannie on the head. "I have to get going. Tell your brother to remember to bring in the recycling bins."

"He won't listen to me."

"I don't want to see them sitting out there when I get home," Mom went on, as if she wasn't listening either. "Another nasty note from the community association snootie-patooties is *just* what I need."

"I think that nurse next door is mean to the old lady," Jannie said, partly because she did think so, and partly to see if Mom was paying attention.

"That's nice, sweetie." Travel mug, purse, cell phone, stack of file-folders, car keys. "'Bye, and be a good girl!"

Jannie heard the engine, followed by the garage door rumbling open and shut. The house fell silent except for the burble of the coffee-maker. She sighed and dragged a stool from the counter across so she could clamber up to look in the freezer.

No toaster waffles. Lots of Stouffers-food and the microwave junk Troy lived on—pizza rolls, burritos, pastry pockets. She stuck out her tongue and tried the fridge, but that was mostly leftover take-out containers, two-liter bottles of soda, and about ninety bazillion canned energy drinks. A search through the cupboards finally rewarded her with a variety-pack of healthy cereal bars.

"Bleh," Jannie said.

She thought about knocking and seeing if Troy was awake yet and maybe wanted to drive them someplace but decided against it. Probably, he'd stayed up all night playing video games and drinking SugaRush Ultra-Blue, and would be mad about pesky sisters disturbing him in his basement lair.

Sighing again, she grabbed a couple of cereal bars—granola crunch and yogurt mixed berry—and did her own version of Mom's out-the-door checklist. Change, fanny pack, travel-size hand sanitizer, housekey. No phone. Mom said she was too young for a phone.

Dad said maybe for her birthday. But Dad *also* said

THE HUMMING

maybe a new bike, maybe he'd take her and Troy to Disneyland, maybe they could come spend Christmas with him and Brittnylynne, and yeah as if any of *that* was going to happen.

Outside was just like it had looked from her window. The whipped-buttery sun was warm, the shadowy shade was cool, dewdrops beaded the grass, and everything was picture-perfect, except for the trash cans and recycling bins waiting by the curb, and a couple more crumpled papery-looking wads on Mr. Schromm's lawn.

Mom said that theirs was one of the few families-with-kids who'd been "grandfathered in" when the snootie-patooties made the new rules; all Jannie knew was that it meant there was hardly anybody around to play with. Not so bad during the school year. Summers and breaks sure could be boring, though.

A car turned the corner, but it was just the old lady's frump-a-grump of a nurse. She got out and gave Jannie a squinchy oh-great-*you*-again frown before grabbing her purse and her usual armload of bakery bags and clumping up the walk.

The sight of the bakery bags made Jannie's tummy ping and poing some more, despite the granola crunch cereal bar she'd eaten. Granola crunch *cardboard*, more like . . . and she just knew the nurse was stocked up on glazed donuts, chocolate snack-cakes, maybe those cookies with the frosting.

The nurse wasn't a total *fattie-fat* fattie, but she wasn't skinny either. She always wore stretchy pants with bright floral smock-tops. Today was no different. The pants were lime sherbet green, and the top looked like Hawaii lost a fight with a clown.

Jannie did a cheery smile-and-wave, which the nurse ignored. As soon as her back was turned, Jannie made a face instead, then skipped past Mr. Schromm's house to a little spur of path that cut across to a strip of park following the edge of the golf course.

CHRISTINE MORGAN

They called it a park, though in Jannie's mind, a park—a *real* park!—would have swings and slides, maybe places for soccer or baseball. Playground stuff. Fun stuff. Not a hardly-ever-used jogging trail winding along with only some benches and the occasional drinking fountain. There weren't even any picnic tables.

She searched the grass and poked through the bushes. Most of the golf balls were plain white. Some were neon-colored, orange and yellow. She also found a nickel, three bottlecaps, a pretty rock, and a few things she didn't bother picking up, not even with hand sanitizer. Yuck. Cigarette butts and wads of A-B-C gum.

And a dead hummingbird under a bench, which was sad. Just a bunch of brittle feathers, purple-blue and red, with its long dark beak in the dust and its itty-bitty feet curled up stiff.

Poor hummingbird. She didn't pick it up either, partly because eew-dead-thing and partly with vague Mom-voice don't-touch-that-you'll-get-germs, but mostly because she didn't know what to do with it. Dropping it into a trash can seemed mean, but what else was there? Bury it?

In the end, she settled for sort of kick-scooping a mound of gravel over it, then setting her pretty rock for a headstone. She wondered if it was one the old lady would recognize, if the old lady gave them names, even.

The hummingbird funeral brought an end to her great golf ball hunt for the day. By the time she got back to her street, the neighborhood had reached its maximum normal creepy-quiet levels.

Every day during the week was the same. The grown-ups left, and the houses sat there. Silent and empty . . . but alive somehow, with things on timers and remote control, and the tiny blinky red eyes of security systems. Like a ghost town. A robot-house ghost town of the future.

The only people she mostly saw coming and going were workers, cleaners, deliveries, and snooper-spy snootie-patooties eager to find something wrong so they could leave their nasty notes.

THE HUMMING

"Don't give them any more reason to come after me," Mom often said if Jannie left toys outside or Troy's speakers were too loud. "They still wish I'd been the one to move out instead of your father. A divorced man, that's fine; but a single mother?"

Jannie knew better than to argue or ask, though it did make her wonder what the snootie-patooties would have thought about Dad and Brittnylynne, or Dad and Valerie, or Dad and Monica.

Down the block, someone's sprinklers came on, spitting water with a hishy-wishy noise. A Daily-Maid van and a UPS truck drove past. That was it. No barking dogs, no crying babies. No ice cream man jingling music—she *wished*; they *never* got the ice cream man driving by here. No sirens or explosions. Not even a radio turned way up.

Creepy, quiet, empty, and boring.

If only *something* would happen, something interesting and exciting. When she had to do her "how I spent my summer vacation" paper, it'd be nice to be able to write about more than collecting stray golf balls for quarters or listening to Troy cuss at noobs over the internet.

She went around the side of the garage, thinking to deposit her day's haul in the bucket where she kept them until she had enough to go to the clubhouse. Then maybe she'd see if Troy was awake after all. He didn't have to take her to Becca's, but he could at least drive her to the store for a candy bar.

Her gaze wandered across to Mr. Schromm's yard. Sure enough, now the wheelchair was parked out on the patio. The old lady sat sort of slouched in it, with her head down and her bunched, shaky hands to her face. She looked like she might be crying, or trying real hard not to.

Jannie paused, nibbling on her bottom lip.

Did the old lady know somehow about the hummingbird funeral at the park? No, that was silly; there was no way she could know. But what if she really did recognize them all, even give them names? What if she was worried because that particular one hadn't shown up for breakfast?

The bird-feeders—Mr. Schromm had put them in special a few days after the old lady came to live with him—were clear tubes with bright red horn-shaped fake-flower-looking-things sticking out of the sides. Every morning, the nurse refilled them from a pitcher. The hummingbirds would go zipping from one fake-flower spigot to another, suspended on their blurred-invisible wings, fairy-rainbow-jewels of silver and turquoise, shimmery greens, purples, even gold.

Now that she really paid attention, Jannie saw there weren't very many flitting around the feeders at all. Hardly any, when on another day there'd be a dozen or more. Normally, they flew in smooth, graceful little dances too; a birdie ballet. But today, the few that were there moved in kind of jerky, jittery fits and starts.

Then, even as she watched with a confused frown, a bronzy-red hummingbird just fell out of the air, plop onto the patio, where it lay twitching feebly. The old lady covered her mouth to muffle a sob.

"Omigosh!" Jannie yelped. She dropped her golf balls, dashed to the low fence, and scrambled over it into Mr. Schromm's yard.

The hummingbird twitched again and stopped moving. It looked like a delicate, broken toy. Like a wad of colorful tissue paper someone had crumpled up and thrown away.

Like . . . the things she'd noticed earlier and thought they were discarded windblown wrappers? Which she didn't see now, because probably the nurse had swept them up along with the stray leaves?

The thought of the nurse froze Jannie in her tracks for a second. With a huge guilty trespassing flinch, she stole a glance in the direction of the house. The blinds were partway open on the big picture window into the family room. She saw the TV set—on, tuned to the channel that

THE HUMMING

did game-show reruns from fifty years ago—and the nurse kicked back napping in a comfy chair.

A relieved breath shuddered from Jannie's lungs. She resumed crossing the lawn, making more of an effort to be extra quiet. At the corner of the patio was a plastic yard-waste bin; when she peeked inside, she saw exactly what she'd been afraid of. Five or six brittle, feathery bundles in a drift of leaves and grass clippings. Hummingbirds, dead ones, just like she'd found in the woods, just like the one that fell ker-plop on the patio.

"Jenny?" The old lady's voice quavered.

"Shh!" She flung another flinching glance through the window. The nurse had a box resting crooked on her chest and a partly-eaten glazed donut dangling in limp fingers.

"Jenny, dear, is that you? Jenny from next door?"

"Hi, uh . . . Mrs. . . . Mrs. Schromm?"

"Edith," said the old lady, wiping at her eyes.

"Ummmkay . . . Edith . . . I saw you, and the, um, the birds, jeez, what happened?"

This time, it was Edith who cast a furtive look at the window. "You won't believe me. Nobody believes me. My nephew doesn't believe me. He says it's dementia, paranoia. But I'm *not* senile! I *didn't* have a stroke!"

"Okay, okay, shhh!" Jannie hissed, bouncing from foot to foot as if she had to pee. Which, of course, now she did have to.

"It's that woman! That horrible woman, that lazy, lying, miserable *bitch*!"

Jannie's eyes almost popped. Hearing the b-word from her brother when he was gloating about pwning somebody in a video game was one thing. Hearing it from a nice little old lady in a wheelchair was another.

"Do you see what she did?" Edith went on. "Do you see what she's done?"

"Shhhh! She'll hear you! She'll wake up and we'll both be in trouble!"

"She's killing innocent hummingbirds!"

"Huh?" Jannie said, baffled. The nurse wasn't even out here . . . "Oh, hey, wait, you mean, like, when she refills the feeders? She *poisons* the birds?"

"Poison would be kinder!" Her wrinkled old eyes leaked more tears as she gazed, stricken, at the bronzy-red bird. "It's only supposed to be sugar-water, a simple syrup of sugar and water, boiled and let cool. It isn't expensive. It isn't complicated. But she makes it with *artificial sweetener*!"

"The . . . the diet stuff, the fake sugar? Um, well, so?"

"So? So, they starve! It has the right *taste* and they keep *drinking* it but not the *calories*, and they *need* those for their quick little metabolisms! They *think* they're getting food, but it's a trick, it's empty, and they *die*!"

"Okay, okay, shhh!" Jannie hissed again. "She must just not know—"

"Oh, she *knows*, that crafty bitch! She does it on *purpose*! It's *murder*!"

"But why?"

"Because she's *evil*!"

That was enough as far as Jannie was concerned. "Can't you tell your nephew?"

"I have told him. He doesn't believe me. He believes *her*. I've tried to shoo them away, but the little darlings don't understand, and . . . " She flicked irritably at the armrest.

"Well, we gotta do something!" said Jannie. She went over to the nearest feeder, poked her pinkie finger into one of the trumpet-shaped plastic spigots, examined the clear liquid on the end, sniffed it, and tasted it. Sweet. Not flavored like Kool-Aid, just way-whoa-*sweet*!

Another hummingbird buzzed past her head, so close she felt the whiffy-whirr of its fast-beating wings against her cheeks. The sound was a whispery flutter-hum that reminded her of riffling her thumb along a deck of cards. Its feathers were grey and blue-green, with a ruby-red throat-bib. She even saw the shiny black beads of its eyes.

THE HUMMING

"No, no, shoo!" cried Edith.

Jannie waved at the bird. "Psst, yeah, shoo! Go on, get out, stupid!"

"They won't," the old lady said. "They'll keep coming back, thinking it's food, until they die."

"What if we put in real sugar? Don't you have some in the kitchen?"

"And wake the bitch up?"

"Oh, yeah." Jannie waved at the hummingbird again. "I know! I'll get some from my house!"

Without waiting for a reply, she ran back across the yard, scrambled the fence, and dashed inside. Troy's door was still shut, but he must have been awake because she could hear electronic shooting and death groans from the basement, and the smell of recently-microwaved pastry pockets hung in the kitchen.

Sugar . . . sugar . . . the canister on the counter was empty except for a rock-solid crust at the bottom . . . she found a box of store-brand sweetener in the cupboard but that was the whole gosh-dang problem in the first place . . . Mom used that in her coffee because she said they already put too much sugar in those energy drinks–

Snapping her fingers, she whirled and yanked open the fridge. Not only was it packed full of black-and-yellow cans with jagged white lightning-bolt letters, but a bottle of Troy's SugaRush Ultra-Blue gleamed like a great big sapphire torpedo.

She dumped some cans into a plastic bag, tucked the two-liter under her arm, and bolted back out. Yard-fence-yard and to the patio, puffing and panting for breath. The old lady–Edith–was trying to ward off the hummingbird from the feeders, but it was really seriously determined to stick in its beak.

"Here, here, okay, hang on a second," Jannie gasped. She plunked down the bag of cans and struggled with the twist-cap.

The hummingbird zipped backward and forward and

sideways at angles. It started to go all herky-jerky the way the bronzy-colored one had done right before dropping dead out of the air. Its wings went stutter-flutter. Jannie saw its shiny eyes again and thought they looked desperate.

The cap spun loose and the totally shaken up soda shot everywhere in a terrific, ginormous fizzy-foamy blue spray. A super-soaker blast of it nailed the hummingbird point-blank, knocking it into a spinny somersaulting cartwheel before pasting it to the patio. Jannie lost her grip on the plastic bottle, which hit the ground and skidded, rolling and squirting in a circle.

"Glahgh!" Edith yelled, as she got a faceful of SugaRush Ultra-Blue. Her false teeth landed in her lap.

Jannie, also doused, ran to the spot where the drenched, feathery wad thrashed and splashed in a puddle. "Omigosh I'm sorry little birdie are you all right?"

The hummingbird's long, skinny tongue flicked from its beak. It flipped itself over. It wallowed and rolled. Droplets flew from its wings and tail as it shook off the flurrying way birds sometimes did at birdbaths. Its startled shiny-black eyes blinked a lot. Then its head darted. Its tongue flicked some more—flick flick flick!—lapping at the brilliant blue soda.

"Hey, cool! Look! The—" She broke off, tipping her head to the side. "That's weird."

"What's that, Jenny dear?" Edith asked, her words mushy and slobbery without her teeth. She wiped SugaRush from her face.

"The hummingbird," said Jannie, crouching.

"It isn't dead, is it?"

"Nuh-unh. But . . . it's . . . um . . . bigger."

Spraying more droplets in a sparkling blue mist, the hummingbird beat its wings as it righted itself. Its body, Jannie was sure, had been maybe as big as a fun-sized Snickers bar; now it was—and she was sure of this too!—as big as a Twinkie.

And growing.

THE HUMMING

Growing even as she stared in jaw-drop astonishment.

Tiny feathers fell off as larger ones replaced them, to be in turn replaced by ones even larger. The black beak had been a sewing needle, then a golf-pencil, then a school-pencil.

"Um . . . " Jannie gulped and duck-walked backward a few steps. "Do you see that?"

"Oh my goodness. It's the size of a bedroom slipper!"

And still growing. Growing, blundering around as it flapped clumsy wings that looked like soggy comic-book pages, jabbing its thin spike of a beak–which, Jannie realized, looked really sharp–and flicking its weird string of a tongue to drink up more spilled soda.

The size of an old lady's bedroom slipper, then a football, then the size of one of Troy's huge galumphy high-top sneakers he always left in the hall for people to trip over no matter how much Mom told him not to.

The puddle was almost gone, and the soda that had sprayed everywhere was drying to a sticky mess, but the bottle still had maybe a third of its contents that hadn't gurgled out. The hummingbird lurched for it, poking its beak into the cap-hole, lashing its tongue in the sloshing blue liquid. Its wings and tail fanned out. Where the feathers had been grey with shimmery blue-green before, they now had a sapphire sheen that almost seemed to glow in the sunlight.

"What in the *world* do they put in those sodas these days?" Edith pressed a hand to her chest.

"Chemicals and stuff, I guess?"

The bottle was pretty well empty. The hummingbird was bigger than Jannie's pillow, its shiny black eyes like golf balls. Like mean, mad, crazy golf balls. And that beak . . . that long sharp beak . . . had she actually thought how *funny* it would be for fairies to ride hummingbirds in jousts and musketeer-sword duels?

Not funny, no, not funny at *all*!

"We should maybe . . . " she said, rising from her duckwalk squat to grasp the handles on the back of Edith's wheelchair.

The hummingbird flapped its wings again, and this time they made the kind of brisk whipcrack noises of kids snapping damp towels at each other in a pool-fight. Its body wouldn't have fit into a shopping cart. What had been itty-bitty bird-claws were practically dinosaur feet!

The feathers at its throat, which had been ruby-red but turned a deep, rich pomegranate-purple, quivered. Then the hummingbird chirped, a screechy, squeaky shrill teakettle chirp that hurt Jannie's ears.

"I think it's still hungry," Edith said.

"It drank all the soda."

It screeched louder. It hopped, wings beating the air with wind and a whirring, humming vibration. But it couldn't quite take off and came down stumbling. One of its dinosaur-feet tangled in the grocery bag and a claw punctured a black and yellow can.

"Uh-oh," muttered Jannie as the long-beaked head darted to inspect the leaking dribble of yellowish fluid. She tugged at the chair, but it wouldn't budge; the brakes must have been on or something so that the old lady didn't roll away.

She finally figured out the brakes, but by then, the hummingbird was bigger than a sofa and had treated the cans of energy drink like someone dying of thirst might treat Capri Suns. Punch and slurp, punch and slurp, its beak for the straw, and chug-chug-chug!

Jannie turned the wheelchair toward Mr. Schromm's house and got it moving. She'd only made it a couple of steps when all at once, the patio door slid open.

"What in the hell is—" began the frump-a-grump nurse, stomping out. Her cotton-candy-pink kerchief was crooked, frizzy grey hair going wild. She still had a partly-eaten donut in her hand, crumbs on her chin, and flecks of glaze speckling the front of her bright floral smock-top.

The rest of what she'd been going to say, she didn't.

THE HUMMING

Instead, she made a sound like when a vacuum cleaner tries to suck up a penny. Her eyes went *way* wide and her mouth shaped a big shocked O.

With a piercing shriek worse than a million fingernails on a chalkboard, the hummingbird launched itself into the air. Its wings whirred so hard the wind almost knocked Jannie over. She ducked. It went past–*whoosh!*–in a buffeting rush of feathers and speed.

The nurse shouted the f-word and sprang butt-first through the door. A split-second later, the hummingbird was there, wedging itself at the door, flapping and fluttering, trying to squeeze in after her.

Those bright-colorful clothes, Jannie thought. And the sugar, all that sugar, glazed donuts and chocolate snack-cakes and cookies with the frosting!

She hauled the wheelchair in reverse as hard as she could. Edith was babbling something, but without her teeth, Jannie couldn't make any sense of it, and didn't really care.

A twisting heave, a crunch-rustle, bits of fluff filling the air, and the hummingbird crammed itself into the house. Furniture crashed over. The nurse screamed and screamed. The bird shrieked and shrieked. The half-drawn blinds leaped, rattled, clattered. Feathers bristled against the glass. Wings battered at the window, shaking it in its frame.

Jannie, running full-tilt backward and dragging the old lady with her, didn't even realize they'd gone onto the grass and most of the way across the yard until she bumped smack into the fence. The fence! What was she going to do about the fence?

There wasn't time to think of a plan. Feeling like she, too, was gonzo on sugary soda and energy drinks, she just sort of hauled Edith out of the chair, boosted her over the top with a yelp and a flailing of bony arms and legs, and followed in a vaulting tumble that might have made her gymnastics teacher happy for once. Then she hoisted Edith piggyback like with a toddler instead of an old lady. She staggered for the door, glad she hadn't bothered to lock it again.

Behind them, glass shattered and there was a splintering crackle of wood and another screech that just about made Jannie's head explode. An immense whap-whap-whap, like flat thunderclaps, made everything shudder.

Troy emerged from the basement with a puzzled expression. "Hey, what's all the noise?" he called. "Sounds like a war zone." He saw Jannie, with Edith piggyback, and the puzzled expression switched to one of total confusion. "Sis?"

"It's a hummingbird!" she cried.

"A what?"

"A—" She tripped and bellyflopped, Edith landing on her, both of them going, "Oof!"

Troy did come to help them up, glanced out the window above the sink, and gaped. *He* said the f-word, plus a few others, in a stunned, marveling tone.

"A hummingbird, I told you," Jannie said, panting. She risked a peek out the window herself.

It burst up from the wreckage of Mr. Schromm's house, shedding scraps of drywall and wallpaper, stirring a billowing cyclone of plaster dust. The furious whirring of its wings made a helicopter downdraft, sending ripples across the lawn, flattening chunks of fence on both sides. The next house over had a backyard pool, which whipped into a frenzy from the gales. A pool-cleaner guy had just been bopping along doing his job with earbuds plugged in; he got one look at the massive shape rising out of the debris and dust-cloud, and keeled over on the spot.

"Jannie," said Troy, "that's a hummingbird."

"I *told* you, *duh!*"

A hummingbird as big as an airplane, body arched in a comma-curve . . . wings beating so fast they were half-invisible blue-sheened blurs . . . its long beak a black spear

THE HUMMING

stabbing at the sky . . . the hum and the whirr and the deafening hurricane thunder . . . pieces of Mr. Schromm's house tossed around like playing cards . . .

"Whoa!" Troy seized Jannie and pulled her below the counter as a shiny gold thing smashed through the kitchen window in a hail of busted glass. The shiny gold thing broke off the sink faucet with a clang and a cold gushing shower, then bounced to the floor–a badly bent and dented golfing trophy.

"It's so loud!" Jannie hollered.

"What?"

"It's so *loud*!"

"*What?!*"

She gave up, risking another peek as a huge moving shadow blotted out the sun. More windows all along that side of the house cracked or shattered. The kitchen door banged back and forth. The table made a coin-flip and hit the wall so hard it sprang several years of framed school pictures from their nails. Gritty sandstorm gusts howled in through every gap.

Troy yelled, but she couldn't hear him or anything else through the destruction. He spun her around, pushed her toward the basement door–it was also banging back and forth like it was in a haunted house movie–and went to pick up Edith. Jannie eyed the bangy-slammy door in alarm, then saw the stool she'd perched on that morning while asking Mom about waffles.

Gosh that seemed like forever ago! And to think, she'd been grouchy and bored, wishing for something exciting to happen this summer!

The stool, though . . . Jannie grabbed it by the legs and shoved the seat-end at the basement doorway. The door whammed into it with a crunch, breaking one of the legs and snagging long enough to let her catch the edge and hold it open.

"Go, Troy, go!"

He went, carrying Edith, plunging down the stairs in a

way that would probably kill them both. Jannie didn't even try to take the steps like a normal person, butt-whumping down. She got a brief glimpse of posters, a paused game on the big screen, laundry, clutter, and mess.

A brief glimpse only because there was a sudden pop and the power went out, hurling them into basement darkness.

Troy said the s-word. "I didn't save!" He drew his phone and used it to cast enough light for them to see by, and all three of them crowded into the closet-sized bathroom as the house shook and creaked and groaned overhead.

"My goodness," said Edith. "It's like a tornado."

Jannie's ears felt the way they did during take-off or landing when they flew to visit Dad. She closed the bathroom door—and locked it for no good reason; if the hummingbird came after them, it wouldn't try the knob!

"Are we gonna die?" she asked.

"If it caves in on us, probably," Troy said.

"I didn't mean to! I didn't know!"

"Wait, what? Didn't mean what? Didn't know what?"

"That your soda and Mom's energy drinks would do *that*!"

His eyebrows twisted in a way that said he didn't think he heard her right, but he didn't ask.

"Let's see what's going on out there," he said, waggling his phone. "I can still get online."

The community association might be snootie-patooties about their rules, but they'd had exterior security cameras installed all around the neighborhood that people could log in and look at, even from work. Edith and Jannie leaned close to peer over Troy's shoulders.

They watched in solemn silence, skipping from one view to the next, as the huge hummingbird laid waste to house after house after house. It bashed them apart with the gale-force winds of its wings. Muffled, and from a

THE HUMMING

distance, they heard the destruction. They heard the shrill, piercing screeches and shrieks.

It drove its beak—which was now as long as a telephone pole!—into the wreckage, seeming to go for the brightest houses within the snootie-patootie acceptable paint range, impaling colorful bedspreads and furniture with floral-print upholstery. Epic splatters of blue-tinged whitish bird poop streaked lawns and driveways. And they'd thought the *geese* were bad!

Yard guys, pool guys, Daily-Maids, deliverymen, housekeepers, and golf carts fled in panic. The garbage truck roared down the street so fast it jumped the curb, missed the turn, rolled two complete rotations with trash spewing every direction, and teetered to a smoking stop in somebody's just-trimmed hedges.

"Oh yeah," Jannie said to Troy. "Mom wanted me to remind you to bring in the recycling bins, but I don't guess it matters very much now."

Wings whirr wings blur zip zip zip and sip. Dart head. Beak and tongue. Sip sip. Pulse race flutter flutter. Up down forward back sample sip sip sip. Liquid sweet. Dart and zip. This one. That one. Wings whirr whirr whirr.

Craving hunger craving need. More more. Sweet. Sip and drink. Beak poke. Tongue flick.

Need need.

More-more-hurry-faster.

Zip. Whirr. Up-down. Thiswaythatway.

Faster-faster-faster!

Whirring wings whirring wings frantic.

Hurry hurry!

Sweet need sweet need *sweetneedsweetneedneed!*

EYE SEE YOU

IT STARTED AT Disneyland; how's that for messed-up? Happiest place on Earth, my butt. Thanks, Walt. Thanks a ton.

And no, it wasn't Mickey, or any of the other walk-arounds in their character suits. An aunt of mine, though, used to be so terrified of Chip and Dale she'd nearly wet her pants once during a photo-op.

Nor was it the pitchfork-devils in Mr. Toad's Wild Ride, or the spooky forest in Snow White's whatever-they-called-it. Still, when you think about it, seriously, what the heck? Those were in Fantasyland, for cripe's sake; we're not even talking the Haunted Mansion. Disney was pretty hardcore in the old days.

The old days, yeah, and this will date me as a dinosaur for sure, because the one that wrecked my mind forever hasn't even existed since, what, the mid 1980s? They took it out to make room for Star Tours on the notion maybe this Star Wars thing might really hit it big. And, to be fair, okay, they were right on that one.

But, before then, the attraction occupying part of Tomorrowland was, like Mission to Mars, intended to be all scientific and educational. As such, it rarely had as long a line as, say, the Jungle Boat Cruise or Matterhorn. And, therefore, as such, when my grandparents first took me to the park, they started there because we didn't have to wait.

How would they have known it'd ruin our entire day? How would I have known it'd wreck my entire life?

EYE SEE YOU

Nothing like being four years old and getting a forever phobia for your birthday.

Maybe the seeds had been sown earlier, I'm not sure. I seem to remember already being anxious, after hearing so many parables and proverbs in those formative preschool years.

Someone would always be "keeping an eye on you," and I suppose it was meant to be reassuring, but it always struck me as a threat. Even Santa got in on that one. Or your nice babysitter might have "eyes in the back of her head." Warning, foreboding. Or the mean lady in the house on the corner might "give you the evil eye." Or, if they thought you'd fibbed, "look me in the eye and tell me that, young lady."

Or you'd be instructed to "look with your eyes, not your hands." Or they'd chide you for taking too big a helping with "your eyes are bigger than your stomach." In the car, packed into the back of that old yellow wood-sided station wagon like sardines, my cousins would play "eye spy with my little eye." On the news, traffic reports came from "eyes in the sky."

Eyes, there were eyes everywhere, eyes constantly watching. Judging. Missing nothing. Doing so much more than simply looking. People would "eat with their eyes first," or in some grownup movie they might talk about "undressing her with his eyes." You could keep things in "the eye of the beholder."

I even thought they could make decisions and vote—I was twelve before I realized the phrase was "the *ayes* have it" as in aye-or-nay.

So, yeah, a layer of underlying groundwork may have already been in place before my grandparents took me to Disneyland. I'd been promised a ride on the flying Dumbo elephants, and a mouse-ears cap embroidered with my name, and it was going to be the best day ever.

Starting in Tomorrowland. Starting at Adventures Thru Inner Space, walking a path winding amid scientific wonders. Sitting between Nan-Nan and Pop-Pop in a swively dark blue ride-car where the front folded down to put a safety bar across our laps, my feet not reaching the floor, just so agog and excited . . .

Then they shrinked us.

Shrunk. Shrinked, shrunk, shrunked, does it matter? I was four. I was four and little already, reminded of it every day. The littlest of all the cousins. I didn't want to be any littler! I couldn't afford to be any littler!

But Nan-Nan patted me and told me it would be okay. That there was nothing scary in here, nothing scary at all.

I believed her, and they shrinked us.

They shrinked us smaller than a snowflake. I knew what snowflakes were from that past Christmas—when the ominous Santa kept his eye on me to make sure I was a good girl or else I wouldn't get toys and candy in my stocking. I'd get dead bugs and dog poops instead, my cousins said.

I *was* a good girl, extra super duper good, but I worried that whole December. When Christmas morning finally came and I did dump out my stocking, my tummy felt so sick I couldn't eat a single bite of candy.

As for the snowflakes, before then, I'd only seen them on tee-vee, in the cartoons and holiday specials. When it happened at our house, everyone rushed outside and it was falling thick and white. I remember it fluffy on my mittens, making tiny cold kisses on my face.

Now that we were all shrinked down, the snowflakes loomed enormous. Like giant tinker-toy constructions or Spirographs of ice. So big, and intricate, and delicate, and beautiful, and it made me sad we'd smushed them into snowballs or tried to catch them melting on our tongues.

They shrinked us more, a doctor-sounding man's voice talking about molecules, while Nan-Nan and Pop-Pop went ooh, went ahh, and we were the teensy-weensiest ever, and what if they couldn't un-shrink us?

The doctor-sounding man sounded scared too . . . but

EYE SEE YOU

then he sounded not so scared and said we were getting un-shrunk again, big enough for microscopes, and that was when it happened.

When I saw the Eye.

I saw it. It was real. It was huge. The Eye that I'd been warned about. The terrible, terrible, all-seeing Eye. In the sky, bigger than my stomach, eating first, the beholder.

How it stared!

Wide and blue, ticking back and forth, never blinking!

Oh, and I was so very small still. I was shrinked down teensy-weensy, helpless in the cold hard gaze of the glaring, staring Eye!

I started screaming then. I kicked and shrieked and cried.

Nan-Nan jumped and hissed at me to hush. Pop-Pop went for-God's-sake-Ethel-quiet-her-down! Other voices called out, alarmed and startled, from the dark all around us. The doctor-sounding man kept talking about science and the wonders of Inner Space, but I couldn't listen.

We came out into the light again, our ride-car in a line with the others, and the world seemed like its regular size and normal, but I couldn't stop crying. People looked. Other kids, bigger kids like my cousins, laughed and pointed, what a scaredy-baby!

Pop-Pop got growly-mad and said he'd give me something to cry about if I didn't stop it, and Nan-Nan jumped quick out of the ride-car when the folding bar lifted and picked me up, and I clung to her with my face buried in her neck.

The Eye, the Eye, I'd seen it, and I knew it had seen me too.

It had seen me, and it was terrible and cruel.

It would *always* see me.

I cried so hard I threw up. I only wanted to go home. Nan-Nan said maybe we should leave, but Pop-Pop just got madder. We'd driven all this way, and paid admission. He had bought these ticket books. We were by-Christ going to use them.

CHRISTINE MORGAN

They must've calmed me somehow. I've seen the pictures in the family photo album, me wearing my mouse-ears, me and Nan-Nan on the flying Dumbo ride, me shyly shaking Mickey's white-gloved hand, me on Pop-Pop's lap gawping with amazement at a baby elephant taking a waterfall shower, a snapshot taken by a helpful stranger of the three of us in front of Cinderella's castle.

But I don't remember any of it. I only remember the Eye.

I saw it in my nightmares. Even when I slept in Mommy and Daddy's bed or left my bedside light on. When I was awake and couldn't see it, I still knew it was there. Seeing me. Watching me. Judging me.

Then I realized it could see me in other ways too. Through the eyes of other people . . . someone might be walking by and glance my way, and there it would be again, that cold-hard-terrible-cruel Eye. Through eyes on the tee-vee—I used to love the Romper Room lady, used to jump around and wave and hope she spied me in her magic mirror to call my name; now I hid from her.

All my dollies and stuffed animals, I turned to face the wall. I scribbled with black crayon over the eyes in picture books or Mommy's magazines. I shut my own eyes when put in front of a regular mirror, like when they were brushing or cutting my hair, because what if I saw the Eye there in *my* eye, seeing *me*?

When someone talked to me, I wouldn't lift my gaze higher than their chin. I got taken to a bunch of doctors for that, and it was awful. Doctors with bright lights and stern demands, doctors who said they only wanted to help but it was all a trick to try and make me look at them.

Look me in the eye and tell me that, young lady.

The eyes have it, keeping an eye on you, the eye of the beholder, looking with eyes and not with hands.

The Eye. Seeing me.

My cousins, how they teased and sneered! Sometimes, they'd draw eyes on things and leave them for me to find:

EYE SEE YOU

wide round eyes with long eyelashes, crazy-eyes popping with red veins, evil green and yellow monster eyes. I spy with my little eye! Sometimes, Cousin Mikey would flip his eyelids inside-out and chase me around and hold me and push his face close to mine, then call me a tattle-taler and say he was only playing.

There are eyes on dollars, you know. Not just president eyes; those aren't so bad. But on the back, it's there. The Eye, and it sees you. It sees me. It sees everything and everyone. Pop-Pop used to give us each a dollar when we went to their house for the weekends, joking how he was paying us to leave. After Cousin Bess showed me the Eye, I traded her all my dollars from then on. She gave me *two* shiny quarters for each, and for a long time, I thought I was getting the better deal.

I was almost seven when Nan-Nan got really sick and the doctors put her in the Eye-See-You.

We went a few times to visit her. I always cried, but they thought I was crying because of Nan-Nan. Partly, I was. I didn't want to see Nan-Nan like that, all grey and shriveled, with hands like bird-claws with spider-legs for fingers and her mouth not working right, until I noticed how *her* eyes had gone so murky and confused, and felt kind of better. If *she* couldn't see me, the Eye couldn't see me *through* her; and that was good, right?

Except then, Nan-Nan died, and her eyes got closed forever. Sewed closed, even–Cousin Mikey told me that; that they sewed her eyes and lips closed so she wouldn't be able to come back and haunt us.

It made me wonder . . . if everybody's eyes got closed forever . . . sewed closed, or glued–Mikey also told me about a kid at his school who used superglue instead of eyedrops by mistake!–would we be safer?

Or if *my* eyes did . . . at least then I'd never know, would I? If anyone was looking at *me*, if the Eye was seeing *me*?

All fun and games until somebody loses an eye. You'll

put your eye out. Better than a poke in the eye with a sharp stick. Aunt Suzanne said that one all the time (she wasn't the aunt who was scared of Chip and Dale, that was Aunt Judith).

But, if *my* eyes got closed forever—sewed shut, glued shut, put out, poked with a stick—and I never knew if anyone was looking at me, if the Eye was seeing me, wouldn't it be even more dangerous? If I *didn't* know?

I didn't *want* to know.

The Eye already saw everything.

The Eye could see the future.

I found out when Cousin Cindy, who was eleven, bought a Magic Eight Ball with her Pop-Pop dollars. She also did fortune-tellings with the foldy paper thing, and at her last slumber party—I didn't get to go; they said I was too much a baby still—they even tried some witch stuff.

But she let me use the Magic Eight Ball a few days later, when we went over there so Daddy could help Uncle Jim work on his car. By then, she was bored with it, saying it only ever told her REPLY HAZY TRY AGAIN and OUTLOOK NOT SO GOOD, and she couldn't wait until she saved up enough more dollars to buy a talking ghost-board.

So, downstairs in the rumpus room while she and Bess and their friends played that stupid *Ungame* where nobody could even win and they only discussed their feelings and giggled about cute boys, I got to try the Magic Eight Ball like Cindy had showed me.

You took it, this smooth sphere all black and shiny-glossy, like a pool-table ball with an 8 in a white circle, and you held it or shook it and asked it a question . . . then you turned it over, and in the bottom, there was a round window into a dark liquid void, and a magic blue triangle would float up from the depths with your question's answer.

Were my cousins *ever* going to stop treating me like a baby?

VERY DOUBTFUL.

EYE SEE YOU

Was Nan-Nan in Heaven, like Mommy said?
MOST LIKELY.
Most likely? What did *that* mean?
ASK AGAIN LATER.
What was I going to be when I grew up?
That time, when I turned the Eight Ball over, the magic blue triangle didn't float up from the depths. There was just the round window, empty, and the dark liquid void.

I righted it, gave it a good hard shake, repeated my question, and upended it again. What was I going to be when I grew up?

A scatter of bubbles like from soda pop had collected in the window, and then in the middle of them, a blue bar appeared. Not a triangle, just a bar, a plain blue line.

I wobbled the ball, wondering what that was supposed to mean, and got YOU MAY RELY ON IT, which didn't make any sense.

Maybe it was broken?
MY REPLY IS NO.
Then . . . it wasn't broken . . .
Was someone, or something, there?
IT IS CERTAIN.

I shivered with thrills and chills, and whispered who-are-you as I gave the ball another shake, flipping it almost immediately.

The window was all full of seething bubbles, then up through them came a blueness out of the dark liquid void to press flat against the plastic glass.

Not a magic triangle.
A single, staring, glaring eye.
The Eye.

Looking right at me. Terrible. Unblinking. Cold and hard and cruel. It had found me again despite all my precautions and best efforts. It had found me, it was looking at me, it could see me.

I screamed. I dropped the Eight Ball. No, more like I threw the Eight Ball, hurled it with a frantic flinging shove.

As it rolled crazily across the rumpus room's burnt-orange shag carpet, for a split-second, the triangle appeared again.

EYE SEE YOU.

Cindy, Bess, and their friends also screamed, half a heartbeat after me in startled surprise, and bumped the table so their game pieces fell over. From upstairs, someone hollered what-the-bleep. I barely noticed.

The Eight Ball clacked against the base of Uncle Jim's stereo cabinet. I was up on the couch by then, somehow, like I had seen a spider. I wish I had seen a spider. I'd have rather seen a spider! Even a great big hairy one!

You-better-not-have-broke-it from Cindy. What's-wrong-with-her from one of the friends, to which Bess went she's-cuckoo-for-cocoa-puffs in this mean and snotty way.

Don't-no-don't-there's-an-Eye! as Cindy rushed to pick up the Eight Ball. It-*saw*-me-it-will-see-you!

Jeepers-what-a-stupid-baby said the other friend.

Did-she-break-it? asked Bess.

Are-you-broken? Cindy asked it, then turned it over to read the reply.

I flinched because I knew what would happen, what would float up to fix her with its terrible staring glare.

Only, she went whew-okay instead and announced MY REPLY IS NO . . . but then *she* shot me a look anyway, a look so vicious and awful I almost screamed again. It was *there*, the Eye, there in *Cindy's* eye, whose eyes had never been blue before but one of them sure was now, and the hate in it stabbed into *my* eyes.

Someone was thumping down the stairs from the kitchen, shouting what-the-bleep-is-going-on, and I heard Daddy calling my name and was I all right, in the exasperated not-again way he did when I woke up with another nightmare, and Bess was shaking her head at the other girls and twirling her finger by her temple, and Cindy was still glaring at me with her new blue awful Eye–

There's a famous story about a man with an eye like

EYE SEE YOU

that, and another man who sees it and knows that it sees him. Someone read it to me when I was older. Kind of weird they'd keep books like that in our library, books where people go crazy and murder other people, chop them into pieces and bury them under the floorboards or wall them up in the cellar or something; I don't know, maybe they thought we could relate?

At the time, though, I hadn't read it. I had no idea. I just saw my cousin hating me forever, holding the Magic Eight Ball curled against her as if it was a kitten or a baby chick or bunny, cradling it, and the Eye was inside, looking out through Cindy, taking over, so I sprang from the couch and ran at her, meaning to rip it out of her grasp.

I'd get rid of it, was my intention. Get rid of it, maybe smack it against the raised edge of the rumpus room's brick fireplace. Crack its glossy black shell like a walnut, grab the Eye, and . . . I don't know, flush it down the toilet, grind it to bits in the garbage disposer, I don't know.

I didn't mean to hurt anyone. I didn't mean to hurt Cindy, even if she hated me right then. I didn't mean to knock her into Uncle Jim's stereo cabinet with its glass door and she fell against it and it fell on her and made such a horrible heavy crash. Bess said I did it on purpose, pushed her, then tipped the stereo, but I didn't, I really didn't!

It was an accident, with so much blood. An accident, that's all.

She went to the hospital. Like Nan-Nan. In the Eye-See-You at first, of course, but I wasn't allowed to visit her. Not then, not ever. Not even later when they sent her home, when she learned to walk again. I wasn't allowed to visit anyone. Though, most of them never visited me either. My parents, a few times; I guess because they felt like they had to. Bess, once, to tell me the whole family hated me and she wished I had cut my throat instead of doing what I did do.

Maybe I should have. Which isn't to say I'm suicidal.

Don't get that idea. It might have been easier on everyone, is all. I wouldn't have ended up here, where they feel sorry for me, where they take care of me.

Where, if the Eye *does* see me, at least I'll never know.

The Eight Ball broke too, when the stereo fell on Cindy. It didn't crack like a walnut but fractured like an egg, its smooth black shell splitting into jagged chunks and pieces. The dark liquid spilled out in a blue weird-smelling gush, staining the carpet.

Something else also spilled out, something white, something both angular and roundish, a smaller ball made from triangles. It bounced and tumbled, flickering messages of evil affirmation.

SIGNS POINT TO YES.

YES.

YES—DEFINITELY.

AS I SEE IT, YES.

The next bounce, I was sure, would come up with the Eye, and the moment I saw it seeing me—EYE SEE YOU—I'd never be able to stop screaming. I'd be small again, shrinked teensy-weensy, caught helpless under its unblinking, unrelenting stare of watchful scientific judgment.

The way, I suppose, the police must have looked at me, and the lawyers, and the actual judges, and the doctors. The way some people probably still look at me. The way you might be looking at me now.

It's all right, though.

Those jagged wedge-shards of black plastic . . . dripping weird-smelling—and, it turns out, really astringent and stinging—dark liquid . . . got the job done.

You may see me, but I don't have to see you. I don't have to see anything. Ever, ever, again.

HAUNTED HEIST

Three slim penlight beams shone through dusty darkness. Motes drifted, cobwebs dangled, grit scuffed and crunched underfoot. Tall, boxy, angular shapes loomed in black shadow, now and then catching a faint sheen as the lights' reflections glimmered across grimy, glassy surfaces.

Like empty mirrors. Like wide, blank, dead eyes. Like dim windows into a void, hollow glimpses of a derelict past.

Shit, for that matter, this place *was* a hollow glimpse of a derelict past.

"Everywhere we could've busted into," Jett said in the whiny way that made Rowder want to pop him across the chops, "why here, huh?"

"Salvage." Jaw tight, teeth clenched, Rowder swept his penlight around.

The windowless room, a converted basement underground afterthought, was L-shaped, with a suspended ceiling from which several tiles had fallen or tilted askew. A nubby durable carpet had held up surprisingly well; the galactic murals painted on dark blue walls hadn't.

"Smells like old hot dogs and zit cream," Sondra said.

Jett snorted. "Smells like nerds."

"That's what I said."

Rowder thought it smelled more like mildew and stale popcorn, but he didn't share this with the others—who, probably in an attempt to cover up their nervousness at a little urban exploring turned B&E, kept bantering.

"Shit, this must've been Nerd Central back in the day."

"Yeah, you can almost still hear them." Sondra cupped a hand to her ear and, with a passable ventriloquism, mimicked dweeby voices. "*Star Wars* is better. No way, *Star Trek* is better. Why do girls only like jock assholes instead of nice guys?"

"Girls *do* only like jock assholes," Jett said.

Before they could start beating that dead horse again, Rowder interrupted. "Can it and get a move on. Our target should be in the back corner."

"Yeah, okay, okay . . . hey, shit, *Eviscerator*? Me and my brother used to play that at the pizza joint by our building all the time!"

Sondra smirked. "Nerrrrrd."

"No way, listen, no freakin' way, *Eviscerator* was brutal, really hardcore! Not one of those nerdy 'elf-shot-the-food' things."

Her smirk became a sneer. "An 'elf-shot-the-food' reference? Nerrrrrrrrrrrrrrrd!"

"Bite me."

"You wish."

Rowder cleared his throat with an ominous growl, and Jett stifled whatever doubtless witty retort he'd been about to utter. Instead, after another longing gaze at the quiescent *Eviscerator*–drippy red lettering, cartoon splatter of organs and intestines–he went back to his original question.

"But why here, huh? Why this? You didn't answer."

"Because, dumbass, those nerds you're talking about? Those nerds are all grown up now, with solid tech jobs and plenty of disposable income."

"Middle-aged virgins with no life," added Sondra. "Still couldn't get laid in a whorehouse with a whole roll of quarters."

"And they love this retro shit," Rowder went on as if

HAUNTED HEIST

she hadn't spoken. "They're collectors. Spend all their money on action figures, comic books, LEGO sets, and—"

Just then, his penlight beam found what it was looking for, a line of pinball machines lurking in the furthest, darkest corner, where the short bar of the room's L-shape led toward a restroom, pay phone, and emergency exit. Some of the machines had been indifferently draped with tarps or plastic sheeting. The others looked even dustier and cobwebbier than their upright video game cousins.

He skated the light along the row. KISS-themed . . . something with buff and rugged barbarians like out of a Robert E. Howard paperback . . . Vegas-themed . . . flying saucers and space aliens . . .

"Help me uncover these." He whisked off one of the tarps, which sent a grainy cloud billowing into the air. Dukes-of-goddamn-Hazzard.

Sondra made with a dramatic cough-and-wave, but did the same at the next one. "Jungle Fury," she announced, squinting her disapproval at some really politically inappropriate depictions of Vietnam.

"Aw yeah," crowed Jett as he peeled back some plastic to reveal a beach volleyball theme featuring busty bikini bimbos. "Hello, ladies!"

"Nerd."

"Too bad the power's out; I'd drop a few coins in their slots."

"Pig-nerd."

Doing his best to ignore them again, and wishing he'd done this job solo—but Jett had the van, and it'd take at least two people to heft their target up the stairs—Rowder reached for the dustiest-by-far tarp . . . which didn't just have cobwebs but the desiccated remains of spiders and cocooned flies, and a dried wasp as big as his freakin' thumb, littering its surface.

Not wanting another cloud—the air in the enclosed basement already pushing the limits of visibility and breathability—and not wanting to fling dead bugs everywhere, he slid the tarp off with slow care. And was rewarded with the sight of skeletal black trees and birds silhouetted against a lightning-shot green sky, with ghosts looming in the weird windows of a classic haunted house.

"Jackpot," he said.

Sondra and Jett crowded close. "That's what we're here for?" Jett asked. "The Munsters?"

"Not the Munsters, dumbass," Sondra said. "Their house didn't look anything like that."

"Oh, who's the nerd now? Nerrrrr—unf!" He doubled over as she slammed an elbow into his gut.

Sudden LIGHT and COLOR, sudden NOISE erupting from the machine in front of them! 8-bit Bach, "Toccata and Fugue in D-Minor!" Flashing LIGHTS and glaring COLORS, spooky SOUND EFFECTS chains and thunder and eerie laughter!

The plunger yanked back of its own accord. A steel ball rolled into position, and *ker-sproing* up the chute it went, into the garish playfield, clanging off bumpers, ricocheting crazily, while the buttons on the machine's sides click-click-click depressed themselves and multiple flippers beat like crazy. Illuminated numbers spun and flickered through impossible scores.

Someone was screaming. Rowder didn't know who. Couldn't tell who. Sondra? Jett? Both? Himself? Someone else? Some*thing* else? Their bodies jostled and caromed into each other, more pinballs and bumpers, more sound effects *clang-jangle-ping* and more 8-bit cacophony with the green sky spilling out its radioactive radiance while the lightning cracked, while hinges squeaked and floorboards creaked—

Then, just as suddenly, it all went dark again, and silent.

Rowder shook his penlight but it was deader than disco. "Sondra?" he said into the darkness. "Jett?" With no reply. He was alone; he *felt* it. Alone in the silent dark.

Except . . . it wasn't entirely dark. On the front of the

machine, next to the coin slots, shone two faint, expectant ruby-red lines.

So, exhaling a ragged breath, he reached into his pocket for a quarter.

For Aaron Halon

DERPYFOOT

WARMS. The warms and the purrs. The milks and the licks.

Others. Squirming pile, furry mewing bodies. The Mother. The licks, wet and rough.

The purrs, rumble rumble, and the heartbeat whump-whumpwhump. Voice and cry, meow, trill, croon. The Mother. Soft tummy, bulgy teats, nipple, push-push-push knead-knead-knead, the milks.

Milks. Purrs. Warms. Licks.

The scruff, the teeth-clamp. Lift. Tuck and curl. Swinging. Squalling. Then drop.

Alone. Cold. New. Strange. Not-fur. Like-fur, not-fur.

Mew and mew, struggle and mew. Legs. Feets. Blunder and bump.

Mother-smell again, fur and milk. The brush of a touch. The Mother comes, the Mother goes. More mewing, more squalling. The Others. One by one. Drop, drop, drop. Roll and squirm. Complaints.

Then the Mother comes, and stays. Curls around. All the warms. All the purrs. Lick-lick-lick. Nose nudging. Milk smells, milk smells. A teat, a nipple, an Other.

Mew. Mew and cry.

Nudge. Lick. Another teat. Another nipple. No Other. Milk and milk, knead-push-purr, milk.

Yawn. Nuzzle. Burrow. Licks. Warm fur-pile, Others, Mother.

Sleeps.

DERPYFOOT

Sounds.

Loud-sounds, strange-sounds.

Strange-touch, not-fur, not-scruff, lift. Cold. On back, belly-up. Mew and wiggle, complain and squirm. Smells, thick not-milk smells, strange.

The Mother, a call-cry, concerned. Mew and mew and mew!

More sounds. Strange-sounds. Not-same-kind sounds. Big thing, strange thing. People-thing. People-thing and people-sounds. Movement, head brought close to warms, to licks, the Mother.

"See? Your baby's right here, your baby's fine. Good kitty, Bella, that's a good mama-kitty."

People-sounds and people-touch.

"How many this time?"

"Eight. Five boys and three girls."

"Eight? Eight more cats? Jesus fuck." Pause. Strange-smells, gusty humid yeasty smell and bitter smoke-smell. "What's wrong with them?"

"Nothing's wrong with them! They're perfect little babies!"

"They don't look right. I seen a shitload of kittens thanks to you, and those do not look right."

"They're fine!"

"And what about *that* one?"

"Runt of the litter, is all."

"Runt, all right. Is all? My ass. Look at its paw there."

People-touch, grab and pinchy. Squall! Bend the leg. Prod the paw. Mew!

"Got one foot a little crooked. It's nothing."

"Nothing? Fucking deformed."

"One little crooked foot!"

"Mutant freak-cat."

"Don't say that! He's a fuzzy sweetie!"

Squall and squall, squirm and mew and squall. Mother-meow, a rustle, the flump and tumble and complaining of the Others.

"Some sweetie. Screaming like the possessed. I never heard no cat sound like that."

"You're scaring him! And he misses his mama. Here you go, Bella. Here's your baby."

Lowered. The smells. Mother and milk. Fur and purrs and warms. Released. Roll and wobble. No more strange people-touch. The Mother. Lick, lick, lick. Pushed over. Lick, lick, lick some more.

"You ought to drown the whole ratty lot of them."

"Caleb Bodean!"

"What? You inbreed 'em so much, now they're all starting to come off deformed. Like that one big bastard with the damn yellow lantern eyes."

"I din't breed him! He showed up a stray and you know it."

"Stray, whatever. I swear that one ain't right, ain't normal. Bet he's the one knocked up your precious Bella, and now she got these mutant freak-cats. Probably ree-tarded."

"Shut your stupid face."

"You shut yours, woman!"

"I don't have to take this from you!"

"Who the fuck else are you gonna take it from?"

"Jackass!"

"Cow!"

Hissssss. The Mother. No purrs. Fur bristling.

"See what you've done, you're upsetting Bella."

"Fuck Bella!"

"Well, fuck you too!"

The Others. Mew and mewl and whimper. Crawl. Teats, where? Nipples? Milks?

Hissssss again. A low, drawn-out yooooowwwwl.

"Listen to that bitch! She's gone nuts!"

"I told you, you're upsetting her! She's a brand-new mama. Never done this before."

DERPYFOOT

"Christ. You and your goddamn cats. I need a beer."
"Then go get yourself one."
"Did I ask you to wait on me?"
"What, you mean you're gonna make your own damn dinner for once?"
"Maybe I'll take myself down to The Wheel for dinner!"
"Maybe you should!"
"Have me a big ol' chili-burger."
"Go right on ahead, and when you get the sizzling shits, don't come running to me."

Stomp-clomp-stomp-thud. A clinky jingle. A slam. A grindy-growly noise.

"Jackass." The people-touch again, stroking the Mother as she settles, brushing over the Others as they clamber and fumble for milks. "There, now, Bella. He's gone. You're fine here with your babies in this nice box, you got your nice towel. That's a girl. That's a good girl."

The purrs. The warms, purrs, and licks. The Others, furry side to furry side, kneady-pushy paws, milk-milk-milk. Lick and lick. Purr, purr, purr.

Sleeps.

Same and same and same.

Sleeps and no-sleeps. Warms and purrs. Milks and licks.

Safe.

The Mother.

Sometimes another Other, an other-Other. Similar-smell but different-smell . . . *strange*-smell. Fur. Warms but no teats, no nipples, no milks. Curious sniffs and licks, quick hiss-and-swat, louder hiss from the Mother.

Gradual understanding . . . that other-Other is the Father; there are more other-Others all around but none quite the same. Hearing them. Smelling them. Meows and meows. Scent-marks and scat-marks. Many, many other-Others.

Brightness. Brightness and blur. Light and dark and shape and shadow. Big-shape people-shapes to go with the people-sounds, touches, smells.

Clumsy legs. Wobbly-weak. Tippy. Tip and tumble, roll, wallow. Ears and fur, whiskery noses, eyes, tails. Milk, milk, milk. Little claws, little teeth, more more more and mew-mew-mew when the Mother goes and more more more purr purr purr when the Mother comes back.

Sleeps.

Waking no-sleeps.

People-sounds, people-voices, loud and angry. Slams and shouts.

"—about goddamn *had* it! For fuck's sake, woman! *Look* at this place!"

"You knew I wasn't no Martha Stewart when you married me!"

"I didn't know I'd be living in wall-to-wall cat piss!"

"Oh, it is not that bad—"

More slams and stomps. Hisses, wary snarls. Ears flat. The Mother hunkered over them, the Others crowding close.

"Take a whiff! Cat piss, cat shit, the fucking hair's everywhere, can't walk across the floor without it crunching like a gravel driveway. You said they'd do it outside!"

"I got the litterboxes so they wouldn't have to go out there and freeze in the wintertime doing their business!"

"That's why you had me saw a hole in the damn door, put in that dumb-ass flap that lets in all the cold air."

"Not my fault you're a sorry excuse for a handyman. Speaking of which, when you gonna fix the—"

"I wasn't finished! I'm tired of smelling cat-piss, tired of stepping on their dried turds, tired of cat hair on everything and in my food. Tired of that yellow-eyed fuck

DERPYFOOT

staring at me all the time. You've seen the damn furniture too, clawed half to crap!"

"What are you saying, Caleb?"

"I'm saying I've had it with these cats. One or two, hell, three or four even, that'd be fine, but . . . "

"You want to get rid of our sweeties?"

"We can't keep 'em all, Doreen. You know that. We can't afford it, especially what with them squeezing out eight and ten kittens at a go!"

"The kittens we'll find homes for soon as they're weaned. Just like always."

"That's what you said last time, and you ended up keeping half of 'em."

"That was Sugar-Pie's litter; it would have broken her heart to let them all go. She's old. She might never have any more."

"Always some fucking excuse. What're you gonna tell me next? That since it's Bella's first batch, you can't bear to part 'em from her? Inbred retards though they are? Even that deformed gimp freak-cat—"

"Don't talk about my sweeties like that!"

"I'll talk about your precious damn sweeties however-the-fuck I please!"

The smells, heavy and strong. Sounds. Shapes, looming.

"What are you doing?"

"Drawing a fucking line in the sand, that's what I'm doing!"

"Caleb! Get away from there!"

The Mother hisses again, yowls.

"Back the hell off me, Doreen!" Shoving movement. Stumble-crash, meaty thud, pained grunt.

"Don't you touch them." Gasping, wet snorts. "You leave them alone."

"Or what?"

Sudden grab. Not-fur. Grime and dirt, bad-smells. One of the Others snatched up, lifted, mewing, thrashing. The Mother screeches. Paw-lash claw-slash. Blood.

"Caleb!"
"Ow! Bitch scratched me!"
"Put down that baby!"
Squall. Struggle.
Snap. Crunch.
People-scream. "Bastard!"
A loose thump as the Other drops. Still. Inert. Head twisted crooked. Tongue poking out.

More screams. More crashes and thuds. Two more of the Others seized. The Mother leaping, a ball of fur and fury, claws, teeth. All the other-Others yowling now, hissing, racing around tails-puffed backs-bristled.

Blood and blood and blood. Thin cuts and deep bites. Screaming. So much screaming, so much yowling and howling and screeching and wailing.

"Fucking bitch-cat!"
Wet cracking sound.
"Bella! Noooo! Bella!"
The Mother, no longer hissing.
The box kicked. The box flipped. Towel whump and darkness, squirming, mewing. Stomp-crunch, stomp-crunch.

"Caleb, stop!"
"Should've goddamn listened to me, huh, Doreen? Bossy cunt!" Stomp-crunch.
"You piece of shit! I'm gonna kill you!"
"Like to see you tr—"
BANG.
Silence.

Silence.
Blood-stink. Smoke-stink.
Sobbing.
"Bella, my poor Bella, my poor sweetie . . . my poor sweetie and your poor sweetie-babies . . . that son of a

DERPYFOOT

bitch, that murdering bastard! He asked for it. I told him to stop. I told him. He didn't have to go and do that!"

Sobbing and sobbing. Snuffles. Snorts.

The towel, sodden, sticky. Blood. The Others. Squashed, broken, limp, loose.

Heavy-dark-wet towel lifted. "Babies? Babies, you okay? Did he . . . oh no, no!" More sobs, wails.

Mew?

People-touch. Cradling. Stroking. "Oh you poor sweetie-baby you poor little thing oh that bastard I should've shot him quicker your poor mama, your poor lost little brothers and sisters!"

Mew and struggle.

The Mother! The milks, the purrs, the licks, the warms! The Mother!

Want-need-want!

No.

People-touch, rubbing on not-fur, leaky salty not-fur and people-breath, sour-sweet not-milk and the sounds the sounds the sounds.

"It's all right now, everyone, it's all right, it'll be all right, I'll make it all right, my good kitties, my sweeties, everyone shhh, just hush now, hush now, let's just . . . come on . . . here, kitty-kitty, come on kitties, everyone over to the kitchen, I'll open up some cans for you how about that nice treat some canned food for you while I clean this mess up, while I take care of it . . . "

Set down. Cold. No fur, no not-fur, cold and flat, hard, claws tick-tick-tick paws slide around.

" . . . shot him, shot Caleb dead as the piece of shit he is and what if someone calls the police on me? Nosy neighbors, damn kids! But maybe they didn't hear nothing, maybe they don't want to get themselves involved. No, sure they wouldn't, not all the times they been in trouble with the law. Calling the police'd be about the last thing they'd do."

The noise. The *rrerrrr-errr-err-click* noise, and the

smells, and the other-Others meowing, jostling, meowing, demanding.

"Just a minute, yes, that's right, just a minute, let me spoon it out, hey, hey, take it easy, nice kitties, enough for everyone, last few cans but I'll go to the store tomorrow and plenty of the dry left. Oh but what am I gonna do with *you*, poor kitty-baby?"

Lifted again, cradled, cuddled, breathed on, not-licked.

"Nowhere near ready to be weaned yet but maybe ol' Sugar-Pie has some milk left . . . her litter haven't been off it that long, and she'll take you in, I'm sure she will, Bella's little orphan sweetie."

A Not-Mother. Strange fur. Wrinkled teats, tough nipples, thin milks. Grudging licks. Different scent. Different purrs. Sometimes rebuffing, pushing away. Tired. Warning hisses. Ear-swats and sharp nips.

The New-Others. Bigger. Jumping-bouncing, pouncing, wrestling. Sit on. Flop on. Step on. Bump aside. Knock over, bowl over, run over.

The Father. Different but familiar. *Strange* but familiar. Sometimes lets huddle close for sleeps and warms. Sometimes grooms. Sometimes growls, eyes narrowed. Eyes yellow. Yellow-yellow. Glow-yellow, even in the bright,

In the sleeps, huddled close in warms, the Father-heart makes slow *strange* whumps. The Father-purr rumbles low and deep. In the Father-dreams are big-*strange* places. Sounds but not like people-sounds. Shrill-trill high high piping sounds. Sense of vastness. Sense of space. Colors/not-colors wheeling in a dark, a forever-dark.

DERPYFOOT

And people-sounds.

" . . . say that we had ourselves another argument, and he walked out on me . . . everybody knows about his drinking and how he feels about the cats . . . not much of a surprise, they'll think . . . he'd just up and take off like that without a word . . . no job anyhow . . . probably owes a bunch of people money too . . . good riddance, I'll tell them . . . not like he had any friends, bad-tempered son of a bitch . . . "

Always the people-sounds.

" . . . grave for Bella and her litter . . . complications I'll say, birth defects . . . all's you got to do is look at you, poor baby with your crooked foot, only instead of being the runt anymore, you're the strong one, aren't you? The lucky one, the survivor . . . terrible thing but small blessings . . . who'd have any reason to think otherwise? Been putting my sweeties back there for years, markers and everything."

People-sounds and people-smells.

" . . . only fair, after the way Caleb treated us. After the way he treated me. All of us. Never was good for a goddamn thing in his life."

Milks . . . and foods . . . soft-wet foods, mmm-smack-smack . . . hard-dry foods, krick-crack-crunch . . . people-foods, warm-salty-meat-juice and sweet-sweet-milky-cream . . . lick and lap, lap-lap-lap.

"Always griping at me how much I'd spend, like I was feeding you out of crystal dishes like on those commercials instead from the grocery warehouse . . . griping how I never changed the catboxes enough, then griping at me for the cost of the kitty litter when I did . . . "

Scent-marks and scat-marks. Dirt for pee-digging, for poo-digging, dig dig dig scratch scratch scratch bury bury bury.

"Might as well be of some use now. Might as well give some back, the selfish greedy fucker . . . and wouldn't he be pissed if he knew? Reason enough right there . . . "

Not-furs to run on. Not-furs to climb on. Play-toy string ball toy-play swat swat chase, swat-pounce-skitter.

" . . . cheapskate ought to appreciate it then, me being all thrifty . . . recycling, like those co-op hippies down the road say we should, them with their organic farm . . . though this not hardly vegetarian, though, not hardly! Ha!"

Strange-foods. Wet but different. Sloppy-messy. Big chunks. Gnaw-gnaw-gnaw. Strange taste. Less-good.

" . . . his truck, might be a problem, loved that damn truck . . . he went anyplace, you know he would've took the truck . . . have to do something about that . . . drive it around to the old garage, maybe . . . "

Itchies. Ear, ear, chin, neck, ear, rump, rump, scritch-scritch. Itchies. Groom-groom-groom. Lick-lick-chew-lick. Itchy furs. Itchy skins.

" . . . nosy damn neighbors . . . mind their own business, why can't they? Saying I don't take care of my precious sweeties? I love my precious sweeties! And you love me, don't you? Don't you? We don't need nobody else."

Sounds and smells.

Getting worse. Oily and sweaty. Bad-fish. Sour-milks.

"Eat up, everybody, here-kitty-kitty chow time. Oh, come on. Who's hungry? Eat it up. I'll get out to the store soon, but, look, only a few bags left . . . good thing I got those gallon-size freezer baggies, knew they'd come in handy . . . scrawny old shit had some meat on his bones after all . . . "

Dig-dirt stinky with pee-and-poo, too stinky, too filled, not-scratch, not-bury. Food spills. Food spoils. Spoiled-foods and spoiled food-spills.

" . . . place getting a little messy, maybe, but so what? My house now, isn't it? All mine and only mine. Told him how I wasn't any Martha Stewart when he married me anyway . . . "

Meows and complains. Many-many. All the Others, all but the Father. Who sits. Who watches. Yellow eyes

DERPYFOOT

shining-shining. Sit with. Watch with. Hungries but sit. Hungries but watch. Watch and wait.

" . . . soon as I'm feeling better, I promise . . . need to get some proper groceries up in here too . . . damn Caleb and all his beers in the fridge, not hardly room for anything else . . . gives me the heartburn . . . really could use a nice dish of ice-cream, take care of that . . . 'bout out of antacids anyway . . . so tired, let me just have a nap first . . . "

People-sleeps.

Foods?

No foods.

Complain. Meow. Others meow. Lots of meow. Want-need-demand.

People-sleeps. Grunts and breaths and sloppy snores. People-sound mumbles.

No foods.

Empties.

Empty where-foods-go. Empty hungry bellies. Growl and snarl. Hiss and fight.

Hungries.

Meows. Yowls. More hisses. More fights. More hungries.

So much hungries!

Then, the Father, no more sit and wait and watch. The Father eyes yellow, yellow glow. The Father high up on the people-bed.

And no more people-sounds.

The Others low-hunker, unsure, afraid. Curious but unsure. Hungries but afraid.

The Father down-hops, scruff-bites, up-climbs.

Mew. Squirm.

Released, high up on people-bed.
Warms, but, fading. People but no sounds, no moves, no touch.
No breaths. No sleeps.
The Father, claw and slice, nudge and push.
Licks?
Tastes?
Mew?
Some Others, boldest, approach and sniff, sniff and curious, sniff and lick.
Foods?
Foods!
Lick and bite, and bite, and chew. Greedy growling noises.
Now all, all the Others, crowding crowding busy claws and teeth.
People-taste. People-taste but hungries, people-taste but foods.
Foods and foods, so much foods, red slick wet yellow globby foods.
Foods!

The Father, the flap-thing. Push and through. Urge. Show. Teach. Push and through, through and out.
Bright-hot hot-bright warms . . . smells, many-many new smells, strange smells . . . outside smells! Big air, wide space . . . the World!
The World but not the vastness, not the strange-space where colors/not-colors, where high shrill high trill sounds in the Father's deep-low-rumble purring dreams.
Dirt-real-dirt for scratch and digging. Grass to chew. Chew chew chew. Hork. Chew. Leaves for chase-pounce. Crawly bugs. Birds whoosh so fast so high! The heat-warms, sun-warms, roll and stretch, sun-warms on the tummy!

DERPYFOOT

The Others climb and climb, trees to climb. Try but no, try but fall, try but some paws claw-catch-hold, one paw not. The Others run and run, dash this way that way spring leap bound around around. Try but slow, try but clumsy-stumble. The Others chase and swat, swat and tussle, wrestle wrestle.

The Father, tail twitch twitch get it get it fierce hunter. Yellow eyes flash and gleam. Lick and groom, curl for sleeps, purr.

Naps in the sun-warms, in the shade-cools. Water water drip-drip-drips from metal faucet-tube plink into basin always plenty lap lap lap drink.

Inside for foods, slimy less-good foods now. Dark, not red, not yellow, dark and brown. Buzz-buzz flies and squirmy grub-worms. Soon be bad-foods, sick-make not-foods, should bury-bury kick the dirt.

Hungries come then?

Empty-belly hungries?

Or more foods?

Eat and eat, gnaw and chew for least-bad not-yet-rot bits, eat and eat. And wash and wash, face wash face wash lick the paw wipe the face. Whiskers. Food-meats stuck in claws, chew and gnaw some more. Lick, wipe, wash, groom and groom.

And push-through outside, for more sun-warms and shade-cools.

Then . . . sounds.

People-sounds?

People-sounds!

Peoples! New peoples. At the stick-fence, at the yard.

"We're gonna get in trouble."

"Daddy promised."

"He also said, after, that he didn't really mean it."

"Which is a super unfair liar jerkface thing to do. You

can't make promises and take them back and be a dirty taker-backer. If he won't get us a kitty, we'll just go get our own."

"Why here, though? This is gross, Hailey. Look at the place, it's trailer-trash city."

"Kim at school told me the lady who lives here always has bunches of kittens, and gives them away for free even."

The Others wary-watching, narrow-eyes, gold and green, orange and blue. Some run. Some slink. Some hiss and hunch and puff the fur.

"Whoa . . . that's a lot of cats. A lot of mean-looking cats."

"Stop it, Justin, they are not mean. They don't know us yet, that's all." The smaller of the peoples, a girl-people, crouches. "Kitty-kitty, hi, kitties!"

The taller boy-people puts a hand toward one of the Others. Hunker, ears-lowered, building rumble-yowl deep in chest. Hiss and claw-swipe. Miss, very near miss. "They're, like, feral or something. C'mon. Let's get out of here."

"But I want a kitty."

"Dad won't let you keep it. Besides, they're all grubby. I bet they've got fleas."

"Ohhh, look, this little grey and white one's got a derpy foot."

Sniff and sweet clean people-smell, and gentle people-touch. Head-pets, soft, nice.

Mew?

"See? This one's not mean!"

Mew and nudge and nuzzle.

"Hailey, watch it, be careful!"

"Aww, Justin, see?"

Hands and lift and hold and cuddle. Snuggle. The Girl!

Another touch, the Boy, hesitant but then under-chin scritches yes yes bliss so good, and purr! "I guess he's not so bad. At least he's friendly. Wonder what happened to his paw."

DERPYFOOT

"Poor little derpy foot kitty, you want to come and live with us now, don't you?"

Purr and purr and purr. The Others still wary-watching, or indifferent. The Father pushes through the flap-thing, messy muzzle, matted whiskers, face-wash time. Stops, eyes yellow, eyes flash, stares and glares and hisses.

"Is that what you're gonna call him? Derpyfoot?"

"Maybe. Hey, he fits right in my hoodie pocket like a baby kangaroo! All snug and comfy!"

Long sighing air-sound from the Boy. "We better go ask the lady who lives here if it's okay. You can't just take him. That'd be stealing, even if she gives them away for free."

Snuggledarks and warms, the Girl, slow-moving, walking.

And the Boy. "Jeez, it stinks."

"Litterboxes maybe?"

"I dunno, worse than litterboxes."

Up and up. Steps. Knock and knock.

Others-meows but no people-sounds.

"Keep trying, Justin!"

Louder-knock. "Hello? Anybody home? Missus . . . uh . . ."

"Bodean."

"Missus Bodean?" Loud-hard knock, and creak. "It opened—oh, man! Whew! What *died*?"

"Eew-yuck-gross."

"Hey wait, I see something—"

Then, people-shouts and people-screams. Then, fast-moves run run run bounce bounce claws-dig-in hang on hang on. Screams and shouts and gags and cries.

Fast run bounce jarring jogging claws-dig hang on.

Scared. Scared. Huddle small be small hang on in the soft warm-darks. No purrs. No yowls. Not even mews. Scared and scared, hold on.

Brights. Brights and lights and new smells, new place, new place-smells.

"You brought him *with* you?"

"He was in my hoodie pocket, I forgot!"

"We have to take him back!"

"No no no I don't want to go back there not back there Justin pleeeease!"

"Well . . ."

"You don't want to either!"

"Yeah, but . . ."

New place. New sounds and smells and feels. New big clean place. Many smells to sniff, to explore.

" . . . when Dad gets here, and the police, they can . . ."

" . . . but we rescued him, we saved him from that awful . . ."

Thirsties, and mew, and mew, and water, bowl water wet-cool wet-clear lap lap lap drink.

" . . . Dad isn't going to let you . . ."

" . . . can't send him *back*, there's nobody . . ."

Foods, hard-dry foods, crunch-crunch-crunch. Tasty hard-dry foods and no pushing-shoving, no shares, no growls, no swats and hisses, no Others.

No Others, but no Father.

" . . . or as evidence or something . . ."

"Evidence?"

" . . . or maybe to the pound—"

"No! Not my Derpyfoot! Not the *pound*!"

Dirt-box, new dirt, clean dirt, no scent-marks no scat-marks, scratch and dig, scratch-scratch, pee and poo, dig-dig-dig bury.

" . . . and look at him, anyway, he's all dirty; what if that stuff in his fur is—"

"It is not don't you say it don't you dare!"

"Okay, okay, but we at least better give him a bath."

DERPYFOOT

White place. Cold hard white place, slippy under paws, shrieky under claws, can't catch can't hold can't climb want out out-out-out.

Soothy Girl-voice.

Not soothed! Very much not!

Runny runny water! Runny splash! Louder splashing rushing roar water water not drink- water! Wets! Not-cold-wets, warm-wets, but still *wets* too much wets wets all over bad bad bad!

Out!

Can't!

Wail and protest. Wail-wail-wail.

Girl-voice. "Derpy, it's okay, it's okay, Derpy!"

Wets. All the wets. Drenchy splashy wets. Feets in the wets, pick one up, shakety-shakety fast but set down again back in the wets!

Wets and scrubs. Soapy smelly foamy on the fur in the fur scrubby-scrubs fur this way that way wrong way, messed and wet and soapy! The back the legs the tummy the chest the neck-chin-head, the tail!

" . . . feel *so* much better . . . "

Suds and tingle, icky smell, icky taste, feets in the wets and cold now cold shiver-shiver and yowly-sad meow.

" . . . rinse you off and . . . "

More wets! Wets everywhere! In the face!

"Sorry, Derpy . . . hold still . . . almost done."

Miserable long-longer-longest-ever yowl.

"Almost done, promise!"

Drip. Drip. Shiver and drip.

"There we go. Good kitty, Derpy, what a good kitty. Okay. Let's dry you off."

Cloth. Swaddle and cover. Rub, rub, rub. Less wets. Less and less wets. Shake the paws. Step, shakety-shakety, step.

And the brush, nice, nice.
Dry fur. Warm fur.
Soft and clean and nice.

Thing! Thing on the neck! Head caught! Stiff band of smelly thing! On neck! Around neck! Caught, caught!

Back up back up back up! Out, out!

Can't! Stuck stuck stuck! Hind paw, snag and grab, push, push hard.

Off-off-off!

"... only a collar, you'll get used to it..."

The Girl, pick ups again, pets. Hugs. Snuggle-nuzzle.

"See? Not so bad. And it'll keep the nasty fleas away."

Hugs and pets. Pet-pet-pet.

Mew.

"It's okay, Derpy. It's okay. You're my kitty now, my good kitty, and I love you."

More sounds, people-sounds. Angry. Loud. Yells and shouts.

"—you'd disobey me like that—"

"—said we could, Daddy, you *promised*!"

Flinch. Bristle. Mew and hiss.

"—told you I'd *think* about it—"

"—means *no*, everybody knows it always—"

"Dad, we only—" The Boy, trying to intervene.

"—start with me, Justin; you're older, you should be more—"

"—not *his* fault; I forgot Derpy was in my pocket when—"

"—your sister to a *crime* scene—"

"—didn't know, and we called the police as soon as—"

"—talking about this; the cat's got to go."

DERPYFOOT

"Nooooo! Derpy's *my* kitty!" Hug, squeeze, hurt-tight this time and more crying, fear-smells tear-smells.

"—with all the other ones they took in as evidence—"

"The ones they didn't shoot, you mean; I heard on the news they killed a bunch!"

"You're not helping, Justin."

"I don't want them to shoot Derpy!"

"Hailey, calm down. They won't shoot him."

"But what if they take him to the pound and gas him to death?"

"—about enough of this from both of you. Even if I was going to let you get a cat, it wouldn't be a . . . a . . . *cannibal cat*."

"Jeez, Dad, it's not even the same species, that's not how cannibalism—"

"Damn it, Justin!"

"But it isn't!"

SMACK.

Silence.

No people-sounds. No people-moves.

The Girl, trembling, hitch-hitch-hitch for breath.

"Justin, oh my god, I'm sorry—"

"Don't touch me!"

"Are you all right?"

"I said don't touch me! Hailey's right! *Mom* was right! You're a liar and a jerk and *I hate you*!"

Girl-room.

People-place is quiet. Mad-quiet, sad-quiet. Closed doors and no-talks.

Sad Girl hugs and hugs, pets and pets. Purr, mew, cuddle. Head-boops. Roll over for tummies. Purr and play. String, swatty-ball, feather, crinkly thing! Jump-chase-tumble-pounce!

Finally, happy Girl. Happy-sounds. Laughs and giggles.

Lots of pettings. Lots of cuddles. Warms and pets and cuddles. Purr-purr. Knead, push, purr.

The darks, warm-darks but not all-darks, soft light low and soft pillow-blankie-bed.

The Girl, slow breaths and sweet smells. Sleepy-pets.

Purrs.

Happies.

Sleeps.

Sleeps.

Sleeps and sleeps.

Sudden grab and lift!

Wakes!

Mew but covered, people-hand, big-people-hand, gripping face, squeezing muzzle. Strong-bad smells, whiskey smells, smoke smells, sweat-sour smells.

Squeal but muffled. Struggle and kick but held. Scruff. Scruff and collar-thing, tight on neck, tight. Half-chokes. Legs uptuck. Tail undertuck. Ears flat.

The Girl turns, sleepy-mumbles, pillow-burrows, breath-sighs.

Carried fast. Away from Girl. Away from room. Carried fast, doors and doors.

Cool air, night air.

Outside. The World.

People-sounds, slurred, grumbling.

"—*have* to do this . . . tell her it must've got out, wandered away . . . upset at first but she'll get over it . . . buy her that phone she's been wanting . . . won't say anything if he knows what's good for him . . . call *me* a liar and a jerk? . . . "

Outside, the night, the night. Wide vast night alive with noises, alive with scents, rustle-rustle bushes, dirt and trees, away from the people-place, away from the Girl.

"—squirming, you little . . . *could* just wring your

DERPYFOOT

mangy neck . . . lucky I'm only dumping you . . . catch mice or birds or something . . . can't with that foot then oh well . . . law of the wild . . ."

Stumble and sway, arm-swing, awkward slip-grip of scruff. No more big hand on face, no more grip-squeeze muffle. Hiss and spit, claws and *swipe*, claws and skin-flesh-snag-drag, claws and *blood*!

"Ow! Son of a—"

Grappling, grappling, caught by tail, caught by leg, wrench-pain, hurts, hurts. But *fight*, bite and fight, screech, claw-scrabble and fight, rip-shred-rip at wrist, teeth sink sharp-deep in soft meat. Sudden taste, people-taste blood-taste food-taste.

Scruff again, held again, clamp-tight fist on scruff, more hurts. More people-sounds, angry-sounds. Faster stumble-walk, stumble-run.

"—ought to throw you against that tree . . . bash your head in with a rock . . . look at this, scratches, bleeding like hell . . . tell the kids?"

Yowl from near.

Wavering, warning, rising yowl from near.

Eyeshine glinting, yellow glow, bright angry-yellow shining in the dark.

People-stops, unsteady, uncertain. "What the . . . ?"

Familiar smell. Familiar shape from the gloom. Head low, body low, tail low. Pad-steps careful. Deliberate. Silent. Placed.

The Father.

Then, more. More-shapes, cat-shapes, Other-shapes . . . but strange. Limp-drag-slow strange. Made from shadow made from mist strange.

"Psst! Go on! Scat! Psst!"

Surrounding. Closing in.

Backward, people-stumble, clumsy-stumble worse than ever, backward, blundering.

"—the hell *away* from me!"

Reel and totter. Crack-snap, wet bone snap, and people-yell, crazy waving arms, topsy-tumble.

CHRISTINE MORGAN

Loose! Loose and dropped, falling, twist in air, land on feet, but leg-ouch paw-bend, oof and thump, mulch-leaves-earth. Grunt-mew.

Bigger thump, louder thump, twig-snap ground-shake thump, and more people-sounds. People pain-sounds, on back rolling, foot crooked, flop-wiggle, wobble-wobble.

"—my fucking *ankle*!"

Helpless, feeble thrashings. A get-up try and fail, more pain-sounds, yelping, word-sounds, swearing.

And here are the Father, the Others.

Not all but some. Many.

Closing in.

Growling.

There are angries, and much hungries.

And blood-smell in the air.

Limps.

Limps and limps.

Limp and hobble.

So far away, so far, when hurt, when scared, when tired. When crooked paw and leg all sore-stiff.

Then, nip and grip, lift, the scruff-carry. No struggles. Hang and rest, swing and rest, sore and stiff and tired.

Through the dark with yellow eyes, glow and shine, yellow through the dark. The Father, carry and purr, low-deep-rumble purr.

To the people-place, to the door left open.

Stop. Un-scruff and down. The Father rough-licks rough-licks and nudge.

Mew?

Nudge.

And go . . . limp-hobble in. While, below, the Father sits and watches and waits.

Limp-hobble in, limp-hobble up. Stairs stairs stairs, up and up.

DERPYFOOT

To the room where soft light welcomes in warm-darks, where soft pillow-blankie bed rises high up above, so high.

So high, and hard climb, hard climb with bent paw and sore leg, when aches and tired. Hard climb, strain and pull, claw-claw pull and pull.

Until, finally.

Until the slow and sweet deep-breaths, the gentle hand to burrow under, the warms, snuggle-warms. The drowsy-pets and murmurs.

The Girl.

"Derpy, here's my good kitty . . . "

Mew and nuzzle. Curl up cozy, purr and purr.

A pause, a half-wakeful stirring. "Uck, why's your fur all sticky? Do you need another bath? In the morning, 'kay? It's sleepytime."

Happies, sleeps and sleeps.

ABOUT THE AUTHOR

Christine Morgan is a shameless Edward Lee fangirl who's been lucky enough to be allowed to play with his toys, as she's done in the Splatterpunk Award winning novel *Lakehouse Infernal* and its sequel, *Warlock Infernal.*

Her works include the deep-sea chompy *Trench Mouth*, the pioneer snow monster *White Death*, the splatter western *The Night Silver River Run Red,* and enough short stories to fill several collections with everything from Vikings to steampunk to really nasty smut.

She currently lives in Southern California as her mother's full-time caregiver, where she also reviews, takes on edit gigs, gets bossed around by her cats, and makes weird crafts.

Printed in Great Britain
by Amazon